PUFFIN BOOKS

Dan Abnett is a multiple *New York Times* bestselling novelist. He is the fan-favourite author of over thirty Warhammer and Warhammer 40,000 novels, and has sold nearly three million copies in over a dozen languages. He has also written for franchises such as *Torchwood*, *Primeval* and *Doctor Who*. When he's not being a novelist, he writes screenplays and video games.

In collaboration with Andy Lanning, Dan has scripted some of the most famous superhero comics in the world, including *Iron Man*, *Thor* and *The Guardians of the Galaxy* at Marvel, and *Superman*, *Batman*, *The Legion of Superheroes* and *Wonder Woman* at DC Comics.

Dragon Frontier is Dan's first series for younger readers.

DRAGON FRONTIER
DAN ABNETT

BURNING MOON

PUFFIN

For Evan and Amber 'Bamberlina' McNeill
with fond memories of our trips together
into the Canadian Wild West

PUFFIN BOOKS

Published by the Penguin Group
Penguin Books Ltd, 80 Strand, London WC2R ORL, England
Penguin Group (USA) Inc., 375 Hudson Street, New York, New York 10014, USA
Penguin Group (Canada), 90 Eglinton Avenue East, Suite 700, Toronto, Ontario, Canada M4P 2Y3
(a division of Pearson Penguin Canada Inc.)
Penguin Ireland, 25 St Stephen's Green, Dublin 2, Ireland (a division of Penguin Books Ltd)
Penguin Group (Australia), 707 Collins Street, Melbourne, Victoria 3008, Australia
(a division of Pearson Australia Group Pty Ltd)
Penguin Books India Pvt Ltd, 11 Community Centre, Panchsheel Park, New Delhi – 110 017, India
Penguin Group (NZ), 67 Apollo Drive, Rosedale, Auckland 0632, New Zealand
(a division of Pearson New Zealand Ltd)
Penguin Books (South Africa) (Pty) Ltd, Block D, Rosebank Office Park, 181 Jan Smuts Avenue,
Parktown North, Gauteng 2193, South Africa

Penguin Books Ltd, Registered Offices: 80 Strand, London WC2R ORL, England

puffinbooks.com

First published 2014
001

Written by Dan Abnett
Story and concept by Dan Abnett and Andy Lanning
Text copyright © Dan Abnett and Andy Lanning, 2014
Chapter-head illustrations by Benjamin Hughes
Chapter-head illustrations copyright © Penguin Books Ltd, 2014
All rights reserved

The moral right of the author and illustrator has been asserted

Set in 13/16pt Baskerville MT Std
Typeset by Jouve (UK), Milton Keynes
Printed in Great Britain by Clays Ltd, St Ives plc

British Library Cataloguing in Publication Data
A CIP catalogue record for this book is available from the British Library

ISBN: 978-0-141-34298-6

www.greenpenguin.co.uk

PROLOGUE

Jake Polson was falling through the air, and he was afraid. The sky lit up around him with great sheets of flame so bright they stung his eyes, but he didn't dare blink.

He was falling very fast, and he was desperate to see where he was and what was happening. He didn't dare think about how high in the air he must have been thrown to be falling for so long. He didn't dare think about the hard landing, the broken bones or his inevitable death, because, of course, he was afraid of dying.

More than that, Jake was afraid for his ma and his pa and for Emmie. He could see his sister in his mind's eye as he blinked, clutching her rag doll with its yellow wool hair.

Then the image was gone, and the sky glowed suddenly bright yellow with flames that spread like a comet's tail, lighting up a huge black beast. It breathed fire from its flaring nostrils, or was it from its great maw? Even with his eyes open, Jake couldn't tell where the flames came from. Besides, there was more to see and remember as his body plummeted through the air.

He blinked again, and suddenly all he could see was the cold stare of the mind behind the beast's horrifying magenta eye with its fathomless black pupil.

Jake was overwhelmed. He wondered what had befallen the wagon train. It seemed like only seconds since he'd woken to the sound of animals screaming and stampeding.

He had too much momentum as he began to fall faster. His body rolled and turned as he lost control of his flailing limbs, and his mouth gaped in a howl of utter panic.

Jake's eyes widened as his panic turned to horror. Where there had been one creature he now saw a great swarm of beasts in the sky, silhouetted against the misty yellow light. Everything was illuminated at the glowing edges of the great trails of flame exhaled by the vast beast.

They were smaller than the Thunderbird that had attacked him. They looked solid black as they dipped and dived, but their shapes were unmistakable. Their impressive wingspans, their whip-like tails, their clawed legs and their proud heads became clearer as they soared closer.

A dozen or more dragons circled the campsite where Jake's family and friends had been sleeping, peacefully, until the animals had begun their terrible stampede at the sight of the flying creatures.

What are they doing? he thought, fear threatening to overwhelm him once more. *Why have they come?*

Then Jake landed, hard, his limbs jarred and the wind knocked out of him. For a split second, he thought that he had landed on hard-packed earth. There was a sudden rush of cold, and Jake continued to fall, more slowly. He could no longer see or hear clearly, but he was definitely falling.

The cold quickly became a deep, penetrating sensation, and Jake knew that he was sinking into water. His eyes, still wide open in shock, adjusted to the murk as a flash of yellow flames blazed across the surface, above him. The shot of fire was matched by the burning in Jake's chest as his lungs ached to take a breath. Then Jake saw the dancing green and brown tendrils of waterweeds, and the motes of dirt that had been disturbed when he'd landed in the water, and he knew what he must do.

He kicked frantically, thrusting for all he was worth. Suddenly, just as he thought his lungs would burst, he broke the surface, using the last of his ebbing strength. Gasping for breath, Jake coughed and heaved. Black spots danced before his eyes as his oxygen-starved brain threatened to black out. He fought against the darkness, but his body refused to obey him.

As his eyes began to close, he caught one final glimpse of the dragons swarming overhead, and of the great black beast launching into the air. It cast one last, great blast of flaming light into the sky, illuminating the cargo that hung from each beast's strong back legs.

Then Jake could no longer fight sleep.

Jake Polson sat bolt upright in bed, clutching the patchwork quilt in his white-knuckled fists. He gasped for breath, and was dripping with sweat.

A moment later, he was startled again when David and Michael Garret jumped on his bed. Then Eliza lit a candle and came to sit on the blanket chest. They were followed quickly by the sound of muffled footsteps, and Jake saw first Elizabeth Garret and then her husband appear at the top of the loft ladder. Pius was holding a candle to light their way.

Jake didn't even realize that he'd cried out in his sleep.

'What are these interruptions?' asked Elizabeth Garret. She placed the back of her small, strong hand against Jake's forehead. 'You don't have a fever.'

'He was shouting, "Emmie",' said Eliza. 'Isn't that your sister?'

'It was a dream,' said Jake, trying to rub the sweat off his forehead with the sleeve of his pyjama jacket before Mrs Garret noticed. He was too late.

'You're soaked through,' said Mrs Garret. 'Those nightmares must have made you sweat. You'll need clean pyjamas.'

'It was just a dream,' said Jake, again, not knowing what else to say.

Pius Garret placed a calming hand on his wife's shoulder. He put down his candle and sat on the edge of Jake's bed.

'Off you go, boys, and let Jake talk,' he said to the twins. 'Then we can think about fresh pyjamas and a good night's sleep. Everything will look better in the morning, just so long as you get it out of your system, heh, son?'

'They're alive!' said Jake.

'Well, that's a blessing,' said Mrs Garret, 'and nothing to get in a sweat about.'

'Who's alive?' asked Pius.

'Emmie, of course,' said Eliza.

'And Ma and Pa,' said Jake. 'I saw them, or at least I think I saw them. Except . . .'

'What is it, son?' asked the blacksmith.

'Whatever it is,' said Mrs Garret, leaning over to wipe a fresh drop of sweat from Jake's face, 'I fear there'll be a lot more interruptions before this is over.'

'When I blamed Yellow Cloud and Tall Elk and Chief Half Moon . . . When I blamed the dragons for the fire and for what happened to my family, I was right,' said Jake.

'But the Native people have been so kind to you,' said Pius.

'I saw the dragons in my dream,' said Jake. 'They flew away with my family and friends and all their belongings on the night of the fire. Where did they take them? How am I ever going to find them again?' he wailed.

'I don't know, son,' said Pius, soothing the boy.

'I found Pa Watkiss's wagon in the Land of the Red Moon . . . The dragons lifted it away in their claws, and they did the same with the people. I saw it in my dream. I must go after them.'

'I don't know about that,' said Pius, 'but I do know that, whatever happens, it can't happen in the middle of the night. It can't happen on an empty stomach, either.'

'Mr Garret's right,' said Mrs Garret, rummaging in the chest for clean pyjamas. 'Now get changed and get to bed, and we'll talk about it in the morning.'

Jake got out of bed, and Pius Garret turned to make his way back downstairs. Suddenly, the boy grabbed the blacksmith's arm.

'You will let me search for my family, won't you?' Jake begged. 'You will let me talk to the Natives, won't you? They might know about the evil dragons that did this!'

Pius Garret took Jake by the shoulders, looked him squarely in the eyes and said, 'I'll do whatever's best for you, Jake, just as if you were my own son.'

1

Match, with his forest green patches showing dark against his lighter green scales, flew wing tip to wing tip with Yellow Cloud's larger, older dragon. He was called Gale, because he'd hatched during a wind storm. Match and Jake made spiralling circles in the sky to begin practice. They were training alone, and the dragons had already bathed in the hot pools. It was cold, and they needed to warm their blood for the practice session.

The winter weather was setting in, and the cold-blooded creatures were growing sluggish. They could only fly for short sessions between bathing in the warming mud. If they stayed at the Native settlement for much longer, they wouldn't be able to fly at all.

Jake used the time while the dragons bathed to talk to Yellow Cloud about his lost family. He often talked about finding Pa Watkiss's wagon in the blue sand dunes of the Land of the Red Moon, but, recently, he'd tried talking about the strange and frightening dreams he'd been having about his family being carried away by the swarm of black dragons. They came regularly, but were often hazy and full of confusing images.

Jake tried to forget about his search for Ma and Pa and Emmie, and concentrate on his training as he and his teacher flew out over the plains.

Yellow Cloud smiled at Jake, and peeled off, allowing his student to make a manoeuvre on his own that they had only practised together. Jake was making extraordinary progress, and his teacher was very proud of him, and of Match.

Jake dreaded the day when the Natives would leave for their winter home in the Land of the Red Moon. He knew the Garrets expected him to stay behind in Prospect, but, ever since he'd found the remains of Pa Watkiss's wagon, he'd been desperate to search for clues of his family. Staying behind would also mean being separated from Match for several months, and he knew that he would miss him terribly. It was not natural for riders to be separated from their dragons.

Jake had stayed in Prospect for six weeks, since the great, black dragon had burned down the mercantile and attacked the school. He'd been living with the Garrets, and he'd continued to attend school, taking lessons with Miss Ballantine.

He couldn't thank the Garrets enough for

accepting the responsibility of becoming his foster-parents, and Jake couldn't have asked for a more caring home.

He really loved the weekends, though, when he returned to the native settlement to be with Match and his mentor, Yellow Cloud. Today was more difficult, because today Jake had his dreams on his mind.

He pulled Match up so that his body was almost vertical and his wings beat long and slow through the still, cold air. He hovered, gracefully, at the top of the spiral, while Yellow Cloud demonstrated the move they'd practised on the ground.

Yellow Cloud's mount tilted its body and stretched its wings. Then the beast brought its alula joints close to its back, folding its wings, and flipping its head and tail. Suddenly, it turned its body in a barrel roll, spinning through the air, once, twice, three times.

Jake could see the whole process happen in slow motion in his mind. He concentrated on where the pressure in his hands and legs needed to be to steer Match in the same manoeuvre.

It was a difficult trick, and Jake knew, instinctively, that Yellow Cloud was testing him. He knew that he would rarely need to use the manoeuvre. He also knew that the three rolls that Yellow Cloud managed on Gale were nearly impossible to perform safely.

This wouldn't just be a test of Jake's skills; this would be a test of his good sense.

Yellow Cloud rode Gale in a steep curve back to where Match and Jake still hovered. Then he gave the boy the signal to begin.

Jake began a sweeping descent. Then he picked up speed and flew in a straight line across the sky. He took a firm hold of the feathers at the nape of Match's neck. He adjusted the pressure in his thighs at Match's shoulders and his feet at the joints of Match's legs, steering the little dragon into a half-turn. Match tilted on to his side with his wings at full stretch, above and below his body.

It was not Match's favourite position. On their first flight, into the Land of the Red Moon, they had made the same manoeuvre. Jake had panicked and accidentally injured his friend. The little dragon loved his master, but it had taken time to rebuild Match's trust in Jake.

Jake blinked long and slowly, as he always did when he was preparing to enter Match's mind. It was a wonderful sensation when he felt utterly free and at peace with Match, and with the world around him. Unfortunately, right now, he couldn't do it. Match was too nervous. All Jake could feel was the tremble in Match's body, and, when he opened his eyes, all he could see was the desperate little puff of yellowish grey smoke that came from the dragon's nostrils.

Jake turned Match back to his upright position, and flew around to try the manoeuvre again.

The second time Jake turned Match on his side, the little green dragon made the move effortlessly, and the boy, blinking hard again, eased into his mind.

When he was seeing through Match's eyes, Jake could feel the calm, even pulse in the little dragon's neck and the warm rush of air in his throat. There were no nape feathers in his hands and no scales in the grip of his knees, for he was Match and Match was him, and they were flying as one being. He didn't feel the cold air on his skin and he didn't feel breathless in the thin air. He felt exactly as he had the first time he'd become one with Match, and it was just as wonderful.

Match instinctively folded his wings as his body began to spin. The world in front of their eyes began to turn. Suddenly, the ground was above them, and the grey sky, and Yellow Cloud and Gale, were tumbling beneath their feet.

Jake felt Match's tension, and he knew that he must release his friend from the stress of the manoeuvre. He didn't want anything to go wrong, as it had on their first, fateful flight.

Jake reached deeper into the little dragon's mind as he sought to calm Match's growing panic, but his concentration was broken by his own thoughts.

Jake was reminded, once again, of the first time he'd guided Match into this manoeuvre. He couldn't help the terrible crash. He couldn't help remembering Pa Watkiss's wagon and all of his belongings, and he couldn't help wondering when he would ever find his family.

Jake dwelt too long on his sadness, and, suddenly, Match was halfway into a second barrel roll before Jake knew what was happening. Jake squeezed his eyes tightly shut, instinctively, and he felt a jolt and a rush of wind against his face as his mind was forced back into his own body.

There was no time for Jake to ease the pressure in his legs, or to straighten his hands in the feathers at Match's nape.

Disoriented, Match levelled off upside-down. Jake found himself clinging on to his mount, his hands clasped together, his legs dangling, hanging from Match's neck with nowhere to sit, since his dragon was flying the wrong way up.

'Steady . . . Steady, boy,' he said.

Jake concentrated. He needed to find his way back into his friend's mind before it was too late. He couldn't hang on for long, so he cleared his mind, and, very deliberately, he blinked.

Jake didn't have the correct physical contact with Match's body, but his calm and concentration were all he had ever needed to make a good connection with his mount. Match allowed Jake to slip back into his mind without a second thought, and, within moments, they were flying upright, sweeping together through the sky, following Gale's lead.

Jake blinked and was soon back in his own mind, clambering on to his friend's back. Moments later, Match landed safely close to the corral and the hot pool.

Yellow Cloud had made his point: some risks just weren't worth taking. It was crucial never to lose concentration while riding, especially during manoeuvres. Jake had also proved, to himself and to Match, that he could assess risks and act accordingly. More importantly, he had made an even deeper connection with Match, his best friend in the whole world.

'You did well,' said Yellow Cloud.

'I can do better,' said Jake.

'There is time,' said Yellow Cloud, gazing at the dragons wallowing in the hot pool of purple mud where they warmed their blood in preparation for the short flight back to the plateau.

'No,' said Jake.

Yellow Cloud turned his head to look at Jake with a stern expression on his face.

'You tested me,' said Jake, more defiant than confident. 'I passed your test.'

'You took a risk,' said Yellow Cloud. 'You did not need to try to roll your Thunderbird.'

'You call him a Thunderbird, but that isn't the Native word,' said Jake. 'Call them dragons . . . That's what they are.'

Yellow Cloud looked at Jake, and sighed.

'You could have passed the test by refusing to roll Match,' he said.

'Then I wouldn't have learned anything,' said Jake. 'I need to learn, and I need Match to learn, too. I need to go back to the Land of the Red Moon and search for Ma and Pa and Emmie. I need answers.'

'The blacksmith is my friend,' said Yellow Cloud. 'He is your father too, now. You must do as he guides you.'

'What do you guide me to do?' asked Jake.

'You are my brother,' said Yellow Cloud.

'I'm more than that,' said Jake.

He stood and took a couple of steps towards the pool, not waiting for Yellow Cloud's answer. He took the Native bead bracelet with its large red gem from his wrist. He held it in his left hand and swung it in tight circles over his head until it sang a long, high note.

Match looked up, climbed out of the pool, and

allowed the mud to run off his scales. Then he trotted over to Jake. The boy mounted his dragon in one move. Then he took a firm grip of Match's neck feathers, tugging on them until the dragon stepped on to his hind legs. Match spread his wings and walked into the air.

Yellow Cloud followed suit, and the two dragons made their way back to the Native settlement.

2

Match and Jake flew over the Native settlement at dusk on Sunday afternoon. The sky was streaked with pink and orange as the sun struck the horizon.

As he descended in lazy circles over the settlement, Jake could only count about half the usual number of teepees, and his heart sank. He feared that it meant the Natives were preparing to leave for the winter. There were more fires dotted around the settlement than usual, too, including several in the corral where the dragons lay huddled together in groups. Some of them even had blankets and hides draped over them to keep their cold-blooded bodies warm.

Yellow Cloud descended faster than Jake, landing before him. He was quick to remind the boy of his dragon when Jake dismounted.

'Lead Match into the enclosure and cover him quickly. He must not get cold,' said Yellow Cloud. 'Lay him by the fire with his brothers, and feed him before he falls asleep.'

'I need to speak to you,' said Jake urgently. 'The teepees . . . the extra fires . . . What's going on? Are you leaving?'

'Look after your Thunderbird first,' said Yellow Cloud. 'Then we can talk about the settlement. Patience, Dragon Sight, all will be well.'

Jake did as he was told. The two days a week he spent with the dragon meant more to him than anything . . . except finding his family.

By the time they'd finished tending to the animals, the orange-and-pink-edged clouds had drifted away, and the sky was clear and black with a host of glittering stars. The Native settlement bustled with activity. Some of the women prepared a meal, while everyone else shared the tasks of securing the settlement for the winter. Half of the teepees had already been dismantled and stored, along with tools, clothes, blankets, skins, weapons, and baskets and cooking vessels.

'You're leaving, aren't you?' asked Jake.

'We must,' said Yellow Cloud. 'The Thunderbirds cannot live through a mountain winter. They need the sun on their backs.'

'What about the hot pools?' asked Jake. 'What about the extra fires? Don't they keep them warm?' he asked, even though he already knew the answer.

'They are not enough when the earth freezes, when the snows come, when ice covers the water.

Then the Thunderbirds die,' said Yellow Cloud gently.

'So you're abandoning me?' asked Jake.

'I know you have much on your mind, Dragon Sight, but you must think about Match,' said Yellow Cloud. 'The time will come to look for your family. First you must train, and become a rider worthy of your dragon.'

Yellow Cloud seldom used the name that Chief Half Moon had given to Jake when they had become brothers. When he did, Jake knew it meant something special, and he'd used it twice since they'd returned to the plateau.

'You don't understand!' said Jake, his voice rising steadily. 'My family was attacked and taken from me. I have to do something!'

Yellow Cloud laid a hand on the boy's shoulder.

'Not everything is as it seems,' he said. 'Your journey cannot be the same as other men's, but I will help you to make it in any way that I can.'

Jake looked up into Yellow Cloud's kind face, and his mentor held his gaze for several long seconds.

'Tell me, what do you dream, Dragon Sight?' he asked.

3

The whole Native community gathered in the Lodge that evening to eat. It was the biggest teepee at the centre of the settlement, and all the most important business of the tribe was done under its shelter. During the meal, Yellow Cloud retold the story of Jake's dreams to Chief Half Moon. The two men talked seriously for some time about what must be done for their little brother.

Masefield Haskell, the geologist, sat on Jake's other side. Haskell, with his curly, floppy hair, still wore his English tweed suits, and still sketched birds for a hobby. Jake and Haskell had met the first time Jake had run away to the Native settlement. They'd got off to a rough start when Jake had run away from Haskell too, but had become firm friends since. Masefield Haskell was fascinated by the Natives and by the Land of the Red Moon with its strange landscape and extraordinary rocks.

'Why are they talking so earnestly?' Haskell asked Jake.

'I had a dream,' said Jake, 'about the black dragons. I dreamed about the fire and about my family being stolen away.'

'They tell me you had a terrible fever when Yellow Cloud first brought you to Prospect. Are you sure it was just a dream?' asked Haskell. 'It might not sound at all scientific, young man, but, sometimes, dreams are memories.'

'I wish you'd tell that to Yellow Cloud and Chief Half Moon, and to the Garrets,' said Jake. 'I'm sure my dreams are very important. I think Yellow Cloud is beginning to think so too, but they're bound to take you seriously.'

'In that case, I shall,' said Haskell.

'Thank you,' said Jake.

'Are you thanking me for the science or for speaking up for you?' asked Haskell. 'Because I should think you might thank me for both, given the circumstances.'

'I do,' said Jake. 'I thank you with all my heart.'

'Well, there's no need for that, dear boy,' said Haskell, blushing slightly.

Suddenly, Chief Half Moon raised his hands, and silence fell on the lodge. The old Chief of the Natives in his tall top hat, adorned with dragon feathers, his silvery hair falling in long strands from under it, began to speak. Jake had learned the Natives' language, but White Thunder, his best friend, or

Yellow Cloud still translated whenever their Chief spoke.

'Our little brother Dragon Sight has a head full of dreams,' said Yellow Cloud. 'The sleep takes him, and the pictures come.'

Chief Half Moon gestured at one of the old women, sitting half a dozen places to his left. She waved to White Thunder, who crossed the Lodge to do her bidding. Then Chief Half Moon said, 'He dreams of the rogue Thunderbirds and their masters. He dreams of his lost people and of the Land of the Red Moon. Dragon Sight, special among us, sees through the eye of the dragon, and through the vision of his dreams.'

The Chief bowed his head for a moment to allow for a ripple of gasps to pass through the Lodge. Much was expected of Dragon Sight, but no one anticipated that one so young would develop his skills so fast.

'We must help Dragon Sight to see in his dreams what is good and pure and right,' he continued. 'We must help him to banish from his mind his fears of what is evil and rotten and wrong.'

White Thunder, who had crept out of the Lodge while Chief Half Moon was speaking, returned. She walked quietly around the edge of the large teepee, hardly noticed by anyone, except her friend Jake. When she reached the old woman, she handed her a small parcel.

When Chief Half Moon had finished speaking, he gestured again to the old woman, who rose and shuffled over to the Chief.

Yellow Cloud leaned towards Jake, and said, 'Stand before Chief Half Moon.'

Jake hesitated for a moment while the Chief and the old woman exchanged a greeting, and she handed the old man the parcel. Once she turned away, the boy stood and walked the few paces to stand before Chief Half Moon.

'The dreamcatcher is an ancient tool of our people,' Yellow Cloud translated. 'Hang it above your sleeping place, and it will reveal your best and truest dreams. It will also banish your worst and most evil nightmares.'

Chief Half Moon held out the little parcel to Jake, who took it and bowed his head. It was hard to look at the Chief when he was being so serious, but Jake also wanted to examine the parcel. He dared not unwrap it, though, at least not yet.

Chief Half Moon laid a hand on Jake's shoulder, and Jake lifted his eyes to the old man's face. His black eyes glistened in the firelight, and the corner of his mouth lifted slightly, as if he might smile. Jake smiled back, clutching the dreamcatcher to his chest. Then he returned to his place in the circle.

*

Jake was supposed to return to Prospect before dark, but it had grown late. Yellow Cloud wouldn't risk flying in the freezing cold.

As many of the teepees had been dismantled, most of the Natives were sleeping in the Lodge, and Jake was happy to join them. When it was time to bed down, Jake unwrapped his dreamcatcher.

The small, wooden hoop had a lattice of strong sinew strung across it like an elaborate spider's web. Several polished blue beads were sewn into the web, and three little twists of bright blue feathers hung from more beads at the bottom of the hoop.

'It's so pretty,' Jake said to Yellow Cloud.

'Blue Jay makes the finest and most beautiful dreamcatchers,' said Yellow Cloud. 'They are rarely given, and you are lucky to have one.'

'Will it truly help?' asked Jake.

'It will help you to learn the truth,' said Yellow Cloud. 'Truths are often hidden in stories or even in feelings, and it is difficult to know them.'

'The dreams are frightening,' said Jake, his head bowed. He hated to admit that he was afraid, but he also wanted to know what had happened to his family.

'There is nothing to fear,' said Yellow Cloud. 'The dreamcatcher will see to that. Everything will become clearer, and you will know the truth, in time.'

The Native took the dreamcatcher gently from

Jake's hands. He twisted a section of the Lodge's lining and tied the dreamcatcher to it so that it hung above where the boy would be sleeping.

'Sleep well, little brother,' he said.

'Thank you,' said Jake. As he lay down and pulled his blanket up to his chin, he felt calmer than he had for weeks. He looked up at the little dreamcatcher above his head. The only thing he didn't know for sure was what his dreams would reveal to him.

4

A cool, watery sun rose over Prospect. The ground was hard and white with frost, and the sky was steely grey. The water of the river was darker and deeper and ran faster as the year came to an end. The last of the trade boats had come and gone, and the landing stage on the bend of the river would be idle until the spring.

At the forge, the cock crowed later every day. That didn't stop Pius Garret rising early every morning to light the furnace and set to work making the goods that the townsfolk needed.

Just as the Natives were packing to move for the winter, the people of Prospect were battening down the hatches. They were maintaining their wooden buildings, fixing shutters at the windows, and cutting logs for their fires. They were killing livestock for salting meat, and filling their root cellars with fruit and vegetables to last the winter.

The days to come would be short and the nights long. They would need candles and lamp oil, and lots of layers of warm clothes. They would need strong boots and winter coats to keep out the damp and chill. There was much darning of socks, and blankets and quilts were taken out of chests and aired in the last of the sunshine.

Winter was just around the corner, and the people of Prospect were determined to be ready for the hardest of seasons.

'There you are! Thank goodness you're safe!' said Elizabeth Garret as Jake walked through the door. 'Now, hurry up or you'll be late for school. Eliza and the twins have already left.'

Then Yellow Cloud followed Jake into the kitchen, and Mrs Garret stopped washing dishes and wiped her hands.

'Run and get Mr Garret, Jake,' she said. Jake did as he was told, and Mrs Garret gestured for Yellow Cloud to sit down. 'How can we help you?' she asked.

'I've come to talk about Jake,' said Yellow Cloud.

'He should have come home last night,' said Mrs Garret. 'Thank you for bringing him, but he really mustn't be late for school.'

'As you wish,' said Yellow Cloud. 'If I could talk to you and Mr Garret?'

At that moment, Jake returned with Pius. The blacksmith had taken off his leather apron and was wiping the sweat from his brow with a large handkerchief. When he'd finished, he held out his hand to Yellow Cloud, who shook it.

'Straight off to school now,' Mrs Garret told Jake, handing him his lunch, 'or Miss Ballantine will keep you behind for being late.'

'But –' began Jake.

'Do as Mrs Garret tells you,' said Pius. His voice was firm, but he put a reassuring hand on Jake's shoulder, nevertheless.

Jake didn't want to go to school, but he had no choice, so he said his goodbyes, and ran out of the forge house. He wanted to hear what the Garrets and Yellow Cloud had to say, but he guessed that he would know soon enough. He also knew that, whatever was said, he didn't have the power to change their decisions.

5

On Wednesday, at lunch time, Masefield Haskell rode into Prospect on his mule, Jenny. The mule was heavily laden with rolls of paper, wrapped in canvas and tied with leather thongs. It was also loaded up with canvas bags full of rock and soil samples. As a geologist, Haskell was fascinated by the Land of the Red Moon, which he had spent every waking moment of the last six weeks mapping.

He had sketched and taken samples of the flora and the soil, and of the sand, rocks and gems that he had found. He had even taken samples of the water and of the mists. He had recorded the weather and sketched the strange creatures and the dragons. He had even collected feathers and scales shed by the Thunderbirds.

Masefield Haskell was a very thorough and capable scientist. He had done an excellent job of mapping and recording the Native lands, if he did say so himself, but winter was coming, and it was time to go home. Besides, he needed to sort through the information he had gathered and put it all in order.

Haskell had returned to Prospect, because the weather was bitterly cold, and, once the Natives left for the Land of the Red Moon, no one would come back until the spring. It was easy to fly in and out, but during the winter the Thunderbirds remained in the Land of the Red Moon.

Haskell's maps would, no doubt, bring him back to Prospect, eventually, but it would be a long and difficult journey, on foot. Besides, he had to go back to town. If he wanted to be paid by the Hudson's Bay Company, he must report to the new boss of Prospect, who was reputed to be even fiercer than the old one.

McKenzie, who had once given his name to the town, had done all his business sitting on a stool in the mercantile store, or sitting in the saloon, both of which he owned. He also did most of his business with his old friend and general dogsbody, Trapper Watkiss, hovering close by.

People didn't like Nathan McKenzie very much, but most of them were still a little afraid of him. Some of them still worked for him too, fixing up the ruined saloon and rebuilding the mercantile, which had both been attacked by the great black dragon.

Since the dragon had done its damage, everyone

in Prospect was aware that Nathan McKenzie had been busy trying to rescue his businesses and his reputation. He was a proud man, and everyone could see that one day he'd make his move to rename the town McKenzie's Prospect once more. So, when Masefield Haskell had asked for instructions, McKenzie had waved him away, telling him that he was far too busy and to get on with things.

Haskell knew that it would take weeks for the new man to arrive from the Hudson's Bay Company. He was more than happy to use that time to research the areas inhabited by the Natives . . . In fact, it was a dream come true. Besides, he wasn't sure if anyone was paying him, and he wasn't the sort of man who wasted an opportunity.

Horton Needham had rolled into town in the second week of November with all the fuss and bother that a portly man in a formal suit and a tall hat could muster. He had a large, round face with no hair on it, and he had very little bristly grey hair on his great, domed head. It was almost entirely visible because his too-small hat was perched very high upon it. He also carried a black walking cane.

The coach that Needham and his fellow travellers arrived in creaked under the weight of an abundance of monogrammed luggage. The brass label on his suitcases read:

H. M. N.
HUDSON'S BAY COMPANY,
ROCKY MOUNTAINS, WEST

Horton Michaelmas Needham was a man who insisted on grand titles. He'd worked for Hudson's Bay for nearly twenty years and he was every inch a 'company' man.

Needham had been sent to Prospect for three reasons:

1. to investigate the gems that McKenzie had found;
2. to straighten out the problems with the Natives; and
3. to make a lot of money for the company.

In short, Horton Needham had been sent to Prospect because he was a tough, no-nonsense sort of man who would get the job done without any fuss or bother.

The new boss had brought with him his very own secretary and geologist. He had never heard of Masefield Haskell and he had no reason to trust

McKenzie's geologist over his own hand-picked expert.

On Horton Needham's arrival, Nathan McKenzie had given up his house. He'd had no choice, since he couldn't house his guests in the upstairs rooms of the saloon, which were still undergoing repairs. He also had to close the bar to give Needham office space. Tables and chairs were arranged and other furniture was brought in especially. The Hudson's Bay Company offered a miserly rent for the saloon, and McKenzie had no choice but to accept it.

Soon the saloon was full of Boss Needham's account books and ledgers. He even hired a local clerk to take over the secretarial duties. There were also piles of papers and writing equipment, chairs and desks and record cards, and a number of boxes marked 'miscellaneous'.

Needham was a man who liked to keep records. He liked to know whom he was talking to and why, and exactly who knew what, and he liked to know everything that anyone else knew. Most of all, Horton Needham liked to know what was the truth and what was rumour. He soon decided that Trapper Watkiss, with his red beard and barrel chest, was an old fool who talked a lot of nonsense. In fact, it was Horton Needham's opinion that Watkiss talked so much nonsense he needed locking up for it.

He didn't trust Sheriff Sykes either, because, if he

didn't recognize a madman like Trapper Watkiss when he saw one, what use would the sheriff be to the new boss? No use at all, that's what!

Needham soon banished Trapper Watkiss from his office altogether. He didn't like the way the old mountain man looked, or spoke, or, for that matter, the way he smelled of the outdoors. Of course, the fact that Needham banished Trapper Watkiss from his office didn't stop McKenzie using his old friend to run Needham's errands, and he was soon sending Watkiss all over Prospect to do his bidding.

Overall, though, Horton Needham quickly decided that life in Prospect could be perfectly comfortable. He had a secretary and a geologist, and he had Nathan McKenzie's house to live in and Nathan McKenzie's saloon to work from. What's more, he thought smugly as he put his feet up on his new desk, Needham had Nathan McKenzie at his beck and call from dawn till dusk and for many of the hours of darkness.

6

'What you doin' in these parts?' Trapper Watkiss asked Haskell as they met at the edge of town on the third Wednesday of November.

'Returning to Prospect from the Land of the Red Moon,' said Haskell. 'Doesn't that sound like a wonderful place?'

'I s'pose,' said Trapper Watkiss, not sure what to make of the young man.

'Well, I can tell you that it is the *most* wonderful place,' said Haskell.

'What you doin' back here then?' asked Trapper Watkiss.

'I've come to take up my position as geologist to the Hudson's Bay Company,' said Haskell.

'Don't you know when you ain't wanted, professor?' asked Trapper Watkiss. 'New boss has got a jolly-gist of his own.'

'So, the Hudson's Bay Company has sent the new boss,' said Haskell. 'When did he arrive?'

'A week since . . . ten days, maybe,' said Trapper

Watkiss. 'Terrible busybody. Don't like no one. Took over the McKenzie house and the saloon. Got a secker-tree and a jolly-gist. Big head, bigger belly, and a tiny top hat. Foolish he looks.'

'The geologist has a top hat?' asked Haskell.

'No,' said Trapper Watkiss, 'the new boss has a top hat . . . and a jolly-gist, too.'

'So, he won't be needing my services?' asked Haskell.

'Not a bit,' said Trapper Watkiss.

'Well, we'll just have to see about that,' said Haskell, patting one of his canvas bags. 'He might change his mind when he discovers that I've made a full geological and cartographical survey of the extraordinary lands presided over by the Natives.'

'What's that when it's a summink or other?' asked Trapper Watkiss.

'What the land's made of and where everything is,' said Haskell. 'That's the something or other it is, and no mistake.'

'Well then, you'll find him at the saloon,' said Trapper Watkiss. 'Needham, they call him.'

'Tomorrow, perhaps,' said Haskell, 'once I've unpacked and settled in.'

'Shall I tell Mr McKenzie you're back?' asked Trapper Watkiss.

'No need,' said Haskell. 'Everyone will find out soon enough.' With that, he raised his hat to Trapper

Watkiss, turned Jenny on the spot, and took the shortest route to Pius Garret's forge.

Jacob Polson had been in Prospect for three days and he wasn't glad of very much at all. He wasn't glad of the cold winds and the hard ground and the icy puddles. He wasn't glad of the bare trees and the grey skies and of walking to school and home again in the half-light.

He was glad of Miss Ballantine and her library. He was glad of the latest H. N. Matchstruck novel, *The Plateau of Raging Tempests*, which his teacher had lent to him. He was glad of his dreamcatcher, which made going to sleep so much easier. He thought that, one day soon, he might even understand his dreams. He knew they were about his family, but he still wasn't sure of the details.

He was also glad when he arrived in Mrs Garret's kitchen, on Wednesday afternoon, to find Masefield Haskell.

Haskell was sitting at the table drinking milk and eating cookies. Jake was so glad to see the scientist that he almost blushed as he talked too fast and asked too many questions.

'Mr Haskell!' he exclaimed. 'Are you back for good? Have the Natives gone? Did you find anything in the Land of the Red Moon? Did you see Pa Watkiss's wagon? Did you meet anyone there who could have been Ma or Pa? Did you meet a little girl with a rag doll? Are the Natives hiding things from me? Tell me everything!'

'Slow down, Jacob,' said Mrs Garret, 'and show some manners.'

'I'm sorry, Mrs Garret,' said Jake, 'but it's very, very important.'

'Let Mr Haskell drink his milk and eat his cookies,' said Mrs Garret, 'and wash your hands, so you can have some too. Eliza and the boys are home, and there's time before supper for a nice chat.'

When he had drunk half his glass of milk and had two cookies left, Masefield Haskell wiped his mouth with his napkin and started counting things off on his fingers.

'Yes,' he said, and then, 'No. Yes. No. No. No. No. I should think not. That would take a terribly long time and require feats of memory beyond my abilities, I'm afraid.'

'What?' asked Jake, putting down his half-finished glass of milk, and reaching for his second cookie.

'The answers to your questions,' said Haskell.

'Oh,' said Jake. 'I'm not sure which answers went with what questions.'

'A scientist should always be sure,' said Haskell.

'I'm not a scientist, though,' said Jake. 'I'm a boy.'

'You should think about that,' said Haskell, very

serious. 'You should wonder whether *others* would call you a boy.'

Jake did think for a moment.

'Thank you,' he said eventually.

Haskell had picked up his glass of milk again, but hesitated before taking another sip.

'Are you thanking me for suggesting you think about how others see you?' he asked. 'Or for suggesting you might wonder whether people think you're still a boy? Because I should think you might thank me for both, given the circumstances.'

'I do thank you for both,' said Jake, smiling at Haskell's little habit of thinking about everything from two directions. 'Although, they're sort of the same thing. Plenty of boys my age work on their father's farm or else at some job or other.'

'Plenty,' agreed Haskell, putting down his glass and picking up a cookie. Jake clearly had something to say, and Haskell didn't in the least mind listening.

'All of the Native boys who become riders are men just as soon as they first sit on a dragon,' said Jake.

'That's true,' said Haskell, between bites.

'They don't treat me like a man, though,' said Jake. 'They tell me what to do, and they don't allow me to make my own decisions.'

'They respect the decisions of their elders,' said Haskell, putting down his cookie. 'Plenty of grown men do as they're told. Doesn't Yellow Cloud do what Chief Half Moon tells him? Doesn't Tall Elk?'

'I suppose so,' said Jake.

'There you have it then,' said Masefield Haskell.

'I want to spend the winter in the Land of the Red Moon,' said Jake. 'I told them about my dreams, but they said I must do as Mr Garret wishes.'

'And so you must,' said Haskell.

'So you won't help me either?' asked Jake, suddenly impatient.

'I answered your questions, didn't I?' asked Haskell, frowning. 'There's no need to be so ungrateful, you young pup.'

'Actually, you didn't,' said Jake. 'Not so that I could understand the answers.'

Haskell popped the last of his cookie in his mouth and drained his glass. Then he rested his hands on the table.

'What do you want to know?' he asked.

'Everything!' said Jake, wringing his hands. 'Most of all, though, I want to know if you found Pa Watkiss's wagon. I want to know if my parents could be in the Land of the Red Moon. I want to know if the Natives are truly my family or if they're deceiving me.'

By the time he'd finished, Jake was talking very fast, and the last of his milk and cookies were completely forgotten.

Haskell reached out, tentatively, and patted Jake on his left arm, the one that had been burned in the fire all those weeks ago. Jake stopped wringing his hands. He opened his left hand, palm up, and looked at it. He saw the circular scar in the shape of scales wrapped around a dark, round scar in his palm. It itched and throbbed slightly. He placed his right hand over it and squeezed his palms together.

'What's the matter?' asked Mrs Garret, leaning over to try to take a look at Jake's scar. She'd first seen the injury when it had been infected, and caused the fever that had nearly killed him.

'It's nothing,' said Jake.

Mrs Garret tutted and walked away to continue making supper.

'I'll tell you whatever you want to know, if you'll tell me one thing in exchange,' Haskell said to Jake, leaning forward.

'Anything,' said Jake.

'What's wrong with your hand?' asked Haskell in a whisper.

'When it itches, it's always because it's trying to tell me something,' said Jake. 'I just don't know what it is.'

'Then we should find out,' said Haskell. 'Now, whatever you want to ask me, you can rest assured, I have all the answers in my notes and maps and samples.'

'It's not that so much,' said Jake. 'I've been to the Land of the Red Moon, remember? I want to know if you saw Pa Watkiss's wagon, and his meat barrel and his fiddle. I want to know if you met anyone there who wasn't a Native.'

'How could that possibly be?' asked Haskell. 'No white man ever had the privilege of passing into the Land of the Red Moon before you. You know that!'

'I know,' said Jake. 'I was allowed in because I'm one of them, because of my burns, and because of this.' He thrust his hand out again, spreading his fingers so that his palm was broad and flat, the round scar purple and bulging in his skin.

Haskell reached his hand out over Jake's, and let it hover there, without quite touching it.

'It feels warm,' he said.

'Yes,' said Jake, 'and it itches.'

'Why do they call you Dragon Sight?' asked Haskell.

'Because I see through the eyes of the dragon,' said Jake.

'Which means?' asked Haskell.

'When I ride Match,' said Jake, 'it's as if I'm inside his head, as if we're the same thing. I see through his eyes. I think with his mind. I control his body with my thoughts.'

'How extraordinary,' said Haskell, leaning forward

43

to peer into Jake's eyes. Jake held his gaze for a moment, and then blinked and sat back in his chair, breaking the stare. 'It's really quite hard to believe.'

'What is?' asked Jake.

'That you could become so much a part of them, so quickly,' said Haskell. 'It's almost as if you don't belong in Prospect at all.'

'I belong with Match,' said Jake, rising from his chair to look out of the kitchen window into the darkness.

'You want to go back to the Land of the Red Moon for the winter,' said Haskell. 'You want to leave Prospect and live with the Natives.'

'I want to find my family,' said Jake with his back to the geologist.

'Didn't they die in the fire at the fording place upriver?' asked Haskell gently. 'Wasn't that the great tragedy everyone was talking about last summer?'

Jake slowly turned to face the Englishman, and said, 'That was when there was no other explanation, before I started dreaming, before the black dragon came to Prospect and set fire to the mercantile and the saloon bar, and attacked the school.'

'And now?'

'Now we know there are dragons,' said Jake, 'and I know what I dreamed.'

'Has the dreamcatcher shown you the truth?' asked Haskell.

'I don't understand everything it's shown me,' said Jake, 'but I do know that I must search for my family.'

'You believe they're in the Land of the Red Moon!' said Haskell. 'That's why you asked if I'd seen them?'

'Yes,' said Jake. 'I believe that something in the evil dragons' minds made them steal my family away.'

He frowned and then buried his face in his hands. When the boy lifted his face again, Haskell could see real pain and frustration in his eyes.

'But you don't know?' the geologist asked.

'I don't know what it all means,' said Jake.

'Then we must find out,' said Haskell. He sounded determined, and he banged his fist down hard on the kitchen table. In fact, his fist landed so hard, so close to his glass that it seemed to hop into the air and then land again, slightly askew.

Mrs Garret turned away from the stove where she was basting a joint of meat for supper.

'What must we find out, Mr Haskell?' she asked. 'I'm not sure you should be putting ideas in Jacob's head.'

'No need, madam,' said Haskell. 'Jake's got plenty

of ideas in his head, all of his own thinking . . . Or should I say he dreamed them up?'

Jake smiled slightly. Then Haskell threw back his head and laughed heartily, making Jake jump.

'Dreamed them up!' exclaimed Haskell again, between guffaws.

7

The townsfolk of Prospect had a meeting, and decided that they would celebrate Thanksgiving on November 28th that year, 1850. Many of the towns and cities in many of the States celebrated Thanksgiving on that day, and Prospect was no exception.

It was a cold, clear, crisp Thursday morning. The ground was hard and white. Every blade of grass, every leaf, every twig and rock was covered in a film of frost that glinted and twinkled in the morning sunshine.

The sky was a sharp, bright blue and utterly cloudless. Every chimney sent curlicues of pale grey smoke into the blanket of blue above, which disappeared almost as soon as they hit the cold air, as if they'd never existed. Little gusts of steam streamed from breathing, pink noses and warm mouths as neighbours greeted each other. Feet stamped to keep warm, and hands clapped in their knitted mittens.

It could not have been a more perfect day for the

people of Prospect to gather in the church to give thanks for their safe passage through the old year, and to pray for the year to come.

It was the first time that the front pew, usually taken by the McKenzie/Sykes family, was shared. Nathan McKenzie and his son Horace, and Nathan's sister Mrs Sykes and her son, Sheriff Lem Sykes, were accompanied by Horton Needham. It was his first appearance in Prospect's church, and he insisted on taking the end of the pew closest to the aisle. He wanted the town's people to know exactly how important he was.

The Garrets' pew was filled up with Masefield Haskell and Merry Mack, who had offered the geologist lodgings while the saloon was repaired, since there was no one there to cook for at present. The tiny little old woman, who was always as neat as a new pin, and as busy as a bee, lived in the middle of Main Street, next to the mercantile, so it was most convenient. Besides, she had the freshest eggs and the best home-smoked ham, which was Haskell's favourite.

The only person not in church on Thanksgiving was Trapper Watkiss. He didn't like the preacher, and he didn't like the old woman who played the piano. He never tired of observing that he preferred the nuns that had looked after him when he was a child in the convent back east, even if they had boxed his ears at the slightest provocation. He'd never taken much to religious ways, but he liked to be able to call his preacher Father.

When he did go to church at Christmas, Easter and Thanksgiving, Trapper Watkiss would sit in the pew behind his old friend Nathan McKenzie. However, he had no intention of sitting breathing down Horton Needham's pink neck.

So it was that Trapper Watkiss walked briskly up and down outside the church, breathing on his hands to warm them, while everyone else in Prospect sat inside, in the warm. He'd just stopped at the end of his walk to turn to walk the other way when a huge shadow swept over him, blocking out the sun, which was as high in the sky as it was going to get.

Trapper Watkiss tilted the brim of his hat and looked up into the bright blue sky, only to be confronted by the sight of the dappled green belly of a large dragon as it flew right over him, wings spread wide as it glided past.

Trapper Watkiss cursed and spat. He jumped up and down, cursed again, and then he ran up the church steps just as the bell began to ring for the end of the service.

The church doors opened wide, and the preacher stepped out to bid farewell to his congregation. The men and women, and boys and girls of Prospect were gathered behind him, making ready to wish each other a happy Thanksgiving.

Several of the townsfolk turned as Miss Ballantine, the school teacher, in her good, wool coat asked, 'Goodness, Mr Watkiss, are you quite well?'

A hush fell over the crowd at the extraordinary sight of a white-faced, wide-eyed Trapper Watkiss, standing facing them on the church steps. He spread his arms wide, and, aware that he had everyone's attention, he made his first ever public declaration.

'THERE BE DRAGONS!' he cried.

Jake didn't need to hear Trapper Watkiss's words twice. He jostled and nudged his way to the front of the crowd, with David and Michael ducking under elbows and diving between legs to keep up with him. Eliza managed to stay close by too.

Jake, Eliza and the twins trotted down the church steps, past Trapper Watkiss. They peered into the sky, and watched Gale fly in the direction of Garret's field. Then they waved as Yellow Cloud made Gale bow in mid-air and breathe a little flame.

'There's only one dragon,' said Pius Garret, coming up beside Trapper Watkiss.

The old man was so nervous he was wringing his scruffy hat in his grubby hands, and peering nervously at the congregation, obviously looking for someone.

Horton Needham strode purposefully over to Trapper Watkiss, determined to put a halt to things, immediately. Nathan McKenzie fell in step with him as soon as he realized what was afoot.

'Stop making a fool of yourself,' said Needham, looking down his nose at Watkiss. 'And you are?' he asked Pius Garret.

Garret held out his hand. The Hudson's Bay Company man looked at his own white gloves and then at Garret's calloused workman's hand, and decided against shaking it.

'Pius Garret,' said the blacksmith, 'from the forge.'

'Indeed,' said Needham, turning away for lack of interest.

'There be dragons!' said Trapper Watkiss again.

Needham turned on his heel, and stared.

'Say that again,' he said.

'I don't like dragons, nor Injuns, neither,' said Trapper.

'One Injun . . . Native, and one dragon,' said Garret. 'He's my guest for lunch. More will arrive later to do some trading. Perhaps you'd like to join us, Mr McKenzie. You must have stock to trade?'

Horton Needham spun to face the blacksmith and stepped in before McKenzie could answer.

'The Hudson's Bay Company has stock to trade,' he said. 'McKenzie can no doubt show me the place.' Needham took out his pocket watch on the chain that looped across his striped waistcoat. 'Three o'clock sharp,' he said, and snapped the watch case shut.

'We must go,' said Elizabeth Garret, 'or our guest will arrive before us.'

'Yes, we must,' said Pius Garret, not making the mistake of offering his hand to Needham a second time. He didn't make the mistake of pointing out that the Natives had no pocket watches, either, or that three o'clock sharp meant nothing to them. He simply turned, took his wife's arm, and started down the church steps. 'Where are the children?' he asked her.

'They couldn't wait for us,' said Elizabeth. 'I don't think I've ever seen Jake move so fast.'

'Do you think he's guessed?' Pius Garret asked his wife.

'Not for a single moment,' said Elizabeth. 'I heard him talking with Mr Haskell only yesterday. I suspect our plans will come as a total surprise to him.'

'All the better,' said the blacksmith, smiling gleefully. 'I do love surprises.'

'Rest assured,' said Elizabeth, 'Jacob Polson is going to love this surprise just as much as you're going to love the look on his face when we tell him.'

'I hope you're right, Elizabeth,' said Pius.

'When am I ever wrong?' she asked, laughing her high, tinkling laugh.

8

Yellow Cloud arrived at Garret's forge a few minutes ahead of Jake, Eliza and the twins. The children were all puffing and panting by the time they got there, breathing swirls of curling white steam into the chilly air. David and Michael pretended they were dragons, snorting and huffing as they caught their breath. It was a fun game to play, but, when it came to standing face to face with the beast, only Jake was brave enough.

After giving Gale a welcoming pat and nodding to his teacher, Jake hurried into the forge and collected a pile of warm blankets from behind the furnace. He stepped back into the crisp air and started spreading them over Gale to keep him comfortable. Yellow Cloud's mount had already found the cosiest place outside, huddled against the chimney wall of the forge, where the bricks were warm from the furnace inside.

After a few minutes' watching Yellow Cloud tending to Gale, Eliza walked slowly over to him.

'Hello, sir,' she said.

'Hello, Eliza,' said Yellow Cloud, who had grown to like Pius Garret's feisty daughter almost as much as he respected the blacksmith. 'Your father invited me to your special feast today.'

'Thanksgiving,' said Eliza.

'I don't understand,' said Yellow Cloud, frowning.

'You said it was special,' said Eliza, 'and that's because it's Thanksgiving. We went to church to give thanks for our health and well-being throughout the year.'

'And for the harvest,' said Michael. 'That's what Miss Ballantine said.'

'And for family, and our friends,' said David.

'I gave thanks for you,' Jake whispered, so that only Yellow Cloud would hear him, 'and for Match.'

Yellow Cloud turned to look at Jake, reading the sadness on the boy's face.

He does not know, thought the Native, and decided that he must keep the Garrets' secret.

A moment later, they all heard Elizabeth Garret's tinkling laugh. David and Michael ran to meet their parents, full of the excitement of seeing the dragon. Eliza walked slowly up the lane, and Yellow Cloud and Jake hovered over the dragon for a minute more before stepping towards the kitchen door. It was time to share a Thanksgiving meal.

*

Mrs Garret had done a lot of preparation the day before, but there was still gravy to make and green beans to boil and beets to finish off. The sweet pumpkin pudding had been steaming while everyone was in church, and the turkey was roasting nicely. There were potatoes and cranberries, and thick cream to go with the pudding. There was milk for the children and beer for Pius, and even a bottle of sweet wine. She had also made savoury biscuits to soak up the gravy, even though she thought it was extravagant to serve potatoes and biscuits on the same plate. It was quite a feast.

The table was covered with the best linen cloth and napkins. It was laid with the best dishes, and Mrs Garret's wedding silver, which Mr Garret's granddaddy had sent all the way from Ireland. The kitchen was warm and welcoming, and everyone was happy.

Jake wondered about his own happiness. He wanted to give thanks for the Garrets and for Match and his friends at the settlement, but he was torn. He just knew that he needed to be in the Land of the Red Moon rather than in Prospect over the winter. He needed to search for his ma and pa, and for his sister, Emmie. If he was allowed to do that, he'd really have something to give thanks for.

It was too late, though. He'd tried to persuade them that he must go, and he'd failed. There was nothing more that he could do.

'Jake,' said Pius Garret, cutting through his thoughts. 'Would you say grace for us, please?'

Jake looked from Pius Garret to Mrs Garret, and then at Yellow Cloud. Why was he being asked to say grace? Pius Garret usually led the prayers at suppertime. On Sundays, the children took turns to say grace, and they each took a turn on their birthdays.

Jake reached out his hands to Michael, sitting on one side of him, and Yellow Cloud, on the other, and he bowed his head. Everyone sitting around the table held hands as Jake began to speak.

'Come, Lord Jesus, be our guest;
And bless what you have bestowed.
O give thanks unto the Lord, for He is good:
For His mercy endureth forever.
Amen.'

'Amen,' said everyone together.

'What a lovely prayer,' said Mrs Garret. 'Where did you learn it, Jake?'

'My father would say it on Sundays and holidays,' said Jake. 'I thought I should say it today, as it's Thanksgiving.'

'Of course you should,' said Mrs Garret.

Jake looked down at his plate and reached for the nearest dish to serve himself some food. He'd taken the beets, which Mrs Garret knew he would usually avoid if she let him.

'You don't have to have beets today,' she said gently.

Jake knew that Mrs Garret was trying to be kind to him, and he could almost feel the sympathy in her eyes. He wasn't sure he could quite bring himself to look at her, though.

'Oh,' he said, finally, putting down the beets and looking up. He could feel tears prickling at the corners of his eyes, but he blinked them back.

'Eat up, everyone,' Mrs Garret said, changing the subject swiftly, 'and pass Jake the potatoes. There's hardly anything on his plate and he must be starving after Reverend Varvel's sermon.'

'We're all starving after Reverend Varvel's sermon,' said Pius Garret. 'Did you ever meet such a –'

'Not in front of the children,' said Mrs Garret, before he could finish his sentence.

Jake didn't want to think about Reverend Varvel's sermon, but at least the conversation gave him a chance to swallow his tears and compose himself.

'I can guess,' said Eliza.

'I wish you wouldn't,' said Mrs Garret.

'Bore?' asked Eliza.

'Worse,' said Mr Garret, half-smiling.

'Blowhard?' asked Eliza.

'Worse,' said her father.

Jake sat back and thought about how very normal his adoptive family was, and how very normal his own family had been, once upon a time. All he wanted was a chance to be part of his very own normal family again, with Pa and Ma and Emmie.

'Don't encourage her, Pius,' said Mrs Garret. 'Besides, Eliza, I don't think that word means what you think it means. Methodists don't boast, Eliza, they serve.'

Jake heard the low rumble of Pius Garret's laugh, and, as always, he marvelled at how such a low note could come from such a compact body. It brought him back into the conversation that he'd only been half-listening to.

'He isn't the most humble man, though, is he, Elizabeth?' asked Pius.

'I suspect that's because he's trying to impress a certain young woman,' she said. 'I have to say that long, dull sermons aren't going to win *that* girl's heart.'

'Oh?' asked Pius. 'Then what might?'

'I'm not saying anything,' said Elizabeth Garret, 'but, if that young lady's choice of books is any indication, she'll want a man with a bit more adventure in him than our Methodist preacher.'

'A sheriff, perhaps?' asked Jake.

'Sheriff Sykes and Miss Ballantine!' gasped Eliza.

'Well, that's let the cat out of the bag,' said Pius.

'But at least it stopped her guessing what terrible things you were thinking about poor Lawrence Varvel,' said Elizabeth.

'You really are a very clever woman, Elizabeth Garret,' said Mr Garret, smiling.

'Why else would you have married me?' asked Mrs Garret, her eyes twinkling at her husband.

Pius stuck his fork in the beets on his plate. He laughed and, with hardly a hint of sarcasm in his voice, he said, 'Because you make the finest beets for a hundred square miles, and no mistake.'

'Fine,' said Elizabeth, her cheeks flushed, 'no one has to eat beets today.'

Everyone laughed. Everyone except for Jake.

'Right, Jacob Polson,' Mrs Garret said suddenly. 'I can't bear to look at your sad face any longer, and I can't bear to watch you pushing your food around your plate when you've got more good reasons than most to give thanks. Now listen carefully, because Mr Garret and I, and Yellow Cloud too, have got some news for you.'

9

Mrs Garret didn't get any further. There was a clattering of hooves in the yard outside the forge, and David and Michael were out of their chairs and at the kitchen window in no time. Eliza tossed her napkin on to her empty plate and joined them.

'The Natives are here,' she cried as she looked out of the window.

'Lots of them,' said David.

'On lots of Appaloosas,' said Michael.

In no time at all the whole family was putting on coats and pouring out to meet Yellow Cloud's brothers, neighbours and friends.

The Natives had done regular trade with Prospect for as long as the town had stood on the bend in the river. Yellow Cloud visited most often, but, from time to time, others would come with him. At this time of year, the Natives came in a large group to trade with the people of Prospect, before they left for the Land of the Red Moon.

Much of that trade was with the blacksmith as the

Natives were always in need of well-made horseshoes, cooking vessels and nails, as well as knives, axeheads and even stirrups. It had become the custom for the Natives to visit the forge when trading with the townsfolk, so Michael and David had spent all of the previous Saturday collecting wood to build an impressive bonfire at the end of Garret's field to welcome their visitors.

In return, the Natives rode down from the plateau, bringing skins and baskets and decorative feathers in saddle bags and panniers. They also brought strings of small, polished blue and green gems, similar to the ones they wore around their wrists and ankles.

On this occasion, Yellow Cloud had brought the dried, salted fish that Elizabeth Garret was so fond of, and had given it to her as thanks for her hospitality.

The Natives also brought lumps of fine quality pitch that could be melted and used to waterproof canvas wagon covers. It was of a far better quality than anything the townspeople could manufacture, and was popular with wagon-trainers passing through.

As Pius Garret lit the great bonfire to signal the start of trading, the people of Prospect walked to his field or rode on horseback, or in their carts and buggies. Soon, trading was well under way. Yellow Cloud bartered chickens for Merry Mack and corn for one of Garret's farming friends for the nippers, horseshoes and nails that he needed to keep his horses shod. Pony skins and furs were bartered for rifles.

Horton Needham had insisted that Nathan McKenzie load his cart with the boxes marked 'miscellaneous' from his office. The new boss had brought them all the way from back east, and now everyone would find out what they contained.

Horton Needham stood in the centre of Garret's field and clapped his hands, waved his arms and began to talk far too loudly and slowly. Most of the Natives could understand the new boss from the Hudson's Bay Company very well, but he assumed that they must be stupid.

Needham opened his boxes on the back of McKenzie's cart and began to wave around the things that were inside. He thrust them into the hands of the Natives, who looked at one another and then thrust the objects back at him. They didn't appear to be impressed. Horton Needham had brought cheap glass beads, bolts of lightweight cotton cloth and horse tack. The Natives had their own gems, the cloth was of poor quality compared to the fabric that McKenzie traded, and the horse tack was shoddy. Besides, Garret made all the buckles, bits and stirrups they needed.

More traders arrived in the field. Farmers brought

the last of their autumn produce, and some of the women brought cloth they had woven, and clothes and even baked goods to trade among themselves. They ate and drank, and continued to share the day's celebrations.

As the afternoon wore on, Needham became impatient when the Natives did not want what he had to offer, and he began to open some of the smaller, heavier boxes on the cart. They were full of bottles.

'No!' said Tall Elk.

'What does he mean?' asked Needham, his face turning an angry red.

Jake, who was making the most of the company of his brother riders, did not hesitate. He turned to Needham and said, 'When Tall Elk says no, Mr Needham, I believe he means no.'

'This is good rye whisky,' said Needham, holding up a bottle.

Jake took the bottle from Needham's hand, looked at the label, and said, 'This is the cheapest rye whisky for sale at the saloon, Mr Needham. The Natives have no use for it.'

'Every man has a use for a drink, you rude boy,' said Needham, taking the bottle from Jake. He tried to thrust the whisky into Tall Elk's hand, and, when Tall Elk would not take it, the bottle fell to the hard earth and smashed. The sour smell of alcohol rose in the air, and Needham began to shout and shake his fist.

'What a waste!' he bellowed.

Tall Elk stood firm, but said nothing. Yellow Cloud stepped up to his friend's side.

Needham's face turned from angry red to puce pink, his thin lips puckered and his nostrils flared.

'Look what you've done! How dare you?' he fumed, flecks of spittle forming on his bottom lip as he spat out his words.

'How dare we have no need of whisky?' asked Yellow Cloud.

'How dare you insult me?' asked Horton Needham.

Pius Garret, who had noticed what was going on, stepped up to him.

'Offer them fair trade in goods they need,' he said, 'and they'll gladly barter.'

'You show as little respect as they do,' sneered Needham, turning to face the blacksmith.

'My father taught me that respect has to be earned,' said Jake, angry that the Hudson's Bay Company boss could treat his friends and family so badly.

'Are you going to let them talk to me like this?' Needham asked Nathan McKenzie, who five minutes earlier had been standing next to him. When there was no reply, he turned to glare at McKenzie, but the owner of the mercantile and the saloon had disappeared.

'You'll pay me for the whisky,' said Needham, glaring from Garret and Jake to Yellow Cloud and Tall Elk.

It was dusk, and the bonfire was sending great orange flames into the grey sky. The flickering light danced across Needham's red face. It made his eyes sparkle with an evil light that made him look like a fat devil.

'*You* dropped the bottle,' said Jake.

Needham shifted his glare from Jake to Garret.

'There's nothing more to be said on the matter,' said Pius. He didn't want to get in an argument with Boss Needham, but he wouldn't allow him to bully Jake either.

Yellow Cloud and Tall Elk stood firm, unmoved by Needham's rage.

'PAY ME!' screeched Needham, his spittle frothing and spraying in a bright arc of white droplets in the firelight.

The Natives and townspeople had been talking, laughing and bartering, until Needham's voice cut through the air. Then the crowd suddenly fell silent.

There was a sound of leather reins whipping a horse's back, and someone saying, 'Yah!' Cartwheels creaked into action, and Nathan McKenzie's cart pulled away from Horton Needham. The new boss of the Hudson's Bay Company was left standing without his stock. His small eyes widened a little further, his cheeks turned purple, and his lips tightened into an even rounder pucker in fury at the defiance of both Natives and townsfolk.

Jake wondered whether the man was going to burst.

A crowd had gathered, and everyone waited with bated breath to see what would happen, as the bonfire flames flickered in the darkening sky. Pius Garret and Jake, Yellow Cloud and Tall Elk calmly stood their ground, and Horton Needham stood opposite them. Anything could happen, but no one expected what did.

No one expected a rolling rumble like distant thunder, no one expected the ground to start to tremble beneath their feet, and no one expected the sky to light up with flames that weren't coming from Pius Garret's bonfire.

10

Gale's huge form hurtled into view, and the ground shook violently as he lumbered across Garret's field. Yellow clouds of sulphurous smoke puffed from the great beast's nostrils, filling the air with the smell of rotting eggs as the dragon rushed headlong in the direction of Horton Needham.

As the flames from the bonfire lit the boss's face, Jake, Pius, Yellow Cloud and Tall Elk watched Needham's eyes widen. His mouth, which had turned into a tiny, puckered circle, suddenly grew slack, and his bottom lip dropped wetly on to his chin. Needham's skin, which had gone from red to puce-pink to purple, turned a yellowish white all the way to the brim of his top hat.

Jake, Pius, Yellow Cloud, Tall Elk and all the Natives knew what was coming. Most of the townsfolk had a pretty good idea too, and began to shuffle away from the fire.

Gale had seen the bonfire from where he'd been resting under the blankets and, sensing a better source of heat, he was merely ambling over to warm his chilled blood and loosen his aching limbs. The problem was, Boss Needham was standing directly in his path.

Several of the townspeople gasped at the sight of the dragon, and leapt out of Gale's way. Needham, though, stood rooted to the spot, his eyes bulging with terror.

For a moment, Jake had a vision of Gale trampling straight over the Hudson's Bay man, but then Yellow Cloud took two long strides towards his dragon. He planted his feet firmly in the earth and held his arms out towards the beast in a commanding fashion.

Gale saw his master for the first time. He reared on to his hind legs, expanded his chest and spread his alula joints to slow himself down. The flames from the bonfire flickered, casting their yellow light in bursts across his iridescent scales. If anything, the glow made Gale look even more terrifying as he kicked his forelegs high in the air. He looked like the dragon from every myth that any of the townsfolk had ever heard or read.

Obedient though he was to his master, Gale hated being kept from the warmth of the bonfire, and he couldn't help casting a frustrated stream of orange flames into the late afternoon sky.

A moment later, as if in answer to Gale's, another stream of bright, orange flames cut the sky in two.

Every person still gathered around the bonfire at the end of Garret's field turned to watch.

Then a third jet of flames filled the air, and then a fourth. The dappled bellies of three more Thunderbirds were clearly visible as the dragons flew in wide circles over the bonfire.

The Natives had formed a barrier across the field to reassure the townspeople, who were still apprehensive about the dragons. Behind it, Yellow Cloud had soothed Gale so that he was standing ready with his rider at his left shoulder and Tall Elk at his right. Jake had taken up a firm stance in front of the dragon, his feet slightly apart.

Although Gale belonged to Yellow Cloud, and the closest bond was between a dragon and its rider, Jacob Polson, with his dragonsight, had the understanding of all dragons. Jake was not yet aware of all of his powers. Riders with dragonsight were so rare that there was no one to teach him how to use them, and only time would reveal the extent of his abilities.

Jake already knew, though, that his power over the dragons was somehow magical, that it was, somehow, as strong as Tall Elk's or Chief Half Moon's power over men. He'd been told by the Chief that one day he would be the most powerful medicine man of them all, that he would be the Thunderbirds' medicine man.

Jake put his scarred left hand on the dragon's

head, and the warmth penetrated into the creature's mind and settled him. Jake didn't know how or why, but he knew that it made Gale better.

Jake didn't hear the thud as Needham fell to the ground, and, if he had, he would not have cared that the new boss had fainted clean away.

He felt the movement in the air, and he felt their presence. When Jake looked into the night sky, beyond the bonfire, towards the bend in the river where Prospect stood, he saw three dragons flying towards the field.

When Jake turned his head, it wasn't to look at the boss, or at the townspeople, who were rooted where they stood. They were equally fascinated by and afraid of what they saw making a web of flame trails in the sky around them.

Jake ignored them all and concentrated on the creatures making lazy circles in the sky above the bonfire, drawn to the light and the heat. They knew that their masters were there, that it was a safe place, and they knew that they needed the warmth of the flames to keep them alive.

Jake removed his bracelet of Native gems from around his left wrist. He held it high above his head, in his left hand, and he began to swing it in small tight circles in the air. After only a few moments, the large red gem at the centre of the bracelet began to sing out a high, clear note.

The crowd had seemed silent before Jake had begun to swing his bracelet, but, like most crowds of people, there had been a shuffling of feet and sniffing, and one or two people had whispered to each other. When the bracelet began to sing, the townspeople really did stop making any noise whatsoever.

Jake watched as, one by one, the dragons peeled away from the bonfire to land beyond the line of Natives.

He and the Garrets stood on the strip of fallow field that separated the townspeople from the Natives and their creatures. Eliza, David and Michael stood close to the fire, because their mother had run to help rouse Needham.

Jake knew that Pius Garret didn't like the new boss, but everyone admired Mrs Garret's sense of charity, and the whole family stood beside her, ready to help, while she tended to Needham. The boss was still out cold and his sleeve was covered in blood where he had cut his hand on the broken whisky bottle.

Once Jake had fixed his bracelet back around his wrist, it was Elizabeth Garret who broke the silence.

'Eliza,' she said, 'fetch me a bowl of water and my medical tin . . . Quickly.'

At the sound of her voice, the crowd began to relax.

'You can all go home,' said Pius, speaking to the townspeople. 'There's nothing to see here, and no more trade to be had. Off you go and Happy Thanksgiving.'

He spoke with such authority that no one dared to defy him. Slowly, the people of Prospect began to gather the belongings they'd traded and set off back to town. Most wanted nothing more than to drink, and to gossip about what had happened in Garret's field that afternoon.

Nathan McKenzie knew that, if the saloon had been open, he could have made a pretty penny. He'd lost money because Horton Needham had taken his trade with the Natives, and his cart too. He'd lost money because Horton Needham had turned his saloon into an office.

When things had gone bad with the trading, McKenzie had ordered Trapper Watkiss to take the cart, and the cheap whisky, and drive them away before Boss Needham could do any more damage.

Nathan McKenzie had stood in the shadows all afternoon, watching Horton Needham trying to control Jake Polson and the Natives. He had watched Horton Needham getting more and more angry, and, finally, he had watched Horton Needham growing terrified of the dragons.

McKenzie strode towards the bonfire, watching

as Elizabeth Garret took the bowl of water from Eliza and put it on the ground. As he drew closer, he saw her open the medical tin, and take out the smelling salts.

Just moments after Elizabeth Garret put the little bottle of foul-smelling liquid under his nose, Needham woke suddenly with a cough, and struggled to sit up.

'Don't worry, Mrs Garret,' McKenzie said, crouching beside her. 'I'll get Mr Needham home safe.'

'Not until I've dressed his injuries,' said Mrs Garret. 'Thank goodness that bottle was full of whisky; at least the wounds will be clean.'

Nathan McKenzie squatted beside Horton Needham, who was still terribly pale, but had stopped trying to sit up. Elizabeth Garret pushed back the blood-soaked sleeves of his jacket and shirt, and uncovered the boss's right hand and arm. They'd been cut to ribbons by the broken glass of the whisky bottle that Needham had tried to force on the Natives. He would have permanent scars.

Elizabeth Garret cleaned and bandaged Needham's wounds, working quickly so that he and McKenzie could leave as soon as possible.

Finally, McKenzie nodded his thanks to the blacksmith and his wife, and helped Needham to his feet. The new boss of the Hudson's Bay Company didn't even thank his nurse. He simply pushed his too-small top hat back on to his head. Then he put his arm around McKenzie's shoulder and allowed himself to be half-carried back to the road where Trapper Watkiss was waiting with the cart.

11

Once Horton Needham and Nathan McKenzie were safely on their way, the Natives began to relax. They loaded their horses with the goods they'd traded, and thanked their hosts. Then they each threw a log on the bonfire, and took their leave.

The bonfire roared and the flames leapt high into the night sky. Gale and the three dragons that had flown in later gathered around the bonfire to warm their cold-blooded bodies.

Jake had been so concerned by the situation in Garret's field, and so keen to use his dragonsight, that he hadn't identified the three dragons. As he watched them approach the fire, and saw the flicker of the flames lighting up their faces, he quickly recognized Match among them.

'Match!' he cried, striding towards him. He patted his friend on the shoulder, and rested his cheek on the smooth scales of his neck.

Yellow Cloud and Pius Garret came up beside Jake.

'Why did you bring him here?' asked Jake. 'What's happening?'

'We meant to tell you at Thanksgiving dinner, before they arrived,' said Pius.

'It's about the Land of the Red Moon,' said Yellow Cloud.

'I don't understand,' said Jake. 'You decided I had to stay in Prospect.' His heart was suddenly beating very fast.

'Even Irish blacksmiths change their minds,' said Pius.

'And fussy foster-mothers,' said Mrs Garret, stepping up as close to Jake as she dared, still in awe of the Thunderbirds.

'It's a good job we changed our minds too,' said Pius. 'It looks like you might have made an enemy of Boss Needham.'

Jake looked from the Garrets' concerned faces to Yellow Cloud's serious one. Then Yellow Cloud nodded too.

'I'm coming with you?' asked Jake. Yellow Cloud smiled broadly.

'I'm really going to the Land of the Red Moon?' asked Jake, just to be absolutely clear.

'You're really going with them,' said Pius.

'You've got to do everything you're told, and stay safe,' said Elizabeth. 'I want you home in one piece in the spring.'

'I promise,' said Jake. 'This is the best Thanksgiving ever!'

Eliza Garret stood a little way away, in the shadows. She didn't want anyone to see how angry and jealous she was. She'd been jealous of Jake once before and it had ended badly, but she couldn't help herself.

She crossed her arms, bowed her head and scuffed her feet in the hard ground. *If Jake can go to the Land of the Red Moon, why can't I?* she wondered. She was White Thunder's best friend, and Jake's too, and she was old enough to leave school. Everyone knew that Jake was special, but she was his sister now, and she wanted an adventure just as much as he did.

At that moment, Eliza Garret thought she was more jealous of Jake Polson than she'd ever been. Why couldn't she have what Jake had?

12

There was no time like the present.

Night was drawing down fast. The stars were coming out in the clear, black sky, high above Garret's field, and the dragons had warmed themselves at the bonfire. It would burn for some time to come, but the great surge of heat caused by the extra logs that the Natives had thrown on was already dying down. The flames that had rushed so high into the sky only minutes before were already dancing to a slower beat, pulsing and waving, the woodsmoke curling away in grey wisps.

Jake didn't need to pack a bag or take anything with him on his journey. He lived a different life with his brothers at the settlement from the life he lived with the Garrets in Prospect.

In Prospect, he lived at the forge, went to school, did his chores and read the H. N. Matchstruck books that he borrowed from Miss Ballantine. At the settlement, he lived in a teepee, wore traditional

Native clothes, and, with Match, he knew that he'd always have adventures of his own.

Then Jake remembered that there was something that belonged in both of his worlds, something that he couldn't imagine ever being without.

'You must say goodbye to your family,' said Yellow Cloud, putting his hand on Jake's shoulder.

'Not yet,' said Jake. 'I left something in the house.'

He walked through the kitchen door, into the quiet house, sure that he was alone. Then he realized that someone had lit the stove, and he turned to see Eliza, sitting in her mother's little armchair in the warmest corner of the room.

'What are you doing here?' she asked crossly. 'I thought you were going away with your friends.'

'I came to get my dreamcatcher,' said Jake. 'It helps me to sleep, and makes me dream more clearly, so that I understand my memories. I couldn't leave without it.'

'You weren't supposed to leave at all,' said Eliza, crossing her arms.

'I know,' said Jake, 'but all the dreams I've had tell me that the clues to finding my family lie in the Land of the Red Moon, and I can train with Match while I'm there.'

'You're always so lucky,' said Eliza.

'It's not about luck,' said Jake. 'This way, I

have the chance to find my family. Emmie could be alive.'

'You never think of us!' said Eliza. 'My brother died, and now you're leaving, and it's not fair!'

Her words stunned Jake. She clearly didn't understand what he needed to do, despite his explanation.

'I'm sorry, Eliza,' he said.

Eliza turned her bowed head away from Jake so there was no chance she'd catch his eye.

Jake knew that Match was waiting for him. They didn't have much time to fly back to the settlement before the dragons would need to warm their blood again. He walked past Eliza and hurried up to the loft. He took his dreamcatcher down from where it hung above his bed, tucked it securely into his jacket and hurried back downstairs. He paused at the kitchen door, and looked back at Eliza.

'I wish you understood, Eliza,' he said. 'I wish you could at least say goodbye.'

Eliza looked up for just a moment, and glared at Jake.

'Goodbye, Eliza,' said Jake. 'I'll be back in the spring.'

Eliza said nothing.

'I'll miss you,' said Jake quietly. Then he left, closing the kitchen door behind him.

'I hate you, Jacob Polson,' said Eliza, under her breath. 'I hate you, and I wish I could go with you.'

Yellow Cloud and the two riders who had flown in with Match had already mounted their dragons when Jake ran back to the bonfire.

'We must return to the settlement and prepare to leave for the Land of the Red Moon,' said Yellow Cloud.

'Where's Eliza?' asked Elizabeth Garret. 'You can't go without saying goodbye to her.'

'She's in the kitchen,' said Jake. 'We've already said our goodbyes.'

'Oh,' said Mrs Garret, surprised. She looked at her husband, who took charge of the situation.

'The animals mustn't get any colder,' said the blacksmith. 'Give the boy a hug and send him on his way, Elizabeth, for goodness' sake.'

Mrs Garret kissed Jake on the cheek, and the twins gave him very serious handshakes. Pius Garret, who was no taller than Jake, clapped the boy firmly on the shoulder and then gave him a bear hug that took his breath away.

'Off you go,' said Pius, 'and happy hunting.'

'Mind your manners,' said Elizabeth Garret, 'and be sure to come home to us in one piece.'

'I will,' said Jake. 'I promise.'

As Jake prepared to mount Match, he felt something land on his cheek. He pulled himself on to the dragon's back, and adjusted his hands in Match's neck feathers.

The light from the bonfire picked out tiny white specks in the air all around them, and Jake felt a cold spot on the back of his hand. The first of the winter snow was beginning to fall. Tiny snowflakes were drifting down out of the starry, black sky, dancing in the firelight.

One by one, the dragons lifted their front legs, unfurled their wings and took the two or three steps on their hind legs that walked them into the air.

Seconds later, the four Thunderbirds circled the bonfire in Garret's field, before they peeled off into the night, breathing great streams of fire to light their way home to the Native settlement.

13

'They made a fool of me,' said Horton Needham.

He was sitting on the bench seat of McKenzie's cart, between Trapper Watkiss, who was driving, and Nathan McKenzie.

'They made a fool of me,' said Horton Needham again, 'and they're going to pay.'

The cart was travelling back to Prospect in the dark, as the first of the winter's snow began to fall. Trapper Watkiss had lit the cart lamp, and tiny snowflakes were caught drifting in the small pool of yellow light that it shed. They were moving at the horse's walking pace, on an empty road, and no one had said a word until Boss Needham spoke.

'Trapper was the first man to know the Natives,' said Nathan McKenzie calmly. Boss Needham looked from Nathan McKenzie to Trapper Watkiss.

'True,' said Trapper Watkiss. 'Injuns called me "Flame Beard" twenty, maybe thirty years ago.'

'Trapper was the first to know about the gems in the mountains,' said Nathan McKenzie, in the same calm tone. Boss Needham looked from Trapper Watkiss to Nathan McKenzie, and then back to Trapper Watkiss.

'True again,' said Trapper Watkiss. He took the cart reins in one hand and jiggled his other hand close to Needham's face. The bracelet of gems that he'd been wearing since he'd been saved by the Natives fell out of the cuff of his jacket, and rattled.

'And the beasts?' asked Needham.

'They're like horses,' said McKenzie. 'They do as their masters tell them.'

'They be evil dragons!' insisted Trapper Watkiss. 'I've got the scars to prove it.'

'That was your own fault,' said McKenzie, and Trapper Watkiss knew when to shut up.

Of course, Nathan McKenzie didn't remind Horton Needham about the dragon that had set fire to the saloon, blown up the mercantile and almost destroyed the school. Nathan McKenzie wanted the Hudson's Bay Company and Horton Needham on his side, and he wanted Prospect to become McKenzie's Prospect again some day. Besides, that dragon had been nothing to do with the Natives. He didn't know why the black dragon was different, but he knew that it was.

'I can help you make the Natives pay,' said McKenzie. 'When the Natives return in the spring, I *will* help you make them pay.'

'Why wait?' asked Needham. 'They must pay now!'

'They leave their summer home on the plateau,' said McKenzie. 'No one knows where they overwinter.'

'The Land of the Red Moon,' said Trapper Watkiss. 'That's where they take them dragons for the winter.'

Horton Needham and Nathan McKenzie both turned to Trapper Watkiss.

'Where did you learn that?' asked McKenzie.

'That jolly-gist,' said Trapper. 'The young fella, talks in a funny voice, told me.'

'You've spoken to Masefield Haskell?' asked McKenzie.

'That's the one,' said Trapper Watkiss. 'Excited, he was. Said he'd been there.'

'To the Land of the Red Moon?' asked McKenzie.

'Knows what it's made of, drawn maps,' said Trapper Watkiss. 'That young jolly-gist says he knows more about them lands than any man for a thousand miles. Boasted, he did.'

'Does he?' asked Nathan McKenzie, smiling.

'I've got my own geologist,' said Horton Needham.

'It would seem that Professor Haskell has done his work for him,' said McKenzie. 'Besides, the Hudson's Bay Company is paying Haskell. You might as well get your money's worth.'

'We're paying two geologists?' screeched Horton Needham.

'What price knowledge?' asked Nathan McKenzie.

'Especially when it's the sort of knowledge we've been desperate to get our hands on for over twenty years!'

Nathan McKenzie turned and smiled at Trapper Watkiss.

'Isn't that right, Trapper?' he asked.

'That's right,' said Trapper Watkiss. 'Couldn't get back to the settlement without that damned boy that runs with the Injuns and rides one of those evil dragons.'

'The blacksmith's boy?' asked Horton Needham. 'When I get my hands on him, he'll pay too.'

'Not quite the blacksmith's boy,' said McKenzie. 'He was orphaned.'

'Never been to the Land of the Red Moon,' said Trapper Watkiss. 'Been around these parts more than half my life, and never even heard of it till that jolly-gist made mention.'

A slow smile spread across Horton Needham's face, and his little round eyes began to disappear into his cheeks as they puffed up to make way for his mouth to grin.

'We'd better make an urgent appointment with your Professor Haskell, then,' he said.

'Not *my* Professor Haskell,' said Nathan McKenzie. 'He's paid by the Hudson's Bay Company. He's *your* Professor Haskell, and I'll be happy to arrange a meeting for you.'

'Do it soon,' said Horton Needham.

'There is just one more thing,' said Nathan McKenzie as the cart drew up outside his house, where Needham was staying.

'What is it?' asked Needham.

'I think we need to come to some new arrangement about how we're going to work together,' said Nathan McKenzie, holding out his hand for Needham to shake it.

'I'm sure something can be arranged,' said Horton Needham. He looked down at his bandaged right hand and then held it up to show McKenzie that it was impossible to shake with him.

'Since we can't shake on it,' said Needham, 'you'll just have to trust me.'

With that, Horton Needham climbed down from McKenzie's cart and opened the door to McKenzie's house, leaving Nathan McKenzie outside in the snow on his own doorstep.

'How far do you think I could trust Horton Needham?' McKenzie asked Trapper Watkiss.

'About as far as I could throw him,' said Trapper Watkiss, 'and he's a big man even to pick up.'

'With or without his handshake?' asked McKenzie.

'That's with it,' said Trapper. 'Without, you've got no hope.'

14

It wasn't a long walk, along Main Street, from Horton Needham's office in the saloon to Merry Mack's cottage. Trapper Watkiss made the journey in a minute or two when he was sent to summon Masefield Haskell.

Merry Mack answered her door to Trapper two minutes after she'd served Haskell with his favourite bacon and egg breakfast.

'What do you want with me?' she asked the scruffy little man standing on her doorstep.

'The boss wants the jolly-gist,' said Trapper.

'He's not *my* boss, not Nathan McKenzie, nor the new man,' said Merry Mack, making ready to close the door.

'Wait a minute, Mrs Mack,' said Trapper Watkiss, sniffing the air. 'Is that bacon?'

'What if it is?' asked Mrs Mack, holding the door open just wide enough for Trapper to be able to see one of Merry Mack's bright blue eyes. Sadly for Trapper, that wasn't wide enough for him to push the toe of his boot into the jamb to keep her from closing the door.

'Best bacon in Prospect,' said Trapper Watkiss.

'Which is why I keep it for the deserving, the paying and the righteous,' said Mrs Mack, 'and you, Ignatius Loyola Watkiss, are none of those things.'

Trapper Watkiss stepped away from the door, which he clearly had no hope of passing through. Only two people in Prospect, and probably only three people in the world, knew the name bestowed on him by the nuns. Everyone who called him anything always called him Trapper, and Trapper was always shocked when he heard his given name.

Merry Mack closed the door, briskly, and Trapper Watkiss stood outside, collecting dry, cold snowflakes in the brim of his hat and the cuffs of his coat, waiting for Masefield Haskell. He didn't know for sure that Haskell would appear, but he hoped for his own sake that he might.

Nathan McKenzie and Trapper Watkiss had sat up late into the night in the deserted saloon, plotting. McKenzie was determined to get his town back, so he had to give Horton Needham and the Hudson's Bay Company what they wanted. Needham wanted revenge on the Natives, on Jake Polson and on the dragons, and the Hudson's Bay Company wanted to make money.

The first step to getting those things was to bring

in Haskell and his maps, which was why Trapper Watkiss was standing in the snow, on Main Street, first thing on Friday morning, the day after Thanksgiving.

Twenty minutes later, Merry Mack opened her front door. Masefield Haskell stepped through it, and turned to thank Mrs Mack for the wonderful breakfast. He pulled up the collar of his coat against the snow, and looked around.

Trapper Watkiss stepped forward. For the last ten minutes, he'd been sheltering in the alley between Merry Mack's cottage and the mercantile. He'd been trying to avoid the worst of the snow, but he was, nonetheless, covered in a fine, white dusting of the stuff.

'You were looking for me?' asked Haskell.

'The boss wants to speak to you,' said Trapper Watkiss. 'Says it's a "matter of urgency".'

'Two days ago, you told me I wasn't wanted,' said Haskell. 'I imagine I don't have a boss. Besides, there are two bosses in Prospect. So, Mr Watkiss, are you asking me to see your old boss, or your boss's new boss? Because neither of them can rightly call himself *my* boss.'

Trapper Watkiss looked utterly confused by Haskell's little speech.

'I was told to bring you to the saloon,' he said. 'Mr

Needham and Mr McKenzie want to talk to you. Is that simple enough?'

'I should imagine that would be simple enough for anyone,' said Haskell. 'The question is, why should *I* want to talk to *them*?'

'Don't ask me,' said Trapper Watkiss. 'Except it don't do to cross 'em. So, are you comin' or what?'

'Very well,' said Haskell.

Trapper didn't mind his job as an errand boy so much when he was dealing with such a civilized gentleman.

15

Jake was sitting in the corner of the tiny forge, wondering why he was there, wondering why Pius Garret had allowed him to watch him work. The little Irish blacksmith usually kept his children out of his forge, because it was hot and dangerous, and because there was only room for himself and his tools.

Jake looked around the tiny room. It was too bright and too clean, and Mr Garret hadn't stoked the fire in all the time that he'd been watching him. Jake glanced towards the solid, brick-built furnace, and was surprised to see that it was pristine. There was no dust or soot, and the fire was being fuelled by a little blue-green dragon curled on the floor beneath the chimney, who was lazily producing flames that Mr Garret heated his metals in.

Pius Garret wasn't wearing his usual heavy leather apron, and his bench was arranged with delicate, handmade tools, the like of which Jake had never seen before. He wasn't making the horse shoes, nails and axeheads that were his stock-in-trade; he was making something very small and delicate on a tiny, odd-shaped anvil that sat squarely on top of a work bench that Jake had also never seen before.

Jake looked around again, and realized that he wasn't in the forge at all, but in a well-lit workshop with sunlight streaming in through tall windows.

Jake walked up to look over Pius Garret's shoulder, and he realized that his foster-father wasn't aware that he was there. The little Irishman was working on a small object; it was star-shaped, could easily fit in the palm of Jake's hand, and was made of what appeared to be a dull, grey metal.

Jake turned to look around and saw a glass-fronted cabinet at one end of the workbench. He walked over to it and looked down on the objects inside.

The little cabinet was full of jewels. There were pocket watches with chains, like the one that Horton Needham wore, and there were cufflinks and tie pins like the ones that some of the society gentlemen in St Louis owned. There were wedding rings too, as worn by lots of the married women that Jake knew.

Suddenly, the room lit up, and Jake turned to see the little dragon spray a burst of flames over something that Pius Garret was holding in a pair of tongs, at arm's length.

Then, something happened. Jake didn't know what, but the room was suddenly dark, and there was a clatter and Pius Garret cried out. Jake lunged to his aid, reaching out to catch the bright object that he saw falling through the air.

'Aaah!' cried Jake as his hand closed around the burning object. He opened his hand again, as fast as he could, and heard the tinkle of the silver sheriff's star falling on to the top of the glass cabinet.

Then, just as if nothing had happened, the room was suddenly filled with sunlight again, and Mr Garret was reaching for a buffing cloth to bring Lem Sykes's sheriff's badge to a gleaming finish.

Jake smiled slightly, and rolled over, unclenching his left hand, which felt hot, as it so often did. He remembered where he was, and he thought it was rather magical that he should dream about his foster-father the morning after he'd left Prospect for the last time for several months. It warmed his heart.

He pushed his blankets away and gazed up at the dreamcatcher above his head. Then he looked at his warm, itching left hand, and traced the odd pattern there. He half-expected to see the sheriff's badge imprinted in his palm.

Why does the pattern look so familiar? he wondered for the hundredth time. *What does it remind me of?*

By the time the sun was rising, the Native settlement was already bustling. A light dusting of snow lay over everything, making the last of the teepees sparkle in the grey light of dawn. The earth was hard and white, and only showed its true colour close to the glowing fires that had been kept burning all night.

The Thunderbirds had huddled together, in the corral, for warmth, draped in skins and blankets, which had mostly escaped the frost and snow, because they were so close to the fires. The corners of the blankets that lay against the cold earth, furthest from the flames, were stiff with frost.

The Natives were dismantling the last of the smaller teepees. Only the Lodge would remain standing throughout the winter, with most of their belongings stored inside it. The dragons would carry the rest.

Jake lifted the flap of the teepee and stepped out into the dawn, his breath sending little clouds of white steam into the cold air.

'What can I do to help?' he asked Yellow Cloud. Everyone seemed to have a job, and Jake wanted to show that he was willing to work.

He had not expected to leave for the Land of the Red Moon, so he hadn't thought about the journey and how it must be made. He hadn't thought about how the settlement must be packed up, about storage and transport, or about the horses or the people, or about any of it.

'Today, the riders only ride,' said Yellow Cloud.

'I don't understand,' said Jake.

'You *will* understand,' said Yellow Cloud.

With that, the Native put a firm hand on Jake's shoulder and steered him back into the Lodge. As they entered, Jake realized that Chief Half Moon, Tall Elk and all the other riders had gathered around the fire at the centre of the teepee. Several others, including White Thunder, were serving the riders a hearty meal that more resembled a feast than breakfast.

The riders spoke quietly together while they ate, the atmosphere calm and serious.

Jake ate hot, flat bread, filled with a rich, creamy paste of smoky fish. He'd never eaten the dish before, and it was delicious.

'It's a special day,' he said suddenly, realizing it for the first time.

'Yes,' said Yellow Cloud, smiling. 'Today is the most special day of the year. It is also one of the longest, hardest and most tiring. Are you ready, Dragon Sight?'

'I'm ready,' said Jake.

'Good,' said Yellow Cloud, 'but I am not.'

Jake's face fell, and he thought for a moment that he might panic.

'I need some more breakfast before we get to work,' said Yellow Cloud, grinning at Jake. 'Why don't you have more too?'

Jake breathed a sigh of relief, and held out his dish for White Thunder to refill it with more of the amazing bread and fish.

When the meal was over, two of the older Native women came into the Lodge, carrying piles of beautiful, sleeved jackets made from soft skins. They had no fringing or tassels on them, and no beads. Some of them had heavy, coloured stitching across the shoulders and around the cuffs in various shapes and symbols, which Jake recognized.

White Thunder and another young woman, Fire Ember, took a jacket each from the tops of the piles, and opened them as if to help their wearers into them.

All of the jackets looked the same from the outside, but Jake gasped when he saw the linings of those two jackets.

The Natives made no permanent homes, so all of their art, their stories and their culture had to be carried with them. These jackets, worn on the journeys from East to West, from the plateau to the Land of the Red Moon, told the riders' stories. Each rider had his own jacket, lined with painted and embroidered events from his vision quest and his life as a rider.

The first two jackets belonged to Chief Half Moon and Tall Elk, and White Thunder and Fire Ember held them open as the men put them on.

They wrapped the jackets around their bodies and tied them tightly in place.

Yellow Cloud and Jake were next, but Jake didn't own a jacket. Yellow Cloud stepped forward as Fire Ember held up a jacket, showing streams of fire in the sky across half of it, and a river, and the plateau waterfall in the background. The other half of the jacket depicted the Land of the Red Moon.

Jake wanted to take a long look at the inside of Yellow Cloud's jacket, but this was a sacred moment, and he blushed with embarrassment. He looked away to try to calm himself, but realized that White Thunder was trying to catch his eye.

Jake looked at the jacket she was holding, showing some artwork on the inside. It was not as complete or as colourful as the previous three, but he thought he saw a building. The Natives didn't live in buildings.

White Thunder nodded at him, and Jake stepped towards her, never taking his eyes off the lining of the jacket. Then he realized that it was newer than the others, made from skin that was softer and more yellow than Yellow Cloud's garment. There were no creases in it either, and no wear and tear.

This jacket was brand new, and the building painted on the inside of it was the Garrets' forge house.

'For me?' asked Jake. He could not have felt more surprised or more honoured. His homes and his families had somehow all come together in this one jacket. He could take the Garrets into the Land of the Red Moon with him. Somehow, the beautiful new jacket gave him hope that he would also find Ma, Pa and Emmie there.

'For you,' said White Thunder with a broad smile.

She lifted the jacket higher, and Jake slipped into it. The rest of the riders whooped and hollered, and stamped their feet in celebration.

The riders left the Lodge in a long line, led by Chief Half Moon, Tall Elk and Yellow Cloud. The rest of the riders followed according to their age and status. Jake expected to be one of the last, because he was almost the youngest, and he was still an apprentice. He was also the only rider who had not been born a Native.

Jake was wrong. Dragonsight gave him more status among the riders than age and experience ever would, and he found himself walking out of the Lodge directly behind Yellow Cloud. With his new jacket on, his head held high and his cheeks still flushed, Jake had never felt so proud in all his life.

As they stepped out of the Lodge, the riders were met by the hollering, whooping and stamping of their families, celebrating their departure from their summer home.

A dozen of the strongest Native warriors stood in a line in front of the riders, their heads bowed. They did not join in with the whooping, but seemed to be waiting. Each of the men was dressed in winter clothes with long trousers and similar jackets to those the riders wore. Their hair was plaited in single rows down their backs, and they wore no beads or feathers in their clothes or hair, or on their ankles or wrists. Each man carried an odd-shaped basket with leather straps attached to it.

Jake recognized Pius Garret's work in some of the buckles and fastenings on the leatherwork, but he didn't know what they were used for. They weren't horse tack, and they didn't look like belts or bags.

Chief Half Moon went along the line of warriors, and, as he stood in front of each one, he called out the name of one of the riders. Each warrior then went to stand beside his rider.

Jake's warrior was a young man called Black Thorn. He was lean and wiry, and only an inch taller than Jake. As the Native stood beside him, Jake became aware that he was rocking nervously and squeezing his fists.

'Are you all right?' asked Jake, noticing that the warrior wasn't much more than a boy.

'First time . . . alone,' said Black Thorn.

Jake understood the words, but he didn't know what they meant. Before he could ask another question, the double row of riders with their companions was on the move again. This time they walked towards the corral, where the dragons were standing around the bonfires with blankets and skins still covering their backs.

Chief Half Moon took the bracelet from around his wrist and swung it in the air. At his signal, all the other riders followed suit.

All the beads singing together made the most extraordinary, multi-layered sound. The dragons turned from the bonfires, and each trotted to his master.

Jake was amazed by what he saw next. As each of the riders mounted his dragon, the Native warriors began to strap on the harnesses they'd been carrying. The strangely shaped, tightly woven baskets formed seats that the warriors stepped into and then strapped to their bodies. The harnesses buckled in place around their chests and over their shoulders.

Jake had never seen anything like them. He watched, carefully, as the first warrior took the two longest leather straps and, one at a time, threw them over his shoulders. The Native was standing firmly on the ground, directly beneath and in front of Chief Half Moon's dragon. Chief Half Moon had walked his dragon into the air, and was hovering almost dangerously close to the ground.

The Chief rode rarely, and mostly during the important ceremonies of the year. He was old, but he was also very proud, and he was the most important person in his tribe. He would not be carried by any but his own dragon, and no one but him would ever ride that dragon.

Jake watched, open-mouthed, as Chief Half Moon caught the two leather straps that the warrior had thrown, and began to arrange the buckles and fastenings around his dragon's neck and shoulders. The old man controlled his mount entirely with his knees and feet. His hands should be working the feathers at the nape of his dragon's neck, but they were busy strapping the warrior's seat in place.

Jake suddenly understood why, on their last ride from Prospect, Yellow Cloud had insisted that he practise hands-free manoeuvres. He was preparing Jake for this task.

The plan was to transport everyone into the Land of the Red Moon suspended in harnesses below the dragons. The Natives and their belongings would all be flown from the plateau to the winter training grounds.

For the first time, Jake really understood what it meant to be part of a travelling people. He had experienced a long voyage across a vast country, with Ma and Pa and Emmie, and the wagon train, but travel was central to the Natives' culture.

It was soon time for Jake and Black Thorn to harness Match and begin their journey. Jake walked Match into the air, and held him steady above the ground. Black Thorn had already strapped his seat to his body, but his hands were shaky, and he had trouble throwing Jake his straps.

Jake managed to drop Match a little closer to Black Thorn, and the young warrior tried again. Jake caught one of the straps, but the second fell short. Jake could sense that Black Thorn was becoming agitated, but could do nothing to ease his mind, so he decided to ease Match's mind instead. He took a deep breath, blinked slowly, and concentrated. When Jake opened his eyes, he wasn't looking out over his dragon's head, waiting for the strap to fly into view. When he opened his eyes, he was seeing through Match's eyes. The strap fell short again, but, this time, Jake saw it, and he ducked Match's head on his long, flexible neck and caught the strap in the dragon's maw.

Within a few moments, Jake had buckled the harness securely around Match's shoulders. Black Thorn didn't have time to be afraid before he found himself swinging in a wide circle, climbing into the sky above the Native settlement.

Jake heard a whoop of excitement below him. The harness jiggled, and Black Thorn punched the air in his excitement.

It was the first of several trips that Jake and the other riders made that day. Dragons flew remarkably fast and could travel in a straight line. The terrain below was rugged and dangerous, and paths through and over the land were long and winding, making travel on foot almost impossible.

Chief Half Moon always had to remain in his people's spiritual home, and, in the winter, that was the Land of the Red Moon. He arrived there with a dozen warriors, and with much work to be done in preparation for the arrival of the rest of the tribe.

The dragons returned to the plateau, and the process was repeated. The Thunderbirds rested and warmed their bodies by turns. They carried people in the harnesses, often more than one at a time. Women were carried two at a time, strapped together, and children were strapped to adults. For some, it was a terrifying experience, only to be endured; for others, it was a spectacular adventure.

For some of the travellers, hanging from the harness was as close as they could ever bear to be to a dragon. Others would one day become riders.

At dusk, only four dragons were still making the journeys between the plateau and the Land of the Red Moon. Yellow Cloud and Tall Elk continued to ride, and so did a quiet, stoic, older man, named River Stone, who always kept himself apart. Jake had never spoken to him, or spent time with him.

He had never trained with him either, even though River Stone regularly worked with the other boys.

Jake was a little afraid of River Stone.

The fourth dragon to remain in the sky, as the sun set over the plateau, was Match. Jake watched from his back as the great white sun dropped below the level of the plunging waterfall, disappearing into its grey mists as blackness descended from above.

He knew that he wouldn't see the plateau or Prospect again for several months, and he'd been so excited by the idea of spending the winter in the Land of the Red Moon that he was only just beginning to realize how much he'd miss this place, and the Garrets and school.

He turned Match east, and flew over the waterfall that raged beneath him, sending out a fine mist of spray that seemed somehow warmer than the chilly evening air. He knew that he mustn't linger, that he mustn't allow Match to get cold.

Jake felt Match's exhilaration as they flew at top speed, and, in only a few minutes, they were circling the forge house. The lights were on in the kitchen and smoke curled out of the chimney.

Jake hovered low over the Garrets' house, hoping that someone might come out, but nobody did.

Then Jake turned Match west. He pulled up, suddenly, when he saw the silhouette of another dragon, in front and a little above his position. It was dark, and he thought, for one horrible moment, that one of the evil black dragons had come to hunt him down, to stop him finding his family.

Jake clenched his hands in Match's nape feathers, and urged him to spray the darkening sky with flame-light. As he did so, the other dragon dropped down beside Match and Jake. Riding side by side with him, Jake saw River Stone on his dark blue and green Thunderbird. The old Native nodded once and led the way home.

16

Masefield Haskell walked into the saloon with Trapper Watkiss. Horton Needham, in his striped waistcoat, was sitting in a fancy, buttoned leather chair, while Nathan McKenzie sat on his stool at the end of the bar. He sat taller than Needham, looking over his head, and, somehow, he still managed to look more important than the new boss.

As Haskell strode into the middle of the room, Trapper hung back, standing close to the saloon door to block the exit as Needham had instructed him to do.

'You're the geologist?' asked Needham.

'I am,' said Haskell. He would usually have said something like, 'Masefield Haskell, at your service,' and held out his hand for a handshake. Today he did neither of those things, not because he'd forgotten his manners, but because, today, he was wary.

'You're in the employ of the Hudson's Bay Company?' asked Needham.

'I suppose I am,' said Masefield Haskell, 'although

I was employed by Mr McKenzie, and I haven't been paid for six weeks. I'm quite content to terminate my contract.'

'You can't do that,' said Needham. 'We want you to report on the work you've done. We want your maps of the Native lands, and your samples.'

Masefield Haskell turned and looked at Trapper Watkiss.

Trapper Watkiss didn't like the look that Masefield Haskell gave him. The geologist looked extremely stern, even if he was only a young man, and a scientist. Trapper had always been vaguely intimidated by Haskell's accent, and by his education. Both reminded him of his childhood and the nuns. He hadn't understood them either, and things that he didn't understand always bothered him.

'There's good land to be exploited,' continued Boss Needham, 'and the Hudson's Bay Company has secured the rights to mine that land for gems. The Natives might think they own it, but they haven't got land deeds. They can't *prove* they own the land, can they?'

'They're good, honest people, and they're my friends,' said Masefield Haskell. 'If I spent some time with them, and if I looked around at the land while I was with them, that was my business. If I took a measurement or two of the land, or a sample of the rocks, here or there, it was as a hobby. I've been paid for nothing. My work is my own, and I won't sell it to you, sir.'

'Oh, is that right?' asked Horton Needham.

'I believe I've made myself clear,' said Haskell. 'Good morning to you,' and, with that, the geologist turned to leave the saloon.

Trapper Watkiss, who'd been a little afraid of the clever Englishman, was now also very impressed by him. Trapper would never have talked back to Nathan McKenzie, and he certainly wouldn't have stood up to Boss Needham.

Trapper stepped away from the saloon door as Haskell strode towards him.

Boss Needham turned to McKenzie, and snorted something at him. Then, McKenzie gave Trapper Watkiss a signal.

As the geologist approached the old man, Trapper Watkiss's eyes widened, and he hesitated. He was torn between following his instincts and following his master's orders. With Haskell only a pace or two away, Trapper Watkiss's instincts won the day.

Trapper Watkiss shuffled his feet, watching them as he did so. He did not, however, bar Masefield Haskell's way out of the saloon. He did not look the geologist in the eye, and he did not accost the young man. He didn't hold the door open for him, but he did tug at the front of his hair, as a mark of respect. Trapper was extremely impressed by the young man's actions, and he wished he had the guts to say so.

17

It was a cold, quiet day in Prospect. Snowflakes fell in uneven flurries. The air was chill and dry, and little drifts of snow began to collect along one side of Main Street, against the steps and at the corners of the window panes.

It was the first winter's day. It was the first day without any visitors. No trading vessels, or any other boats, arrived at the landing stage at the bend in the river. No one left Prospect either. Most of the hard work had been done in preparation for the long, cold spell to come, so no one was busy.

No one walking down Main Street on Friday November 29th 1850 could possibly have guessed that men were plotting behind the closed saloon doors. No one walking down Main Street could possibly have suspected that the people sitting eating their supper behind the doors of Mrs Mack's cottage might be in for a terrible shock.

*

Merry Mack never locked her kitchen door. Her cottage was almost too small to need two doors, but, when she'd had it built, she'd been advised that even the smallest home should have an escape route.

Merry Mack had grown glad of the little kitchen door. She liked to sit outside it, in her kitchen chair, feeding her hens and watching the sky. It was a sunny spot, made private by the high wall of the mercantile, across the alley. No one could see her kitchen door or that little triangle of her yard from the street, and she liked the privacy.

The man pushing his way into Merry Mack's kitchen didn't need to break the door down, or smash the glass, because the door was never locked. He was so clumsy and shoved the door so hard that it swung into the cupboard that stood against the wall behind it. It swung so hard that the little brass handle on the cupboard door went clean through the glass in the kitchen door. The glass fell tinkling to the wooden floor, where it broke into even smaller pieces.

Merry Mack put her hand to her face and gasped in shock. Masefield Haskell stood up so quickly that he knocked his chair over in his haste.

'Now look here!' the geologist exclaimed to the man looming over him.

'No, you look here,' said a sinister voice from behind the handkerchief that was tied around the intruder's face. He grabbed hold of Masefield Haskell's shirtfront. 'Hand over your maps and samples, and no harm will come to you.'

The thug didn't see Merry Mack take up the empty casserole on the kitchen table.

As she swung it, with all her strength, she said, 'No harm will come to Mr Haskell in my house, regardless.' The little old woman aimed her improvised weapon at the back of the thug's neck. She was too small to reach his head, and she didn't want to do him any permanent damage, but she'd be damned if she wasn't going to defend her guest.

The thug was taken by surprise, and the blow from the iron casserole was remarkably effective. Merry Mack leaned over the man, who'd slumped to his knees before her. Unfortunately, she'd also disabled Masefield Haskell.

Merry Mack's kitchen was small, with a round table at its centre. Mrs Mack had been sitting on one side of the table when the thug had intruded. Mr Haskell had been sitting opposite her, and they'd been eating the casserole. When Haskell had knocked over his chair, he'd become wedged between its upturned legs, the table and the kitchen cupboard.

The thug had toppled over when Merry Mack had struck him with the casserole, and he had taken Haskell down with him. The unfortunate geologist had hit his head, and was tangled in an unconscious heap among the chair legs.

Merry Mack could not get at Masefield Haskell to help him, and she didn't notice a second man coming through the door behind her.

Suddenly, she felt someone snatch her around the waist, and, when she kicked and squealed, her attacker cuffed her briskly around the side of the head. Then she felt herself fall through the air, unable to find her feet as the brute dropped her. She couldn't help but cry out as her hands were shredded on the broken glass from the kitchen door. Then everything went black as her head hit the floor.

The second man, masked in the same way as the first, pulled the handkerchief off his face. There was no one to recognize him now, and his breath had made the hanky hot and damp.

The man who had hurt Mrs Mack was one of Nathan McKenzie's miners. The man on the floor, who was coming round after the blow from the casserole, was his brother.

'Get up, Marcus,' said Anthony Mimms. 'They're both out cold, and it's time to clear this place out.'

Marcus Mimms pulled his handkerchief down, took a deep breath, steadied himself, and said, 'You'd better let him in then, Anthony.'

After a little persuasion, a man stepped into the

kitchen, and, when he saw the mess and the bodies, he almost stepped straight out again.

'I didn't sign on to the company for this sort of work,' said the new man.

'The only work you've got to do is scientific,' said Marcus. 'Now, find the maps and the samples, and let's get out of here.'

'He'll be staying up there,' said Anthony, pointing to the narrow ladder that led to the loft.

In a matter of moments, the three men had climbed the ladder, and a few minutes after that they were surrounded by Masefield Haskell's treasure trove of belongings.

'I don't believe it,' said Othniel Seeley, the Hudson's Bay Company geologist, sitting on the floor of the loft. 'This is the most extraordinary collection I have ever seen!'

'Well, don't just sit there,' said Marcus, frantically rolling up papers and tying ribbons around them with his clumsy fingers. 'Pack this lot up and let's go.'

'What do we pack?' asked Anthony.

'From a scientific point of view, I want to take absolutely everything!' said the geologist.

'Then we take everything,' said Marcus.

Ten minutes later, Othniel Seeley walked out of Merry Mack's kitchen, while the Mimms brothers struggled down the loft ladder, heavily laden with rolls of paper and bags of Haskell's samples. They'd stripped out the entire attic, leaving only Haskell's clothes and personal belongings.

Marcus was carrying so much of Haskell's research that he closed the door behind him rather clumsily. The sound of more glass breaking as the last shards fell from the door panel roused Masefield Haskell.

The geologist sat up on the kitchen floor, dazed and confused, and put a hand up to his sore head, sure that he'd find a lump there.

Haskell put his chair back on its feet, and used it to help himself back on to his. It was then that he noticed the blood on the floor, and, across the room, partially hidden by the dining table, Haskell spotted the slumped form of Merry Mack.

He rushed to help her, squatting next to the old lady, while trying to avoid the broken glass that she'd fallen into. There was a bright scratch on her pale face, and when he gently rubbed her hand there was no response.

Masefield Haskell tried talking calmly to Merry Mack, but loudly enough to rouse her. That didn't help either, and he had no idea how long she'd been unconscious. He stood up once more, determined to get help.

Then he noticed more blood, and his hand flew

to his face in shock. He was not a man to panic, but he gasped when he saw the gash on Merry Mack's leg from the broken glass. Haskell reached for the basket where he knew she kept her clean rags, and quickly bound the wound.

Still, the old woman did not wake up, and Haskell was beginning to seriously worry for her safety. She'd lost a lot of blood, and she'd been unconscious for far too long.

Masefield Haskell didn't want to leave the old woman, but he knew that he must get help before it was too late. So, he ran out of the front door of Merry Mack's neat little house, his heart pounding. He looked around, but, to his horror, the street was empty. He called out, and, when nobody came, he shouted more loudly. The geologist didn't stop shouting as he ran the length of Main Street, all the way to Doc Trelawny's house.

18

Marcus and Anthony Mimms had pushed the tables together in the saloon, as instructed by Horton Needham, and Haskell's maps were spread out for inspection.

It was not long before Nathan McKenzie beckoned Trapper Watkiss over.

'You know the lay of the land better than anyone,' said McKenzie. 'Could you follow these maps into the Land of the Red Moon, as it's marked down here?'

'Now look here!' Horton Needham objected.

'If you want to get to where the Natives are overwintering, and you want to do it in bad weather,' said McKenzie, 'Trapper Watkiss is the man for the job.'

'I've got my own men, and I plan to lead the party myself,' said Needham. 'Anyone can follow a map.'

The Mimms brothers looked from the maps to one another. Then Marcus stepped over to the sample table. Little piles of rock and soil sat on large squares of the paper they'd been wrapped in. They were all colours and textures, and not like any rocks or soil that he'd ever seen. They were too dry and crumbly and far too yellow and purple and glittery.

'A local man might be useful,' said Anthony, speaking for both of the brothers.

'I ain't doin' it,' said Trapper. 'There be dragons. It's dangerous country too. Just look at that terrain.'

'Talk sense, man!' said Horton Needham, his cheeks turning a florid red. 'What are you saying?'

'I'm saying you need a guide,' said Trapper Watkiss, pointing at one of Haskell's maps. 'Look how close together those contour lines are. Those are mountains. Begging your pardon, sir, but you won't make it without a good deal of help.'

'I'm as strong as an ox,' shouted Needham.

'You ain't fit though, sir,' said Trapper Watkiss, pointing at the bandage around the boss's arm.

'Just scratches,' said Needham. 'They'll heal in no time.'

'That's settled then,' said McKenzie, clapping Trapper Watkiss on the back. 'I can't go because of my leg, but Trapper will get you there, no trouble.'

'There'll be weather,' said Trapper Watkiss, to anyone who'd listen.

'Then there's no time like the present,' said Horton Needham, dipping his fingers into a glittering pile of tiny, bright blue rocks, which looked like rough versions of the gemstones he was greedy to discover. 'We'll leave the day after tomorrow.'

As Horton Needham and Othniel Seeley pored over the glittering samples, and the Mimms brothers studied the maps, Nathan McKenzie took Trapper Watkiss to one side.

'I don't like it,' said Trapper Watkiss.

'You know the Mimms brothers,' said McKenzie, 'and I'll see to it that Needham follows your routes.'

'I still don't like it. I don't trust the new boss,' said Trapper Watkiss, 'and I don't like them dragons.'

'I need someone on the inside,' said McKenzie, winking at Trapper to make sure he understood his meaning. 'After all, who else can I trust?'

If Trapper Watkiss was proud of anything, it was Nathan McKenzie's friendship. When Nathan McKenzie told Trapper Watkiss that he was the only man he could trust, it touched the old man's heart. He squared his shoulders and puffed out his chest, and he turned to Boss Needham.

'Right then, boss,' said Trapper Watkiss. 'Let's get started on a plan. There's plenty to do if we're to leave day after tomorrow.'

19

The great, red moon hung low in a sky that looked like dark green glass, darker than the green beads in Jake's bracelet, and darker than Match's scales. The wisps of cloud were turning purple and the light was fading, but the air was still, dry and warm. The riders and their apprentices were sitting around a small, low fire, built straight on to the flat earth, listening to one another telling stories.

Jake looked out over the land. He could see for miles. To the east, the land seemed to stretch forever, flat and even. Low mists of various colours seeped out of fissures in the ground, cracks that leaked the earth's vapours.

The mists swirled in their various colours, knee-deep. At dusk, they were so thick that Jake couldn't see his feet when he walked through them. He would pretend he was walking through the clouds.

Perhaps that was why the Natives called themselves the Cloud People.

'Dragon Sight . . . Dragon Sight?'

'What is it?' asked Jake when he finally heard Yellow Cloud calling his name.

'Why aren't you listening to Tall Elk's stories?' asked Yellow Cloud. 'We do not talk because we like the sound of our voices. All the lessons do not happen in the sky, on the backs of your Thunderbirds.'

'Dragons,' said Jake.

'You may go and muck out the *dragons*,' said Yellow Cloud. 'You may go and muck out Match and your friends' *dragons*, and you may have the privilege of mucking out your teachers' *dragons*.'

'The apprentices share the mucking out,' said Jake.

'The apprentices do as their teachers instruct,' said Yellow Cloud. 'When their teachers instruct them to muck out, they muck out.'

Grey Wolf could not stifle a giggle, and was soon spluttering into his hand.

'It would appear you will not be mucking out alone,' said Yellow Cloud. 'Grey Wolf would like to join you, mucking out the *dragons*.'

Jake wished that Yellow Cloud would stop saying 'dragons' like that. He only wanted them to use the correct word. Thunderbird was a bad translation made long ago by someone who didn't have the imagination to realize that the Natives lived with dragons. Some old, dull man, who'd first translated the Native word, had thought the Native legend was something that could not be shared. He'd called them Thunderbirds, but dragons were real to everyone.

Grey Wolf stopped giggling and groaned. He clambered to his feet and held his hand out to help Jake up.

They made their way to the corral where the apprentices' dragons ate and slept, and Jake caught sight of the view. From the first time he'd seen the sweep of the mountain range, it had taken his breath away.

The great ridge curved for miles. It looked exactly as if some vast tidal wave of rock had come roaring towards the land, had reached its peak, and had begun to curl over, ready to crash into the flat earth. It looked exactly as a child would draw such a wave. The huge, convex cliff face, which overhung the land beneath, offered the Natives shade from the vast, speckled sun. The plains were flat and the air was dry. There was little wind and no rain at all. Hours of daylight were long and constant, and, when night came, it came suddenly.

The apprentices often slept on the plains. There was no risk of rain, and most of the local animals were small and shy. Fires were kept lit during the few short hours of darkness to keep away bigger predators. Apprentices were not allowed to sleep on the plains alone. Occasionally, a rider might honour one of them with his company, but, usually, three or four boys built a fire together and spent the night stretched out around it.

Jake liked to sleep on the plains. He'd find a narrow crack in the dry earth and drive a stick into the ground. He'd tie his dreamcatcher to it, and spread his blanket beneath it. He never slept without his dreamcatcher.

For the first time since his family had been taken from him, Jake could find some joy in his life. He thought about his family every day, and he longed to begin his search for them in earnest, but he had Match, and he trained with Yellow Cloud and Tall Elk, doing what he loved most.

Sometimes, he thought his life was complicated. Sometimes, he felt as if he was an outsider everywhere. The Garrets had taken him in, but he wasn't really their son, and the Natives called him brother, but he hadn't been born and raised among them. He loved Match, but sometimes the other apprentices appeared to be afraid of him, or in awe, or seemed not to know how to treat him. Mostly, he just wanted his pa and ma and Emmie.

Then, as the old sun set, he would walk out on to the plains with Grey Wolf and Rolling Thunder, who'd been with him the day he'd met Match, and he would be one of them. He would lie under the dark green sky and watch the strange stars overhead, trying to plot them and remember their positions.

Jake dreamed more in the Land of the Red Moon.

One night, he dreamed he was swimming around and around in a lake of fire, as if in a great cauldron of steaming, frothing lava, golden and burning with a crumbling, creasing crust and flashes of red-hot flame. He looked up to find a way out, and saw Pa Watkiss standing over him on the curved, black rim of what appeared to be a great iron pot.

If he'd had the dream before Chief Half Moon had given him the dreamcatcher, Jake would have woken up shouting and sweating in terror. He knew that this version of the dream was symbolic, though. The flames were not hot, but pleasantly warm, and Jake felt no danger. The colours in the dream were bright and inviting, and Pa Watkiss had a broad smile on his face and was clean and smart.

Nevertheless, Jake had rolled around under his blanket, as if swimming, and had called out in his sleep. When he'd awoken, he'd sat up suddenly to find that he was staring at a pair of naked legs. Halfway up the legs was a pair of old knees. They couldn't possibly belong to Grey Wolf or Rolling Thunder, and they were too old for Yellow Cloud or even for Tall Elk. Jake raised his eyes to look up at the Native. It was River Stone.

Jake began to clamber to his feet, but River Stone reached down and put a hand on the boy's shoulder.

He said nothing, but, after a moment, he removed his hand and began to walk slowly away.

Jake sat in the darkness. River Stone moved swiftly and silently, and was out of sight almost before Jake had realized he was gone. Jake stirred the fire, threw a few more sticks on it, and looked deeply into it to try to imagine what his dream might mean. He was too distracted by River Stone to be able to work it out, even though his dreams were becoming clearer all the time. Why was the old Native suddenly taking an interest in him?

Jake knew that if he was patient he would work out what his dreams meant. He knew that they'd already led him to the Land of the Red Moon, and he was sure that one day, soon, they'd lead him to his family.

20

Training always took place beyond the shade of the ridge, out on the plains with their knee-deep, purple and yellow mists. The green sky with its feathery yellow and turquoise clouds seemed to go on forever, meeting the wide horizons a thousand miles away. There was no land so vast as this anywhere that Jake had been, and he had been right across America.

Every morning, the riders and their apprentices first completed a fly-past of the colony, under the great awning of the ridge, north and west of the settlement. To Jake, it was the most magical part of the winter training grounds, because it was where Match had come from.

Match was an easy-going creature, energetic and playful, but he was always most at peace when he was close to the colony. He was young, and he still keenly felt the presence of the mother of all the dragons, the brood queen, and her influence over him. When they flew over the colony, Jake could feel Match relax completely, almost as if the little dragon felt utterly confident, completely secure in his right to fly through the skies with Jake on his back.

The plains were parched and yellow, and crazed with cracks and fissures from which the purple and yellow gases escaped. Where the shade of the overhang ebbed and flowed with the movement of the dappled sun, the ground was smooth and solid. There were no cracks in the earth where the sun shone for only part of the day, and it was a deeper, richer colour. It was less hard and gave more easily underfoot, so that it was possible to make footprints in the earth, and to mould it into clay forms.

Deep in the shade of the overhanging ridge, where no light penetrated, the earth was permanently wet with puddles of sulphur-smelling mud, and pools of oozing purple liquid. The air was thick with the fog of sulphur and the scent of the creatures who lived there.

This was the colony. The old brood queen and her sisters lived comfortable lives deep in the lea of the mountain. They nursed their eggs and the hatchlings that emerged from them. They were also tended by a family of Cloud People. It was their life's work to look after the mother and her nursing sisters, and prepare the infants for adulthood. Some would become mounts, and some would become future brood sisters.

As the riders and their apprentices performed

their daily fly-past, the brood queen acknowledged her offspring's success. The sisters lifted their maws and blew great flares and streaks of flame vertically into the sky. The air around the colony was so rich with sulphur gas that when the flames hit the chemical they turned a rich, vibrant purple.

Jake thought it was the most beautiful colour he had ever seen. Brood sisters must be the only dragons in the world who produced such gorgeous flames.

The riders and apprentices were supposed to fly over the colony in pairs, travelling roughly in a circle, southwards. This particular morning, Jake broke ranks. He was the most highly ranked apprentice, but Yellow Cloud was a hard taskmaster and he had scolded and disciplined his student so often that Jake had been pushed down to third place. Two of the older boys in their third and fourth winters of training held positions one and two.

When Jake pulled up and hovered above the heads of the brood sisters, the apprentices in the ranks behind him didn't know what to do. Their riders hesitated, and the formation was ruined.

Riders and apprentices peeled off in all directions. Yellow Cloud could not have guessed that Jake would stop during the fly-past, and had continued on. He flew a tight circle to return to Jake's side, but it was too late. Below them, the brood sisters were suddenly aware of a change to the fly-past. They stopped breathing fire, and waited for a signal from the brood queen.

On the ground, the Cloud People attending to the colony stopped working, and looked up at Match, aghast.

They had heard rumours about Dragon Sight. He was quickly becoming a legend, but they had no experience of him, except for the fly-pasts in the mornings. Nothing like this had ever happened before, and they didn't know what to do in such strange circumstances. The brood queen was an old and magical creature, not to be disturbed or upset. She was fragile and wise, and revered by all the Cloud People.

Jake hovered on Match, not sure what he wanted to do, but absolutely certain that he didn't want to just fly over the colony. He'd done it so many times, and, every time, he'd felt Match's love for the brood queen, and his own connection to her. Jake felt that he owed it to Match and to the queen to do something special for all of them. He wanted to show the brood queen how wonderful Match was, and how special was their connection. He wanted to show her what she had made.

He saw Yellow Cloud make a tight circle, and realized that he only had a moment to decide. He loosened his grip on Match's neck feathers, and slackened his knees, instructing the little dragon to curl up his wings and drop closer to the colony. Then he urged Match's head forward, so that the little dragon stretched his neck and extended his wings.

They swooped in low, and glided right over the brood queen's head. Her eyes opened wide, and she eagerly followed Match's every move as he swooped and swayed, and performed an elaborate dance.

Yellow Cloud wanted to make Jake stop, but he couldn't do it without checking with the colony caretakers. Jake's teacher signalled to the lead handler, who gestured back from the edge of the colony. Yellow Cloud had to stay clear and allow Jake to continue. It was bad enough that Match was causing a commotion. The lead handler would not allow a second dragon to make things even worse.

Jake and Match performed a series of manoeuvres above the brood queen: a figure of eight, followed by a loop, and then an upright spiral and a circle of the colony to finish.

Then they repeated the manoeuvres, while the brood queen followed Match with bursts of bright purple flame, as if she was lighting his way, dancing with him, filling the spaces in the air that he made for her with light.

The riders had gathered their apprentices and

were making large circles high above the colony, looking down on the spectacle.

The family of handlers watched, mesmerized, and Yellow Cloud hovered as close as he dared. He couldn't help being impressed by Jake, but he was also very angry. Would the boy ever learn that the rules kept them all safe?

Match and Jake, and the brood queen performed the dance again as everyone watched.

When it was done, Yellow Cloud flew up to meet the other riders and apprentices, and, moments later, Jake and Match joined them.

Yellow Cloud led them back to the plains. He and Jake should have formed the third rank, and everyone thought that Jake had won favour once again. They were all wrong. As they landed in silence, all the riders could see the rage in Yellow Cloud's face as he confronted Jake. No one knew what he was going to say, including the Native.

Jake felt very small, and his face grew very red as his teacher stood over him, his hands on his hips, staring hard into the boy's face. Jake waited for Yellow Cloud to speak, but his Native teacher said nothing. Jake realized that his mentor's anger went beyond words. He wanted to drop his face in shame, but he dared not break his teacher's gaze.

In the end, Yellow Cloud cast his eyes to one side in disgust, and turned to walk away.

Jake didn't know what to do, or even how to say sorry, and he didn't know how to explain the connection he felt to the old brood queen. Sorry wasn't good enough. He would have to work harder than ever to earn Yellow Cloud's trust. More than that, he would have to learn to be more obedient.

21

The party was not large when it left Prospect in the pre-dawn darkness, the following Sunday morning, and no one but Nathan McKenzie saw it go.

Trapper Watkiss wasn't at all impressed when he realized they were leaving on a Sunday. He hadn't liked the nuns, but they'd taught him to believe that it was ungodly to begin a grand undertaking on the Lord's Day. He didn't like his luck.

It wasn't a large party. It was adequate, however, for safety's sake. If they were to climb a mountain, Trapper wanted to make sure there were enough men on enough ropes to do it safely. There were supplies to think about too, especially in the winter. Trapper had organized for two mules to be loaded.

Finally, Trapper Watkiss wanted to know there would be men on his side in a fight, should the worst come to the worst. With a boss like Horton Needham, and Nathan McKenzie left behind in Prospect, he wasn't taking any chances.

Horton Needham had his geologist and his

secretary. The secretary, Reginald Pennyworth, was a very big man who never spoke or wrote anything down, and Trapper Watkiss suspected he might actually be a bodyguard. It was obvious that the clerk Needham had employed in Prospect was the only man performing any secretarial duties.

Trapper Watkiss didn't entirely trust Marcus and Anthony Mimms. They were mean men, who would do almost anything for a bottle of whisky. They were miners, not trappers like Watkiss, and they'd only been in Prospect for five years. Trapper never trusted a man he hadn't known for at least a decade. Besides, Needham was holding the purse strings.

Saturday had been spent organizing the men and the mules, and then Trapper had pored over Haskell's maps. They were clever and beautiful and they'd get them where they wanted to be. Just to make sure, Trapper took one of the plain silk handkerchiefs from McKenzie's stock, and drew his own map on it. He'd drawn many maps in his time, but none of them as clever as this one. He wanted to make sure he could find his way back to Prospect if there was any funny business, and he didn't plan on getting lost on Horton Needham's account.

Merry Mack had been installed in her cot bed in the parlour of her cottage on Main Street for some time.

Doc Trelawny had hurried back with Masefield

Haskell to find the old woman still unconscious on the kitchen floor. She'd been very pale and cold, but the doctor had been able to find a pulse. He'd gently felt her head all over and checked for broken bones from the fall. Then he'd looked at the cut on her leg.

'Thank you for helping,' Doc Trelawny had said.

'Are you thanking me for dressing the wound, or for calling you?' Haskell had asked. 'Because I should think you might thank me for both, given the circumstances.'

'Are you *sure* you're all right?' the doctor had asked, frowning slightly at Haskell. He'd heard rumours that the geologist had some funny ways, and he'd wanted to make sure that his odd little double question wasn't out of the ordinary.

'Perfectly,' Haskell had said, 'just a bit of a bump on the head.'

'Let's get Mrs Mack to bed,' Doc Trelawny had said, 'and then I'll take a look at your head, you understand?'

'Very well,' Haskell had said, 'but I really do feel perfectly all right.'

Doc Trelawny had examined Haskell, and had given him a clean bill of health. Then the geologist had sat up with Merry Mack. She hadn't moved all night, although she'd moaned once. The sound had quite startled Haskell, making him jump out of his chair beside her bed. He'd put a gentle hand on her forehead and was pleased that she hadn't been quite so cold.

'How do you feel?' Masefield Haskell had asked. 'Can I get you anything?' Mrs Mack hadn't replied. She'd woken very briefly during Saturday afternoon, and had patted Haskell's hand when he'd reached out for her.

'Can I bring you something to eat, Mrs Mack?' he'd asked. 'Some soup perhaps?'

Again, she hadn't answered. She'd just smiled slightly, and turned her head as if she was saying no.

Mrs Mack was asleep in her bed in the parlour of her cottage when the expedition party left the saloon before dawn on Sunday morning. Masefield Haskell was sitting in an armchair with his feet up on an old gout stool, and a quilt that Mrs Mack had sewn when she was a young woman draped over him. He didn't hear the men in the street outside as they took their leave of Nathan McKenzie, and he didn't hear his mule Sarah as she brayed one short, low bray. He didn't hear them because he was sleeping very deeply.

Haskell was so worried about Merry Mack that if she'd stirred in her sleep he would have woken up without any hesitation, but six men and two mules in the street went totally unnoticed by him.

22

There were no instructions from Yellow Cloud, so Jake began to do what he hoped might make his teacher proud.

After the fly-past, riders and apprentices usually paired up for one-to-one tuition. Each of the apprentices was at a different stage of his studies. They were all good at different things. Grey Wolf was proving to be a fine long-distance rider at high altitude. He had confided in Jake that he was still fearful low to the ground, however, and had trouble taking off and landing. Rolling Thunder, on the other hand, tired easily and lost concentration, and his ground mapping was poor. He was working hard with his rider to improve those skills.

Jake knew that Yellow Cloud had high expectations of him as a rider, because of his spirit quest, because of the unique scar on his hand, and because of his dragonsight. Jake's expectations were all about learning fast so that he could begin his search for his family. It was almost all he ever thought about.

When Yellow Cloud gave him no instructions, Jake decided that he would practise complex figures. They required the most discipline and the best connection between rider and dragon. They were beautiful, but mastering them also meant a lot of tedious, repetitive work.

Jake hated them, and Yellow Cloud knew it.

The art of performing complex figures was to create a series of shapes in the sky to mark out a perfect sphere. The horsemen did something similar on the ground with their Appaloosas. With the horses, it was possible to trace their movements by following the paths of their hoofprints. In the sky, Match would signal certain manoeuvres with bursts of flame.

Jake had completed some of the figures over the colony, but he had improvised, performing the manoeuvres in a random order.

Perhaps, if I perform the complex figures perfectly, Yellow Cloud might not be so angry with me, he thought.

Jake made sure that Yellow Cloud was watching him, bowed his head to his teacher, and mounted Match. He walked his mount into the sky, and flew towards the blue dunes.

The air was totally clear to the south. There were no clouds to obstruct Jake's chance to carve a perfect sphere in the green sky. Most of the apprentices liked to practise in the sky over the plains where there were no mountains and no plants to cast confusing shadows. Jake liked the shadows, and, besides, he liked to be over the dunes, where he'd found Pa Watkiss's wagon.

Jake felt, in every bone in his body, that his parents were somewhere in the Land of the Red Moon, just as he felt Match's cool scales beneath him when he flew, and just as he saw through Match's eyes when the two of them were in perfect harmony.

Jake looked down on the bright, glittering crystal dunes, hoping to see some corner of a canvas wagon cover, or some hoop from a barrel or spoke from a wheel. He saw nothing but grains of sand in every shade of blue.

The dunes shifted and settled with the ebb and flow of the winds, like the tides of an ocean. Pa Watkiss's wagon had been exposed when Match had crash-landed in the dunes on their first flight. Jake had shifted an avalanche of sand, crabbing his way clumsily down the dunes, and exposed more of Pa's belongings. He'd seen Pa's fiddle, and he had known for certain that Pa Watkiss had to be in the Land of the Red Moon. The dreams had told Jake the rest.

Jake traced Match's shadow over the dunes as the two of them made a wide sweep of the area. He concentrated hard, trying to control the anticipation that filled him whenever he thought about the clues. He'd come here for a reason, and, today, the reason was to impress Yellow Cloud by completing the complex figures.

Jake couldn't see Yellow Cloud, so he flew another wide circle over the dunes, and then began to map the sky. He drew an imaginary grid, and curved and moulded it into a perfect sphere in the sky. He looked out to the horizon, up to the cool, dappled sun and across to the mountain ridge. He looked low across the peaks of the dunes and out to where the base of the mountain met the horizon, where the horizontal met the convex curve of the ridge. He looked straight down and then straight up.

Then Jake saw Yellow Cloud, high and to the west, and he wondered why he hadn't spotted him before.

Jake had divided the sky into imaginary sections. He had cut it in half across its centre and then through its core, as if it was an apple. Then he'd done it again, and again, imagining it was the globe in Miss Ballantine's classroom and he was drawing its lines of longitude and latitude. He drew the Greenwich meridian and the equator, and the tropics of Cancer and Capricorn.

All I need do is complete the complex figures. All I need do, to put everything right, is impress Yellow Cloud, he thought.

Then Jake and Match flew inside the sphere, a perfect figure of eight cutting through the equator and touching the edges of the tropics north-west and south-east. He repeated the process with another perfect figure of eight, cutting through the equator again, but, this time, reversing the direction, touching the edges of the tropics north-east and south-west. Match exhaled flames at each of the points where the lines of Jake's globe touched.

The figures were only just beginning, and Jake knew they would become a lot more complex before he was finished. He wasn't sure he could complete them, but he was determined to get as far as he could.

Jake and Match stopped, dead centre of the sphere, and Match hovered, pulling his wings close to his body. He pushed his head low and forward, so that his next puff of flames hit the middle of the sphere. Then, the little dragon brought his tail and then his body around in the southern hemisphere, and rotated and flipped his body, reversing so that he was flying almost upside down for a moment.

It was an almost impossible manoeuvre for the average apprentice, but Jake was different. He looked out through the dragon's eyes, and steered Match with his mind, and not just with his hands, knees and feet. He was also lucky because Match was playful and a natural acrobat, and was never happier than when he was flipping and cartwheeling through the air.

Yellow Cloud hovered in the sky a little above and to one side of Jake's position. He quickly realized what his apprentice was attempting, and understood that the boy's honour was at stake.

Yellow Cloud watched Jake as he made the patterns in the sky, and checked the flames from Match's nostrils. The circles around the sphere were true and good, and the figures of eight were performed at the perfect angles. There were no false moves.

Then Match hovered and spiralled, and the corkscrew motion that formed the second of the complex figures began. Jake had to map a constellation from the night sky over the plateau, and another from the Land of the Red Moon. The first was his birth constellation from April 30th 1837, and the second was the constellation from the first season he was paired with Match.

The constellation from the Land of the Red Moon was particularly beautiful. It was a swooping 'V' shape, like a dragon's wings, with a strike through the point of the 'V' like a thunderbolt.

Every point, every star in each constellation, had to be marked on the surface of the sphere with a puff of smoke from Match's nostrils. Match had to swirl and glide, sweep and turn within the space determined by the diameter of the sphere, and no more. The space was cramped and some of the turns were excruciatingly tight. One mistimed beat of a wing, one badly judged flick of the tail and the pattern would be ruined, and Jake and Match would fail to complete the figures.

Jake looked out through Match's eyes. Inside the little dragon's head, the boy coaxed and cajoled, and calmed and soothed. When Match got it right and graced the air with a puff of yellow smoke at precisely the correct point, Jake praised him. It was so easy for him to tell Match what a wonderful friend he was. It was true, after all.

More than half the figures were completed to perfection.

Jake was aware of Yellow Cloud in the sky. He was aware of every element of the exercise, of all the points in the sky, on the horizons and on the ground that he was using to guide him. He was aware, too, of his perfect connection with Match.

Jake could not feel how tightly his fingers were grasping Match's neck feathers. He could not feel the tension in his legs, or how firmly his knees were pushing into his mount's shoulders. He could not feel the pressure in his heels and feet. He didn't need to feel those things when he was in Match's head, when their minds were entwined, when he was steering the little dragon with his thoughts.

It was the best kind of magic.

The dappled sun was climbing higher in the sky as the morning wore on. Jake didn't know how long he and Match had been airborne, but time mattered less in the Land of the Red Moon where the air was so much drier and warmer than it was on the plateau.

Jake looked out through Match's eyes as they completed the spiral up through the sphere from South Pole to North. Match left a puff of smoke at the North Pole and flew straight up. As his tail cleared the North Pole, Match flipped, ready for the nosedive that would take him back down through the sphere.

The manoeuvre required a barrel roll, so Match tucked in his wings and extended his head and tail. Suddenly, with the sun as high as it could climb, the dragon's shadow was a tiny, hard, black dot on the blue dunes below.

Everything else on the ground was lit bright and blue and stark.

Everything on the ground was blue, except for a sudden, bright flash of red.

Jake knew nothing, except that he was hurtling, head first, towards the ground at breakneck speed. His hands were suddenly sweating as he clutched at Match's neck feathers, and he was frantically squeezing his knees, and kicking his heels into his mount's sides, trying to change their course.

He simply could not remember what they were doing. All thoughts of complex figures, all thoughts of pleasing Yellow Cloud, had left his head. What's more, *he* had left Match's mind suddenly and without warning, and they were both paying the price.

Match was panicking, and Jake was panicking, too. His hair was sticking to the sweat on his forehead, and he couldn't catch his breath. The ground was careering towards them at an alarming rate, and there was nothing on earth that Jake could do about it. He closed his eyes so firmly that he began to see stars. He squeezed his fists so tightly in Match's nape feathers that his knuckles turned white, and he began to pray.

23

During the fly-past, Yellow Cloud had been angry with Jake, and disappointed in him.

He hadn't been surprised to see Jake and Match flying south towards the blue dunes. He'd been disappointed, yet again.

Every day since they'd come to the Land of the Red Moon, Jake had asked when he could go back to the blue dunes to begin the search for his ma and pa and sister.

Yellow Cloud knew that there was a time for everything, and now was the time for Match and Jake to begin their training in earnest. Yellow Cloud understood Jake's yearning to find his family, but he also understood how dangerous the world was, both worlds, and how fragile the life of a young dragon.

Bonds between men and dragons had caused evil in the Land of the Red Moon . . . evil beyond Jake's imaginings, and that evil had begun to spill over into the Land of the White Sun. One day, Yellow Cloud would tell him the legends, and, perhaps then, Dragon Sight would understand what was at stake.

When Jake didn't circle back with Match, Yellow Cloud had followed his apprentice south, and soon found him, exactly where he expected him to be. He assumed that Jake would land in the dunes, or, at the very least, fly over them, looking for clues. He did not expect to find him attempting one of the most difficult lessons a rider must ever learn.

Yellow Cloud was impressed. He didn't like to show it, so he simply took up a position in the sky, and watched. The complex figures emerged below him, performed almost perfectly. Once or twice, Yellow Cloud very nearly whooped with delight.

Then something happened. Yellow Cloud watched as Match dropped out of the sky like a stone. The nosedive that should have taken the dragon and his rider down through the South Pole, and then up and out for another spiralling circuit of the imaginary sphere, was about to end in disaster.

Yellow Cloud realized that Jake had lost his connection with Match, and that the boy and his mount were both panicking.

Yellow Cloud dropped Gale through the air, fast. Then he allowed him to spread his wings and glide low to the ground. Gale had to time his wing beats so that the downstrokes fell in the dips between dunes. Yellow Cloud guided him so close to the tops of the blue dunes that one false move and he, too, would crash.

Yellow Cloud flew across Match's eyeline, and then swung up in a climbing circle, doing his best to urge Jake to follow suit.

Jake did not follow suit.

Yellow Cloud dropped Gale hard out of the circle to get a better look at Jake's face. There was no expression there, and he didn't even appear to be blinking.

Yellow Cloud was so shocked that he suddenly found himself pushing too hard with his feet and squeezing too hard with his hands in Gale's nape feathers. Gale soared almost vertically into another high, wide circle, but the angle was dangerously steep, and Yellow Cloud could not keep his seat on Gale's back. He had no choice but to let go before Gale hit the top of the arc and overbalanced.

The dragon was going to crash; there was no doubt of that. Yellow Cloud had to take his chances.

Jake held his breath for a moment, and closed his eyes. His panic had abated, and he could see the ground coming up towards him so fast that he thought he could almost count the individual blue sand crystals.

He concentrated on Match. He thought of his green scales, his soft feathers, the colour and smell of the smoke in his nostrils and the cool, smooth surface of his iridescent scales, and he was lost in the moment.

Jake heard an odd clicking, purring voice in his head, and he knew that he and Match had connected. He also knew that, if only he trusted him, his little dragon friend could do anything.

Jake didn't open his eyes. He simply put his trust in Match. Suddenly, he felt a strange, unexpected tug, and then a wrench sideways rather than a steep, pressured climb. He felt the turn of a head and a tail, the flex of an alula joint, the extension of a wing. He felt knees pulling up, and he felt Match beginning to roll.

This connection wasn't like the other times when he'd bonded with Match. Before, Jake had entered Match's mind and, somehow, he'd been in charge of the little dragon, seeing through his eyes and controlling his movements. This time Match, with all his animal instincts, was in charge of the bond between them.

Yellow Cloud shouted.

Jake felt as if he was in some kind of suspension as Match's body flexed and turned and spiralled, and then began to climb. Then he opened his eyes and there was nothing. There were no bright blue dunes and there was no cloudless green sky. Jake didn't even know which way was up, but he didn't need to know. Match knew.

Suddenly, with utter clarity, Jake saw Yellow Cloud's riderless dragon plummet through the air in a tangle of legs and wings. It huffed smoke from its nostrils and it pawed the sky. It flapped its wings frantically from their alula joints, because it had no time to expand them.

Yellow Cloud shouted again. Match dropped, spread his wings and glided, slowly, in a tight arc, directly over Gale, who had just dropped through the air.

Yellow Cloud landed, behind Jake, with a jolt.

Match had too much to think about and his connection to Jake was not strong enough. He tried to compensate for the extra weight on his back, but Jake was not ready for Yellow Cloud to land behind him, or for the way that Match's back dropped with the extra weight on the dragon's relatively small frame. Jake's feet bounced out of position, his hands lost their grip and, suddenly, he was thrown off Match's back, and was falling. Match was not in control of Jake, but neither was Jake.

Without Yellow Cloud's weight, and with his mind freed, Gale managed a clumsy, but effective landing. He avoided crashing by choosing a medium-sized dune, and the impact sent out a glittering spray of crystals as he came back down to earth.

The spray of blue sand crystals that Jake sent out spread a much broader arc across the dunes and across Gale, who shook the sand away and puffed yellow smoke at Jake's half-buried, crooked body. The large dragon brought his head down close to where the boy lay unconscious, and the creature stood guard while Match and Yellow Cloud landed.

If there had ever been any sign of Pa Watkiss's wagon among the blue dunes, if there had ever been a flash of red from his long underwear, Jake's crash-landing had moved enough sand to cover it all up two or three times over.

24

Yellow Cloud breathed a sigh of relief as Jake rocked his head gently from side to side and began to open his eyes. The Native took a gentle hold of Jake's left wrist.

'Do not move, Dragon Sight,' he said. 'Tall Elk will tend to you.'

Jake turned his head to face Yellow Cloud and moaned slightly.

'What happened?' he asked, his eyes trying to focus on the walls of the Lodge. 'I ache . . . all over.'

'You had a bad fall. You were unconscious,' said Tall Elk, coming to Jake's bedside. 'You were lucky not to break any bones, but there are bruises.' He touched Jake's head gently, and Jake winced.

Tall Elk turned to Yellow Cloud, and said, 'I know you must talk to him, but talk gently, and do not frighten him.'

'I must do what I must do,' said Yellow Cloud.

Tall Elk sighed and turned away, leaving Jake with his teacher.

'That was not you, was it?' asked Yellow Cloud, his tone very serious. 'Tell me the truth, Dragon Sight.'

'I don't understand,' said Jake. 'What do you mean, it wasn't me?'

Yellow Cloud looked down at Jake. He let go of his arm and softened his voice.

'It's important we talk about this,' he said.

'I'm sorry I'm not like you,' said Jake, closing his eyes.

Yellow Cloud smiled, and said, 'I think you are exactly like me. Chief Half Moon was my rider when I was an apprentice, and I could never understand why I had to do everything he told me to. I spent more time mucking out than I did in the air my first two winters at the training grounds.'

'You did?' asked Jake, shocked.

'Yes,' said Yellow Cloud.

'I'm sorry about the fly-past,' said Jake. 'I just wanted to show the brood queen what she's done.'

'She knows what she has done,' said Yellow Cloud. 'She has been doing it for a thousand years.'

'So long?' asked Jake. 'I didn't know.'

'That is why she must be well looked after,' said Yellow Cloud. 'She is old and tired and fragile. She is losing her scales, and there are only so many more dragons like Match in her. When she leaves us, it will be the end of times.'

Jake looked Yellow Cloud in the face.

'The end of everything?' he asked, horrified.

'No,' said Yellow Cloud, 'only the end . . .' He hesitated, searching for the right words. 'It will only be the end of *our* times,' he said. 'The end of one brood queen and the beginning of a new dragon age. There are legends . . . Before the end of your third winter of training, you will hear them told.'

'I want to hear them now,' said Jake.

'You will hear the legends when it is your time,' said Yellow Cloud. 'There are more important things to talk about now.'

'Could anything be more important than the end of times?' asked Jake.

'This morning you thought there was nothing more important than searching for your family,' said Yellow Cloud.

Jake turned his head away. He knew that it was true, and he knew that the feeling he had about his family would not go away until he found them. He didn't want to think that he might find proof that they'd perished when the wagon train had caught fire.

'Right now, it is important that we talk about what happened up there,' said Yellow Cloud, pointing a finger up into the Lodge as if it was the sky.

'Nothing happened,' said Jake. 'I just wanted to show you that I could do the complex figures.'

'You think I do not know that?' asked Yellow Cloud. There was a long pause. When Jake didn't answer, the Native spoke again.

'You panicked, didn't you, Dragon Sight?' he asked. 'You lost concentration, and suddenly you knew you were in danger.'

'It was the nosedive. The ground was so close. The dunes were so blue, except . . . I thought I saw Pa Watkiss's long underwear. I thought I saw the red cloth.'

'You broke contact with Match, and you panicked,' said Yellow Cloud.

'Yes,' said Jake. 'I thought we were going to die. It doesn't matter, though. It all turned out all right.'

Again, there was a long pause, but, this time, it was Yellow Cloud who was silent. Jake didn't understand why the Native looked so pale and stern.

'I knew it was too good to be true,' said Yellow Cloud.

'What was too good to be true?' asked Jake. 'Match saved us. How could that be bad?'

'Riders are the luckiest of men,' said Yellow Cloud.

'I know,' said Jake. 'Match is my best friend.'

'There is a connection between a rider and his dragon that does not exist even between two men,' said Yellow Cloud. 'I know that you have felt it. It does not come so easily to all men.'

'I understand how blessed I am,' said Jake. 'It's because of the dragonsight.'

'That is part of it,' said Yellow Cloud, 'but it is important that you know the whole truth, now, before you ever sit on a dragon's back again.'

'This really is serious, isn't it?' asked Jake.

'This is as serious as death,' said Yellow Cloud. 'More serious.'

'How could it be more serious than death?' asked Jake.

'Because death is an end of things,' said Yellow Cloud. 'It is neither good nor evil. It is only the opposite of life. Death is to life, as sleep is to wakefulness.'

'Yes,' said Jake. 'There's nothing to fear. So, how could my connection with Match hurt me?'

'When you and Match are one, when you see through his eyes,' said Yellow Cloud, 'that is the connection?'

'Yes,' said Jake. 'That's it.'

'How does it feel?' asked Yellow Cloud.

Jake closed his eyes and thought for a long moment.

'It feels like nothing else,' he said, not sure what his teacher wanted him to say.

'Can you tell me about it?' asked Yellow Cloud.

Jake was embarrassed. He closed his eyes again, and lowered his voice.

'It feels like goodness,' he said. 'I don't know if I

should say it. The Reverend Varvel wouldn't like it. Pa wouldn't like it.'

'You are here to learn and I am your teacher,' said Yellow Cloud kindly. 'You will not be punished for speaking, and, if you are wrong, I will try to guide you.'

'It feels good,' said Jake. 'It feels right.'

He opened his eyes and looked hard at Yellow Cloud.

'Do you know what heaven is?' he asked. 'Do you know what paradise is?'

'I have heard about heaven,' said Yellow Cloud, 'and about hell.'

'When I'm riding Match, and I'm him and he's me, and we're flying through the sky,' said Jake, 'I think that's what heaven must feel like.'

'Then,' said Yellow Cloud, more serious than Jake had ever seen him before, 'I can tell you all about hell.'

25

'Starling was the most promising boy on the vision quest that year. He was strong and lean and joyful. He would fight if he had to and remain calm when it mattered. He could laugh and cry, and he loved to fly.'

Jake listened attentively as Yellow Cloud told his story.

'Starling was paired with an older, larger Thunder . . . dragon that had been waiting for a rider for many years. There was much rejoicing when the pairing was made, for many riders feared the wonderful dragon would never find his man. His scales were like the feathers of a starling, and some of the riders laughed that the dragon was waiting for an apprentice with the right name.'

Yellow Cloud seemed to hesitate, and Jake looked at him for a moment before turning away again. The Native wore a faraway expression that was full of sorrow, and Jake didn't want to intrude on his grief.

'Starling learned his lessons well, worked tirelessly,

listened hard to the stories and legends, and recited them to the younger riders, word for word, when his turn came. He did his share of every job. He was courteous, and he loved his dragon.'

Yellow Cloud swallowed hard to settle his emotions before continuing.

'It was our third winter of training,' he said.

'You were apprenticed together?' asked Jake. 'You were brothers?'

'We were more than that,' said Yellow Cloud. 'We were brothers of the same mother, born under the same sun.'

'I don't understand,' said Jake.

Yellow Cloud looked at him blankly, as if he had no further explanation.

Jake thought for a moment.

'You were twins,' he said. 'You and Starling were twin brothers . . . Born of the same mother, under the same sun.'

'Yes,' said Yellow Cloud.

'I didn't know,' said Jake.

'That is why I am telling you his story,' said Yellow Cloud. 'It is our legend. You would have heard it with the others when it was time. The time has come now.

'He was better than me,' said Yellow Cloud. 'He was more true, more disciplined, more able. Everybody loved Starling. He did everything perfectly.

I was punished and he was praised. I think I hated him, sometimes, for that.'

Jake wondered whether to fill the pause that followed. He wondered whether to admit that he'd hated Emmie when he'd saved her rag doll from the river instead of his book. Now she might be dead too . . .

'He worked so hard,' said Yellow Cloud, while Jake was still thinking about his sister. 'Then, that third winter, suddenly Starling changed.

'He made his connection with his dragon almost as soon as we arrived at the winter training grounds –'

'Why did it take so long for Starling to connect with his dragon?' Jake asked. 'It was his third winter of training. Why didn't it happen sooner?'

Yellow Cloud smiled broadly, and put a firm hand on Jake's shoulder.

'You do not understand at all, do you, Dragon Sight?' he asked. 'Most riders never have a true connection with their dragons. Some take years to develop a bond. A talented rider might make a connection towards the end of his training or in his first years as a rider.'

Jake's eyes were wide and his mouth had dropped open. He couldn't believe what he was hearing.

'So it took Starling until his third winter?' asked Jake.

'Yes,' said Yellow Cloud, 'and that is fast.'

'How long did it take you?' asked Jake.

'We were born of the same mother, under the same sun,' said Yellow Cloud. 'For us, things often happened at the same time.'

'Not sooner?' asked Jake.

'It is almost never sooner,' said Yellow Cloud. 'Will you never know how special you are, Dragon Sight? How important it is that you become the man we all need you to be?'

'I don't know,' said Jake. 'How important is it?'

'Important enough for me to be sitting at your bedside telling you a story even though it causes me great pain and sadness,' said Yellow Cloud.

'But it won't wait?' asked Jake.

'For you, Dragon Sight,' said Yellow Cloud, 'nothing can wait. Now, let me finish the legend.

'Starling never wanted to leave the sky. He was first in the air for practice each morning, and always the last to land. He would volunteer for any errand that required a flight, and would spend hours practising complex figures. River Stone had nothing but praise for him. He would tell all of us what a fine rider Starling would make.'

'Wait,' said Jake. 'River Stone was his teacher?'

'Yes,' said Yellow Cloud. 'His skills as a teacher surpassed those of all the riders. Chief Half Moon was destined to be our leader, but even he was not as wise a teacher as River Stone.'

There was a pause while Jake thought for a moment, and then he nodded for Yellow Cloud to continue.

'As Starling became more favoured, I was less in the sky and more on the ground. In my envy, I behaved even more badly,' said Yellow Cloud. 'I spent more time being punished, and I saw less of my brother. When I did see him, he seemed too thin and his skin had too much of a sheen on it, as if he was feverish.

'I spoke to Chief Half Moon, and, even though he was disappointed in me, he could see that I was worried for my brother. He spoke to River Stone. They argued.'

As Yellow Cloud slowed down, unsure how to explain what had happened between the two men, Jake guessed.

'River Stone thought Chief Half Moon was jealous,' he said, 'jealous of his skills as a teacher, and jealous because he had chosen the wrong twin to train.'

'Yes,' said Yellow Cloud. 'Riders are proud men. There was rivalry between River Stone and Chief Half Moon, so they argued.

'Starling did everything that he was instructed to do, but he stopped talking to the rest of us. He would sit alone and say nothing. He would not look me in the eye. If I approached him, he would walk away.

He spent all his time with his dragon, and most of that time in the air.'

'He frightened you,' said Jake with sudden realization.

'Much of my training frightened me,' said Yellow Cloud. 'Dragons are frightening. Connecting to a dragon, being inside the head of the beast, bearing the weight of its mind is frightening.'

'Not to me,' said Jake.

'Not to Starling, either,' said Yellow Cloud.

Jake looked hard into Yellow Cloud's eyes. His voice when he had spoken his last words was low and cracking, and Jake knew that he was deadly serious. He also knew that he must learn this lesson well.

'Everything he did on his dragon's back was perfect,' said Yellow Cloud. 'He never made a mistake. He could perform the complex figures as if by magic. The rest of us would be made to watch while he demonstrated them, over and over, always the same, always perfect.

'On the ground, he stopped talking, he stopped eating with the rest of us, and he spent his time mucking out the dragons, so he could be close to his mount. One day, I found him eating with his dragon, the same raw flesh.

'I told Chief Half Moon. I told River Stone. They talked about the bond. I told them I felt it too. They said his bond with his dragon was strong, that it felt like that for some riders. They told me that Starling was special.

'One morning, when he flew to the head of the rank for the fly-past, I saw that Starling was naked. He had a layer of purple mud all over his body from the hot spring. He had bathed with his dragon. There was nothing of the man left in him.'

'That's terrible,' said Jake, blushing at the thought of wallowing naked in the mud of the bathing pools, 'but you can't think that I could become like that?'

'You let Match into your head, didn't you? You let him take over your mind?' asked Yellow Cloud.

'We've been connected since the first time we flew together,' said Jake, 'since the first time I blinked and found myself looking out through his eyes.'

'Today,' said Yellow Cloud, 'you were not looking out through Match's eyes. Today, Match was looking out through your eyes.'

'No,' said Jake, 'Match is . . . I was . . .'

Jake didn't know what to say, and he didn't know what to think. He looked at Yellow Cloud, who looked steadily, but kindly, back at him.

'How did you know?' asked Jake.

'I know,' said Yellow Cloud, 'because Starling was my brother and the same thing happened to him.'

'How could you possibly know that?' asked Jake.

'I watched him lead the fly-past over the colony.

I watched him dance for the brood queen. I saw his pride in his dragon. I saw that nothing else meant anything to him. Even the rules suddenly meant nothing to him.

'I watched my brother break ranks and complete the complex figures above the brood queen. I watched her and her sisters breathe the purple flames that made his dragon's scales shimmer and shine. I watched Starling allow his mount to nosedive into the colony so that those flames seared the coat of dry mud from his skin. I saw the mud spark white and yellow and red. I saw it flare on his skin and spark off it.

'Starling was powerless. His dragon controlled him. A rider would never hurt his dragon. A dragon . . .'

Yellow Cloud could not bear to finish his sentence. The riders respected the creatures they rode. They had lifelong relationships with them, and some of them had deep bonds. He could not speak out against them.

'Match would never hurt me,' said Jake fiercely. 'Match *could* never hurt me.'

'They are beasts, with the instincts of beasts,' said Yellow Cloud. 'You have seen how dragons can act towards men. You blame them for taking your family. You fought them when they attacked your town.'

'They weren't Match,' said Jake.

'No,' said Yellow Cloud. 'Starling's dragon was a good beast too. All the riders loved that animal. They had tended it for years and were happy when it finally paired with an apprentice.

'In the end, I watched that dragon dance with my brother on its back. I watched the sparks fly from the mud caked on his skin. I watched his wild, sightless eyes.

'Then it was over. We landed on the plains, and Starling tried to take himself away from us. Then I saw the scorched earth covering his skin in ugly patches. I saw all the new marks on his skin that could never be tattooed. I saw the new marks that meant he did not belong to us . . .'

Yellow Cloud swallowed hard once more before he could continue. It was a difficult tale for him to tell. Jake wondered who would have told the story if it had been recited in front of all the apprentices, at the right time. He wondered whether Yellow Cloud had ever had to tell the legend before.

'I saw all of those things, and I was more angry with Starling than I had ever been with anyone in my life. I called my brother's name, but he did not turn to me. I called his name again. My voice was hard and angry, and I did not recognize it. I called his name, once more, and Starling turned to face me.

'He was my own brother, born of the same mother, under the same sun, but I did not recognize him.

His eyes were as cold as if he was not looking out of them, and his mouth was hard. He was an empty shell.

'He stood looking at me as if he did not know who I was,' said Yellow Cloud. 'I do not think Starling did know who I was. I do not think he knew who *he* was. I strode up to him, I stood as close to him as I could without touching him, and I looked him right in the eye.'

'Who was looking back at you?' asked Jake. 'Someone was looking back at you. Some*one* or some*thing*.'

'What do you know of it?' asked Yellow Cloud.

'I know what I saw at the school house,' said Jake. 'I know what I saw when Match and I brought down the big black dragon. Behind those eyes there wasn't just an animal. It was one mind made of two halves . . . that's the only way I know how to explain it.'

Yellow Cloud held his head in his hands for a moment, and then he looked long and hard at Jake.

'You know too much, Dragon Sight,' he said. 'You must learn one lesson at a time, and you must learn each lesson well. Today you must learn that the rider must control the dragon's mind. If the dragon controls the rider . . . that way madness lies.'

'Madness?' asked Jake.

'Don't you think that Starling was mad to paint himself in mud? Don't you think he was mad to allow his dragon to fly the complex figures over the colony? Don't you think he was mad to allow the brood queen and her sisters to flame away the mud that covered his skin? Don't you think he was mad to be burned?'

'Yes, you're right,' said Jake. He hadn't worked it out for himself, but he could see how serious Yellow Cloud was.

'I could not help it,' said Yellow Cloud, 'I wrestled my own brother to the ground and we fought like dogs. Chief Half Moon and River Stone separated us, and I was blamed, because I had made the first attack. It made no difference. They soon saw the madness, just as I had seen it.

'The winter was at an end, the training over, and we were to return to the plateau. I hoped that returning to our summer home might change Starling.

'The last night in the Land of the Red Moon is very special. No one sleeps. A great fire is built, to resemble a teepee. It reaches up towards the moon, which appears to sit like a great ball on top of it. We celebrate long into the night, whooping and hollering, and dancing and feasting.

'Starling was there that night. He seemed more like himself. He ate with us and talked to some of the other riders, although he did not talk to me. He was not ready to forgive me for attacking him. He did not speak to River Stone either. I will never know why not.

'As the moon rose high in the sky, and the fire burned bright on the plains, Starling sent up a great wail. He threw back his head, and sounded a long call, as if he was crying to the moon.

'Everyone fell silent, and looked up to where he was gazing. We saw his dragon circling low over the fire, its belly shining blue-black in the firelight. It should have been in the corral. There are rules, but no one did anything. We all just watched.

'Starling raised his arms to the moon, or to his dragon, or to both. He cried out again.

'Then he began to walk towards the fire.

'No one knew what was happening. Everyone was quiet, watching. No one knew what to do, so we did nothing. I did nothing.

'We did not realize what we were watching until it was too late . . . until Starling had walked into the fire.

'His dragon circled overhead, adding streams of flames to the teepee of fire that was already raging. Then the dragon threw itself on the fire.

'It was the end of Starling's madness. It was the end of his dragon. It was the end of something that none of us understood. It was the beginning of a legend, and it was a lesson to us all.

'The dragon is our best friend and our deadliest

foe. We must revere him and respect him, but we must not be controlled by him,' said Yellow Cloud. 'The relationship between the rider and his dragon is a partnership, Dragon Sight. Never forget that.'

Yellow Cloud stood up, suddenly, and smoothed the legs of his buckskin trousers. He coughed once, into his hand, as Jake watched him, and he swallowed twice. His emotions were under control once again.

'Will you be ready to ride, tomorrow?' asked Yellow Cloud.

'Yes,' said Jake, solemnly.

'Dragon Sight,' said Yellow Cloud, taking hold of the boy by his chin and looking into his eyes, 'will you be ready to mount Match? Tell me honestly.'

'Yes, Yellow Cloud,' said Jake, unblinking, hoping that his teacher could see that he, too, was in earnest. 'Yes, Yellow Cloud,' he said again, 'I will be ready.'

26

'How do you think Jake is managing in . . . what do they call it? I never can remember,' asked Elizabeth Garret.

'The Land of the Red Moon,' said Masefield Haskell, saying the words as if they were poetry. 'I'm sure he's doing marvellously, Mrs Garret. The weather is warm and dry. The food is rich and plentiful. There are very few predators, and the boy will be learning such wonderful skills. I quite envy him.'

'Well thank you,' said Mrs Garret, not entirely sure that she felt any better. She struggled to think of Jake in a strange land where it was still summer and where there was no rain. She struggled to think of him as a man and as a dragon rider, and she certainly struggled to think of him without a mother. He'd had two mothers. Of course, losing the first had been tragic, but giving up the second might have been foolish. She tried not to remind herself that she was the second mother, and that she'd now lost two boys.

'Are you thanking me for reassuring you or for enriching your life with details of such a wonderful place?' asked Haskell. 'Because I should think you might thank me for both, given the circumstances.'

Elizabeth Garret had built up quite a relationship with Masefield Haskell, and had even started calling him Masefield. She was used to him asking for second helpings of gratitude, so she simply smiled and continued to spoon a little thin soup between Mrs Mack's pale lips.

Masefield Haskell and Elizabeth Garret were sitting in the little parlour of Merry Mack's cottage on Main Street. It was Christmas Eve. It had been three and a half weeks since the incident in Mrs Mack's kitchen, and the old woman was still weak and pale. She was awake for only short periods, and she ate and drank very little.

Haskell wanted to look after Mrs Mack himself, because he felt guilty that the burglars had stolen only his belongings, and he'd decided that the whole thing was his fault.

Haskell was neither a doctor nor a nurse, however, and it had fallen to Mrs Garret and Mrs Wemlow, who cleaned at the saloon, to take it in turns to look after Mrs Mack. Masefield Haskell stayed at her side for sixteen or eighteen hours a day, reading and talking to her, and Doc Trelawny visited most mornings.

There was nothing more to be done for Merry Mack except to keep her comfortable. Masefield Haskell took the task very seriously. He also kept the little cottage as neat as a new pin, and he fed Mrs Mack's hens.

Every two or three days, Masefield Haskell left Merry Mack in the care of one of the women and sought out Sheriff Sykes to try to get justice for her. He was gentle in Mrs Mack's company, moving around the little cottage quietly and speaking softly. In the sheriff's office, he railed and he shouted and he banged his fist on the table to get justice for her. It wasn't fair; the old woman had never done another human being a bad turn, and she'd done plenty of good ones.

Haskell would have liked justice for himself, because he was convinced that Horton Needham had stolen his maps and samples from the Land of the Red Moon, but, first and foremost, he wanted justice for Merry Mack.

As they sat in the parlour on Christmas Eve, Masefield Haskell and Elizabeth Garret heard tapping on the kitchen door and a voice calling out to them.

'Good afternoon, anyone at home?'

Haskell rose from his chair and went to the kitchen, closing the door behind him.

'Sheriff Sykes,' he said, holding out his hand for the sheriff to shake. 'What can I do for you?'

'Nothing at all, Mr Haskell,' said Lem Sykes. 'I just wanted to wish you and Mrs Mack a Merry Christmas and let you know that I haven't given up hope of finding the men that committed this terrible crime. In the season of goodwill, it seems only right that something should be done.'

'And you'd be the man to do it,' said Haskell, gripping the sheriff's hand firmly in his own.

'I hope so,' said Sheriff Sykes.

'Have you questioned your uncle again?' asked Haskell.

'He's staying tight-lipped on the subject of Horton Needham,' said the sheriff, 'but he's an ambitious man, and he'll do anything to get some influence back in Prospect, you mark my words.'

'I never understood that expression,' said Haskell. 'How exactly is it possible to "mark" words? Written down, in a book or letter, I suppose, but spoken words?'

'Take heed,' said Sheriff Sykes. 'If my uncle, Nathan McKenzie, can find a way to win back Prospect, he won't hesitate to turn Boss Needham in to me.'

'Is there any word of Needham and his men?' asked Haskell.

'None,' said Sheriff Sykes.

'Of course not,' said Haskell, leaning heavily against the back of one of Merry Mack's kitchen chairs. 'If they admitted they were off in search of the Land of the Red Moon, they'd first have to admit they'd taken my maps and samples. Then they'd have to admit they'd hurt Mrs Mack, and the game would be up.'

'The game would, indeed, be up,' said Lem Sykes.

'So, we wait,' said Masefield Haskell.

'I'm sorry it's come to that,' said Sheriff Sykes, resting a reassuring hand on Haskell's shoulder.

'So am I,' said Masefield Haskell.

'Have you decided where you'll celebrate Christmas?' asked Lem Sykes.

'By Mrs Mack's side, of course,' said Haskell, straightening up and puffing out his chest, a little indignant.

'Of course you must,' said Lem Sykes. 'Perhaps you should kill one of the chickens for the occasion.'

'Oh, I couldn't possibly,' said Haskell. 'What will Mrs Mack do for money when she recovers if she has no chickens to lay eggs?'

'Miss Ballantine and I are going to share a turkey,' said Lem Sykes. 'Perhaps she could cook it here and we could have lunch together. It might cheer Mrs Mack up.'

Masefield Haskell beamed his wide smile, and his

floppy fringe fell down over his eyes as he nodded with enthusiasm.

'It might cheer up Mrs Mack, and it would most certainly cheer me up,' he said. 'Thank you very much, Sheriff Sykes, and thank Miss Ballantine too.'

27

Trapper Watkiss poked the embers of the fire back into life, and added more of the wood that he'd collected.

Day was breaking in a soft yellow light between the trunks of the trees that surrounded the clearing, and a low mist clung to the undergrowth. Trapper pulled the collar of his jacket a little higher around his chin. The forest was too dense for the frost to have penetrated too deeply, and most of the trees were conifers and kept their needles all year round, so there was plenty of shelter from the harsh winds.

The worst of the cold weather and the heaviest of the snowfall wouldn't happen for another week or two by Trapper's reckoning. He was a tough outdoors man, so he wouldn't suffer much from the weather, but he couldn't say the same for some of his companions.

Horton Needham was beginning to suffer, and Trapper Watkiss didn't have much time for his complaining, but he was the boss, and that was that. Besides, Trapper had promised his old friend, Nathan McKenzie, that he'd keep things right, and that's what he planned to do.

Trapper's biggest skillet was balanced over the fire, filled with thick rashers of well-smoked bacon that Sarah had carried all the way from Prospect. It was Christmas Day, and, for all he could forage better than any man alive, Trapper Watkiss was determined to celebrate with the smell and sizzle of good bacon at breakfast time.

'Why aren't you packing up?' scolded Horton Needham. 'Why is that fire still alight? And where have you been hiding that bacon?'

'And a Merry Christmas to you too,' said Trapper Watkiss.

'Christmas has got nothing to do with anything,' said Horton Needham, sitting up suddenly, with a blanket still wrapped around his almost totally bald head.

Most of the other men were already awake, but had chosen not to stir. It was better not to get into an argument with the boss, or to begin a job before he'd asked for it to be done. Nothing was ever right for Boss Needham, and a great deal of time and energy could be wasted in doing the wrong thing.

'Christmas has got something to do with me,' said Trapper Watkiss.

'And what might that be?' asked Boss Needham, his face turning an unhealthy shade of pink.

'I don't work on Christmas Day, not for no man,' said Trapper Watkiss. 'God Almighty had a day of rest on Sunday, and Trapper Watkiss has a day of rest on Christmas Day.'

With that, he shovelled the first slice of hot, crispy bacon into his mouth. It was still steaming when it left the pan, and the fat was still sizzling. That didn't stop Trapper Watkiss taking a large bite out of it, and, apparently, heartily enjoying it.

There was no bread to go with the bacon, only some hard tack, and no eggs either, but that didn't matter to Trapper.

'We're going to lose a day's progress, because you won't work on Christmas Day?' raged Horton Needham.

'We've been following the jolly-gist's maps for three weeks,' said Trapper Watkiss, 'and I've saved your skin twice, and put you back on the right track four times.'

Horton Needham began to say something, but Trapper Watkiss glared at him, and took another big bite out of his rasher of bacon. It was almost as if he was threatening to bite a lump out of Horton Needham and chew that up for breakfast.

'Even if it wasn't the precious baby Jesus's

birthday,' said Trapper Watkiss, between chews, 'I've still earned a day off.'

'Hear, hear!' said a voice from the other side of the fire. Then, one by one, men began to climb out of their blankets, and, knives and tin plates in hand, they gathered around the fire and Trapper Watkiss's skillet.

'Merry Christmas,' said Othniel Seeley. 'Is it too early to toast the day with a tot of whisky?'

'We could sing a hymn, first,' said Pennyworth, Horton Needham's secretary.

'I'm not much of a man for hymns,' said Trapper Watkiss.

'Something rousing!' said Marcus Mimms.

'I do know one Christmas carol,' said Trapper, and he began, in a low, rumbling voice, to sing. Soon, everyone was joining in with the Latin words to the Christmas carol 'Adeste Fideles'. They all cheered when it was done.

'What does it mean?' asked Anthony Mimms.

'I ain't got the foggiest idea,' said Trapper Watkiss. 'I learned it off the nuns.'

'It means, something like . . .' began Othniel Seeley.

'Don't tell me,' said Trapper Watkiss. 'You'll only go and spoil it. Not much good ever come my way from book learning. I know all I need to know. I know about the land, and about the plants and beasts on it. I know how to get you from Prospect to the Land of the Red Moon, following the professor's maps.'

He thought for a moment and scowled.

'It's the Lord's day, today. I don't want to think about nothing else.'

He couldn't help thinking, though, that he was in the company of bad men. He'd been singing a Christmas hymn with men he didn't trust, and, most of all, he didn't trust Horton Needham, or where he'd come by those maps.

Trapper Watkiss walked west between the trees. He took out the knife that he'd slipped into the top of his boot, and made his familiar mark on a straight tree a foot across. If he left his mark, he'd always be able to find his way home, and he'd never, ever be lost.

Then he took the little silk map that he'd made, and he checked his bearings against it. They had travelled less than half the distance to the Land of the Red Moon, and there was much tougher terrain to come.

28

The machine was like a great, crystal bubble with Jake at its centre. For a moment, he couldn't work out how to handle the controls. Then he realized that he was in the vehicle from the H. N. Matchstruck novel *Fire Beyond the Clouds*. He was under the ocean, saving the great city of Atlantis from the evil captain.

Except this wasn't the ocean. The liquid outside wasn't clear and blue; it was golden.

Jake took hold of a wheel in front of him and turned it this way and that, making the great, crystal bubble sway back and forth in the ocean of golden liquid. Bubbles thundered up past him, and he couldn't tell whether he was rising or falling through the liquid, but he knew that it was one or the other.

Then he noticed a device a little in front of and above him. He put up a hand and pulled a tube towards him with eyepieces. It reminded him of the pair of field glasses that he'd seen hanging around Masefield Haskell's neck when they'd first met. Jake put the eyepieces to his eyes, and more of the golden liquid swirled before him. He turned his head, but his vision was not improved. He could see only what he had seen through the crystal sides of the bubble: a vast expanse of golden liquid.

Then Jake's hand rested on a winding handle close to the eyepieces, and he began to turn it. Something flashed across his field of vision. He turned the handle briskly in the other direction and saw the object again. He stopped and turned the handle back and forth until he could see what was suspended in the golden liquid.

He wanted to reach out and touch the yellow, wool hair of the rag doll that was floating in front of his eyes, but he couldn't. If Emmie's rag doll was there, in the golden liquid, maybe Emmie was there too, and maybe he could save her.

Jake reluctantly took his eyes from the eyepieces, and put his hands back on the wheel in front of him. He soon realized that not only did the wheel turn, but it was also on a column that could be pulled towards and pushed away from him. Jake pulled steadily on the wheel, and he felt the bubble tilt and begin to climb through the liquid.

Jake was convinced that the golden liquid meant that he was not in the ocean, that this was no H. N. Matchstruck novel, and that he was not Julius Greengrass. It was not Jake's job to save the lost city of Atlantis. It was Jake's job to save his sister and his ma and pa.

Once the bubble was on its way to the surface of the golden ocean, Jake put his eyes back against the eyepieces and began to turn the handle attached to them to see if he could find more evidence of his family. He longed to see his mother's shawl spread out around her. He longed to see his father's serious face.

What he saw next was deep and dark and purple. It flashed past in an instant as he turned the handle too fast. Jake stopped as soon as the object passed him by, and began turning the handle in the opposite direction, slowly.

Jake's head jerked back from the contraption, his eyes blinking away from the eyepieces. He screwed his eyes tightly shut, and then opened them for another look. He pressed his eyes against the eyepieces, and he saw the great purple and magenta eyes of the evil black dragon that had set fire to his parents' wagon.

He was not afraid.

Jake's dreams, for he knew that this must be a dream, did not frighten him any more.

With his sights firmly fixed on the huge magenta orbs that filled the eyepieces, Jake grasped the wheel in both hands and pushed hard. The sea of golden liquid flowing all around the crystal bubble seemed to part before him. Hard, purple light spread all around, and the bubble was engulfed, as if by magic.

Jake brought the steering wheel and its column back to the vertical position so that the machine hovered. He was looking deeply into the black pupil of the evil dragon. He channelled his thoughts, pushing into the mind of the beast. Deeper and deeper he went until he found what he was looking for. Tentatively, he touched the minds of the men who shared its existence and its evil-doing. He touched the minds of the men, and he read their thoughts.

They called themselves Dragon Lords.

Jake blinked hard, and turned the handle on the side of the viewing machine by small degrees.

Suddenly, it was as if he was suspended high in the air, looking down on the men. He could see the land they lived on, and the way they lived. He could see the cold, hard stares on the faces of the Dragon Lords. The dragons were not corralled together, but each lived separately, casting a ring of fire around its lonely nesting place.

The dragons lived on the plateaus and ledges of the sheer sides of the mountain that the Dragon Lords lived on top of.

The only way on or off the mountain was to fly.

Jake concentrated hard on the minds of the Dragon Lords. They were used to being open for there'd been no one to read them before, no one like

Jake, no one with dragonsight, for a generation or longer. He knew that the dragons resisted being ridden, that they wouldn't allow men astride their backs. He knew that these men didn't leave their settlement, except in their minds.

Jake adjusted his mind again, and he was flying on Match's back, through the lands of the Dragon Lords and the creatures they ruled.

They crested the western edge of the mountain, at its highest point, and Match spread his wings and glided into a vast cavity. Its glassy, concave walls of polished purple stone glittered with shards of blue, green and red, embedded in its surface, and the ceiling hung with myriad stalactites of gleaming crystal that glowed with inner light.

Jake could sense that this was a holy place, a meeting room where councils of war took place. He landed Match and walked around the vast chamber. Within moments, the space came alive. Each seat at the council was filled with a Dragon Lord. Each man was armed; each wore a hair-pipe breastplate and choker. They were magnificent, warlike men in heavy armour, carrying fearsome weapons.

Then he heard their voices, stentorian tones filled with hatred, rage and misery, and Jake wanted nothing more than to leave.

He blinked the visions away, shook away the sounds, and mounted Match.

They flew out over the settlement.

The Dragon Lords were solitary, living in individual teepees, each one standing on its own piece of land. Each man sat before his teepee in a throne so tall it had its own flight of steps. Jake landed and walked among them. They could neither see him nor sense him.

Jake could feel more misery in the air, more of the negative energy that he'd felt in the council chamber. No one dared leave his throne, unless they all did. There was no trust between the Lords, only suspicion.

Jake looked around, but he could see no women or children. This was not a community.

'What is this place?' he asked. 'What does it mean?'

29

'Dragon Sight, wake up . . . Are you all right?'

The soft voice cut through Jake's dream. He recognized it in another moment or two, and then he remembered where he was.

'I'm fine, thank you, White Thunder,' he said. 'I was dreaming.'

'With your eyes wide open?' she asked.

'I suppose so,' said Jake. 'Is it morning?'

He tried to change the subject. He didn't fully understand what he'd experienced, and he didn't want to discuss it with White Thunder.

He tried to catch a glimpse through the entrance to the teepee to see if it was daylight outside.

'It is very early,' said White Thunder. 'The sun is low.'

'The dappled sun,' said Jake.

She looked at him as if she didn't understand what he was saying, and, of course, Jake realized that she didn't.

'That's what I call the sun, here,' said Jake. 'It's like

the Appaloosas on the plateau, the pale ones with all the spots and speckles. We call horses like that dappled. So, I call our sun, here, dappled. It's silly.'

'It is true,' said White Thunder.

'What do you dream about under Blue Jay's dreamcatcher?' she asked after a long silence.

'Come for a walk with me, and I'll tell you,' said Jake. He was wide awake, and the teepee, full of still drowsing people, smelled of a fuggy, sleepy night. Jake wanted the fresh morning air, the dappled sunlight, and the smell of the sulphur mists.

The riders and apprentices had not been able to sleep out on the plains for almost two weeks. It was the end of the season, almost time to return to the plateau, and it wasn't safe to sleep outside. Breathing in the mists at ground level all night could lead to terrible sickness, so most of the younger people slept in the Lodge.

Jake and White Thunder walked south into the shade and the undergrowth where the groundnuts grew. White Thunder wanted to forage for shed-a-tear cactus to make the sticky, sweet dish that she'd serve at the feast in less than a week's time.

'Your first winter's training is almost over,' she said. 'Was it everything you expected it to be?'

'I've learned so much,' said Jake, in earnest. 'I still haven't learned what I came here to learn, though. I haven't searched for my family. My dreams keep telling me they're here, but they also show me things I don't understand, mixed up with stories from the books I read, with people that I know, and the dragons, and my family too.'

'Dreams are full of mystery and wonder,' said White Thunder. 'Sometimes dreamcatchers have too much work to do. Perhaps your mind is fighting it, or maybe some other force is confusing the dreamcatcher.'

Jake kicked at the groundnuts in frustration as he tripped over a root. He was so busy wondering what his dream might mean that he wasn't looking where he was going. They were almost knee-deep in vegetation as it was only in the thickest nut bushes that the shed-a-tear cactus could flourish.

'Do not kick,' said White Thunder. 'You will disturb the –'

She was interrupted by an odd yelp or yapping noise and the sound of tussling. Jake watched as the Native girl waded quickly through the groundnuts away from the sound. She reached a spot where the vegetation was less thick and nothing could jump out at her from the undergrowth.

'It's nothing,' called Jake. 'Look, there's some of your cactus.' He waved to White Thunder, and smiled at her to reassure her. Jake was enjoying her company, and he was enjoying complaining to somebody.

Jake remembered Starling's legend. It had been a hard lesson for him, and he couldn't bear to let his teacher down. He knew he must do as he was told, and he was determined that Yellow Cloud would be proud of him. He had never realized before that his teacher could be afraid. If Yellow Cloud could be afraid of Gale, anything was possible.

Dragonsight could prove to be Jake's curse, but he was determined that it would only ever be a blessing.

Jake was also aware that River Stone watched him almost constantly. He knew that Yellow Cloud and River Stone spoke often about Jake's progress, and that River Stone was like a silent grandfather watching over him. He hadn't seen it before the morning that he'd fallen from Match's back on to the blue dunes, but he'd been aware of it every day since.

Jake expected that if he put his hand up to his brow to shield his eyes, and looked into the sky, he'd see River Stone watching him from somewhere.

Jake pulled a teardrop-shaped, bright, sappy yellow leaf from a cactus plant, and held it up to show White Thunder as she walked towards him. It began to ooze sticky liquid into his hand, and, when he tried to drop it, he couldn't. His fingers were soon stuck together, and, when he tried to take the leaf out of his right hand, the fingers of his left hand stuck to his right palm.

Soon, Jake and White Thunder were laughing at his predicament. It felt good to laugh for a change.

Jake plonked himself down in the undergrowth,

and there was a sudden squeal as he landed on something that appeared to be alive.

Before he knew what was happening, Jake was on his back with his heels in the air and his hands incapable of doing anything.

'Aah!' he shouted, rolling and scuffling, and trying to turn himself the right way up so that he could get back on his feet. 'Help me!'

White Thunder grabbed hold of Jake's elbows and tried to pull him up as something scurried away on all fours.

Whatever it was that Jake had sat on had tossed him on to his back quite deliberately.

Jake fussed with his hands, trying to free himself from the sticky cactus leaf.

'Can you please help me with this, once and for all, so that we can go after that . . .'

'It's just an animal,' said White Thunder. 'It will not hurt you if you do not hurt it.'

'It's not an animal. I saw something,' said Jake.

An image flashed through his mind, and he knew that he had to go after the creature, but first he had to get the damned sticky mess off his hands.

'Why can't I get this stuff off?' asked Jake.

'I can do it,' said White Thunder, 'but it will sting and it will smell for days.'

'Just do it!' said Jake.

White Thunder strode a little deeper into the

shade to where a tall, grassy plant with fuzzy seed heads was growing. She wrapped her hands in the pouch that she'd brought with her to collect the cactuses, and pulled some of the seed heads off the grasses. Careful not to let the seeds near her skin, she brought them back to Jake.

White Thunder sprinkled a little of the seed on to Jake's hands and told him to rub them. Almost instantly, the sticky mess made by the cactus turned rubbery and began to peel away.

'Work fast,' said White Thunder. 'If you leave that on your hands for too long, it will sting.'

Jake peeled at the rubbery residue as his skin began to turn pink and burn, and then he realized that the most awful smell of rotting teeth was wafting up from his palms. For a moment he thought the stench was going to make him retch.

Jake blinked, and the red of Pa Watkiss's long underwear flashed across his memory. Then he saw, in his mind's eye, the creature that had scurried away from him.

It wasn't a creature. The thing that had scurried away from him had been a small person, wrapped in a large, skin garment, scurrying on all fours, and it had been carrying something. He hadn't seen what it was; he'd only seen a flash of yellow.

Jake blinked again as he let the last of the seeds and rubbery cactus leaf fall from his hands. The yellow was older and dirtier, but Jake was sure it had once been the same bright, corn yellow of Emmie's rag doll's hair.

Jake began to wade through the thick bushes of groundnuts, which grew tall in the shade. He hadn't seen which way the figure had gone, but he could guess.

Then he heard a little girl's scream, and he began to move faster.

'Wait for me!' called White Thunder.

There was another scream. Then there was a shrill bark, and, just as Jake was lurching through dense, waist-high vegetation, something shot between his legs. He didn't stop to see what it was. It had brushed against his ankle and he'd felt the cool, smooth skin of one of the reptilian creatures that lived in the shade of the mountains.

Jake's eyes swept the area. He knew he had to be close. He could still hear a low growl and a snarl, but the sounds were layered, one on top of the other. There were at least two beasts, and one poor child. Jake had to save her, even if he wasn't entirely sure how.

His eyes swept across the area, taking in the common wrapping leaf the Natives used to cook all their soft food in, and to cover and contain anything they wanted to carry or store. Beyond, and taller than them, he could also see the grasses with the seed heads that White Thunder had given him for his sticky hands. He made a note to avoid them. The groundnut bushes were dense and almost waist-high, and there was a flowering plant that was grey and fuzzy. Jake knew that Tall Elk used it in his medicines, but he didn't know what for.

Jake couldn't see the child or the beasts. He heard another snarl and a yelp. Then he saw a flash of yellow, and he surged towards the sound.

'Wait!' called White Thunder. Jake stopped in his tracks and watched as she slowly waded towards him, from further south. He didn't know how she could stay so calm.

Jake had grown used to the land quickly, but he was never quite so calm nor so shrewd as White Thunder. He didn't know the local plants and the earth, or the mists and the fumes that rose from the ground as well as she did. It was White Thunder who had taught him that it was better, when under threat, to be able to see and hear as much as possible.

Jake studied her position, and he knew that she could see more clearly through the undergrowth and over it, because she wasn't wading through it, and, best of all, she could see her feet. He knew that White Thunder must have seen the flash of yellow. She must have seen the hand swinging the roundhouse punch, the hand holding on to Emmie's rag doll. Jake couldn't see what White Thunder could see, and he had to rely on her for instructions.

'Wait!' called White Thunder again.

Jake heard his friend's cry, but he could not wait. He saw the flash of his sister's rag doll flying through the air, and he heard the snarl of animals attacking, and he knew that he had to help.

There was a frightened yelp, and Jake thought for a split second that he was too late as he dived in to scoop up the child still holding tightly on to the rag doll.

A mouth lined with small, hard, white teeth bit down into Jake's right hand, sending a shooting pain up his arm.

The creature snarled as its jaws clamped tighter around Jake's hand, but then Jake saw the rag doll appear again, this time being swung hard through the air. The doll crashed into the reptile's nose, and it let go of Jake's hand with a terrified yelp. In an instant, it skittered away to join the others with its tail between its legs.

Jake snatched up the child, but was afraid that he might get bitten again when she bared her teeth at him and began beating at his chest with one tightly curled fist, and one dirty, battered rag doll with yellow, wool hair.

30

The reptiles gone, and everyone exhausted from the encounter, White Thunder managed to calm the child down, and the three of them sat together on the nearest patch of clear ground.

The child was a Native girl, but not one of the Cloud People. She understood most of what White Thunder said to her, and she was dressed for a journey, wearing a full cloak.

White Thunder reassured her that she was safe, that the reptile dogs were gone, even though she wasn't afraid of them. She also told her that Jake was one of her tribe and that he was called Dragon Sight. She even made him show the girl the burns and tattoos on his arm and hand, and she watched as the mesmerized child ran her fingers over his left palm.

She understood how wary the little Native girl was of Jake. She'd obviously never seen a white man, and White Thunder watched as she ran one grubby hand through his hair while she held the rag doll tightly to her body. Jake's hair was too short, and the wrong colour, because Mrs Garret had cut it for school in the autumn, but now it fell almost to his shoulders. In the dry heat of the dappled sun the top layers had bleached to a streaky, golden brown, but it was still dark underneath.

When she looked at it properly, White Thunder realized that she'd never seen anything like it either. She'd never seen eyes like his before, or skin. She'd got used to him, that was all.

As the girl tugged Jake's hair, White Thunder noticed how thin her arm was. She could clearly see her wrist bones jutting out. The child must be starving. Her skin was a sallow, unhealthy colour too.

She was about to ask the child if she was all right, when the girl slumped over. It was only because she was so close to them that Jake and White Thunder were able to catch her unconscious body.

'What's wrong with her?' asked Jake.

'She is exhausted,' said White Thunder, 'and obviously frightened.'

'She's safe with us, isn't she?' asked Jake, cradling the child in his arms.

'Of course,' said White Thunder, 'but we must take her to Tall Elk. Her cloak will tell us her story. We will find her family, and everything will be all right.'

Jake got to his feet, and, cradling the child in his

arms, he walked on to the plains with White Thunder at his side.

The settlement was bustling, and several of the Natives came to meet Jake and White Thunder when they realized that something had happened.

Minutes later, Tall Elk was tending to the child. White Thunder began to burn herbs in preparation for her treatment. Then she arranged blankets over the child and removed her clothes to make her comfortable. She took the rag doll from the child's limp, pale, dirty hands and held it out for Jake.

'This was your sister's,' said White Thunder. 'You should keep it.'

'No,' said Jake. 'She carried it here. It means something to her, and, when she's awake, I need to know where she got it from.'

'Are you sure?' asked White Thunder.

'Perhaps the doll was in my dreams because I was meant to find this girl,' said Jake, 'and not because of Emmie at all.'

31

'Wait,' said White Thunder, under her breath, clutching the girl's cloak.

'Do you need me?' asked Jake.

'I do not know,' said White Thunder.

'Let Dragon Sight go,' said Tall Elk.

White Thunder looked from Jake to Tall Elk, and the old Native medicine man shrugged.

'She has no story,' said Tall Elk as White Thunder held up the girl's cloak. She was young so there wouldn't be much painted on it, but there should have been a map of her birth place, her name and the names of her ancestors, and the constellation she was born under. However, the skin of her cloak had never been marked at all.

'How do we find out where she came from?' asked Jake. 'What do we do if she never wakes up?'

'I do not know,' said White Thunder. 'I am so sorry, Jake, but we all have our stories painted on our cloaks and jackets. I do not understand it.'

'There is something else,' said Tall Elk. He was

crouching on the floor of the teepee, beside the unconscious child. Her head, arms and legs were all uncovered.

Jake gasped when he saw the Native girl's left arm. He hadn't seen it under her shirt and cloak. He'd only seen her right wrist as she'd reached for his hair.

Her left arm, from the wrist to the shoulder, was covered in burn scars. They extended in flaming patterns up her forearm and over her bicep, and a long, thin scar travelled twice around her wrist, almost like a curling tail.

'She's a rider,' said Jake.

'She is a girl,' said Tall Elk.

'I don't care,' said Jake. 'My hair isn't black, my skin isn't the colour of newly shelled almonds, and my eyes aren't the darkest brown. Those things don't matter.'

'There has never been a woman rider,' said Tall Elk.

'There was never a rider like me either,' said Jake, 'and I'm Dragon Sight. Please make her well, Tall Elk. Do it for her and do it for me. I hope you'll tattoo her arm too. She's been chosen.'

'It would appear so,' said Tall Elk, 'but first I must speak with Chief Half Moon.'

'I know he will decide what's right,' said Jake, and he left the teepee.

32

When the thaw came to Prospect, Masefield Haskell felt sure that Merry Mack would finally recover.

The old woman had been in bed since the burglary at Thanksgiving. She'd managed to eat a little turkey on Christmas Day, and had been delighted by the company, even if she wasn't at all sure that she should be seen in bed by two young men. Miss Ballantine had reassured her that it was perfectly respectable since one of them was a scientist and the other a law man. Even so, Merry Mack couldn't help thinking the nuns who raised her might have had something to say about that.

All through the snow and darkness of January and February, Merry Mack had kept going. When Masefield Haskell had been kind and attentive, and even when Mrs Garret hadn't been able to come out to her for a week, she'd somehow managed to carry on. She'd grown very thin, the colour had gone from her cheeks, all of her hair had turned white, and she'd aged terribly, but Merry Mack had persevered. To Haskell's great distress, however, the spark he'd once seen in her eyes had dimmed.

Then the thaw had come. The sun had shone all day long, one fine bright day at the end of February in 1851, and Merry Mack had smiled and decided that everything would be just fine. Two or three days after that, she stopped eating, and the day after that she couldn't even take a sip of tea. At the end of the first week of March, Masefield Haskell came to tell Mrs Mack that the first lambs had been born at a farm just east of Prospect. He wanted to tell her that it really was spring. He wanted to lift her spirits, to give her the energy to get well, so that she could get out of bed and feed her hens again.

He didn't realize that anything was wrong until he took hold of Merry Mack's hand. That's how she liked to be woken, not with a sound, but with a gentle touch. Merry Mack's hand was cold, much, much too cold.

Masefield Haskell rubbed Merry Mack's hand, gently, but he already knew that he wouldn't be able to warm it. Then he touched her cheek, very gently, and that was cold too.

Masefield Haskell didn't know what to do next. So, he sat down in the chair beside Merry Mack's little bed, as he had every day since Thanksgiving, and he told her what he had come to tell her.

33

Match tipped on to his side as he spread his wings, above and below his body. In a few more seconds, he would pass through the gap in the rock that separated the Land of the Red Moon from the Land of the White Sun.

Jake looked out through his dragon's eyes, and wondered what he could have done to stay at the winter training grounds.

He could see the shadow Match's body cast on the rocks, and he could see the shadow of the harness below, carrying White Thunder. Jake couldn't feel the warmth against his chest of the Native girl's semi-conscious body, because he was one with Match, but he knew that she was there. He had insisted that the girl ride with him, strapped to his body, because she was so fragile, but because she was a rider too. He also knew that River Stone, who'd been watching him for weeks, was flying only a minute or two behind him.

Jake couldn't risk the girl falling out of a harness or off his dragon's back as they flew through the crevice between worlds. She held the secret to where Emmie was and whether she was alive or dead, and Jake was determined not to lose her.

The child had been half-starved and feverish when Jake and White Thunder had found her. She'd been weak or unconscious for most of that first week. White Thunder had been constantly at her side, and had spent time feeding her. Tall Elk had treated her with herbs, lit fires in his teepee and danced his sacred dances.

On the third day, after consulting with Chief Half Moon, Tall Elk began tattooing the girl's arm. He worked as diligently as always, and the results were as beautiful as anything Jake had ever seen. He had thought the markings might be more delicate than those belonging to the men, but they were not. Her burns and the tattoos that defined them were bright and dynamic, full of swirling patterns and scrolls. Narrow, sharply pointed bursts of colour surged up the forearm, following the lines of a pair of spreading wings. Two great sprigs jetted out at the apex, representing the feathers at the alula joints.

The patterns were all so clear to Jake, once they were tattooed, that he couldn't believe he hadn't seen them for himself. He'd complimented Tall Elk on his fine work, and the two men had shared a solemn moment. The girl hadn't seen the work yet, but Jake was sure that she'd be as pleased by it as he was.

Jake had wanted to leave the girl in the Land of the Red Moon for as long as he could, with White Thunder to take care of her. He'd wanted her to stay in the warm, dry climate until the fire in the Lodge on the plateau had heated the teepee, the food was cooked and everything was calm.

He hadn't wanted to bring her to the plateau at all. She didn't belong there; she wasn't ready for it. Jake wasn't ready either.

He'd spent the entire winter in the Land of the Red Moon. He'd grown into a man, both physically and mentally. He even wondered whether the Garrets would recognize him. None of that mattered, though, because the one thing he'd meant to do in the Land of the Red Moon was the one thing that he'd failed to do.

Jacob Polson had not found his pa and ma and sister. He hadn't even found evidence of Pa Watkiss's little wagon. Jacob Polson had found a sick Native girl, who, sometime in the past six months, had found his sister's rag doll. That was all. He might look like a man, with his long limbs and broad shoulders, and with soft hair beginning to grow on his chin and above his top lip. The Natives might even treat him like a man, but he had proved nothing to himself.

Flying east, towards the plateau and the rumble of the waterfall, Jake blinked and allowed his mind to leave Match's. There wasn't far to go and he wanted to check on the child strapped to his chest.

As he returned to ordinary consciousness, Jake was aware of the cold air. He was surprised by how steely grey the sky was and how green the canopy of the forest beneath Match's wings. This world that he'd grown up in for the first thirteen years of his life was so different from the Land of the Red Moon, and it suddenly felt as if he'd never really seen it before.

Jake felt the warmth against his chest, and the shallow breathing of the child strapped there. She was wrapped in her cloak with an extra blanket around her head and shoulders. Jake was suddenly very glad that she couldn't see out. He knew with sudden dread that a shock could kill her, and that the plateau would come as an enormous shock to her. The sky was the wrong colour, the land was too green, and there was water everywhere.

He'd keep her in the Lodge, for as long as it took, and then he'd take her home to the Land of the Red Moon.

These were the thoughts that hummed through Jake's mind as he hovered Match a few feet above the settlement. He safely released the harness, and White Thunder with it, and then he allowed Match to land close to the Lodge.

In one easy movement, Jake dropped from Match's

back, and, with the girl still strapped to his chest, he took her carefully in his arms and carried her to the Lodge. Once there, Tall Elk took the girl from him and laid her on the matting and blankets that he'd prepared for her, close to the fire.

'Keep her safe,' said Jake.

'She will be here with me,' said Tall Elk, and Jake left to tend to Match.

34

It was a fine, chill March day, the sky was blue, and the air was still and cold.

The church had not been so full on a weekday since Thanksgiving. That day in March, everyone had come to celebrate Mrs Mack's life.

Nathan McKenzie arrived at the church ahead of the rest of the congregation to have a word with Reverend Varvel, whom he found adjusting his vestments.

'About Mrs Mack,' said McKenzie.

'Is there something you'd like to add to the service, Mr McKenzie?' asked Reverend Varvel. 'I'm sure young Mr Haskell has done a marvellous job, in the absence of any family.'

'That's just it,' said Nathan McKenzie, 'Mrs Mack wasn't without family, and I wanted to make sure that she was buried using her full name. I think that would be most appropriate.'

'It would indeed,' said Reverend Varvel.

'I know she didn't stick with it, and I know she

was comfortable with our little church, but Mrs Mack was raised Catholic. I don't know if you knew that, Reverend?'

'I didn't know that,' said Reverend Varvel, frowning.

'It shouldn't make a difference,' said Nathan McKenzie firmly. 'She was a fine citizen, after all.'

'A fine citizen, indeed,' said Reverend Varvel.

There was a pause, during which Nathan McKenzie seemed to be considering something.

'Did she have another name?' asked Reverend Varvel. 'Other than Merry, I mean?'

'Mrs Mack's name wasn't Merry at all,' said Nathan McKenzie. 'She earned her name in childhood, if memory serves.'

'Oh!' said Reverend Varvel. 'So, do you know what she was properly called?'

'Mrs Mack was called . . . I've written it down to be sure to get it right,' said Nathan McKenzie, taking a slip of paper out of his pocket. He looked at it, and then handed it to Reverend Varvel.

The Reverend Varvel took the piece of paper, looked at it, turned it the right way up, and looked at it again. Then he coughed, before saying, 'Mrs Mack was actually called Gabriella Lalemant Mack?'

'That's right,' said Nathan McKenzie.

'You're sure?' asked Reverend Varvel, looking from the piece of paper to Nathan McKenzie.

'I'm sure,' said Nathan McKenzie.

'Then I'd better include it in the service,' said Reverend Varvel. 'I might refer to her by the name we all knew her by, though, so that everybody's comfortable.'

'Whatever you think best, Reverend,' said Nathan McKenzie.

'I really think that *is* best,' said Reverend Varvel, looking at the slip of paper once more before tucking it away.

With that, the church doors opened again, and the people of Prospect entered to celebrate the life of Mrs Gabriella Lalemant 'Merry' Mack.

The townsfolk sang their hymns in the church, and listened to Reverend Varvel's sermon, and they were surprised by the unfamiliar sound of Merry Mack's real name. Then they stood around her grave while she was buried. Her body lay in the ground in its plain wooden coffin with its beautiful handles made by Pius Garret. Some people cried, and some prayed, and everyone said that they would miss Merry Mack with her little cottage and her hens.

Most of the townspeople sat in the saloon after the burial and drank a toast to Merry Mack, including the Garrets, Sheriff Sykes and Masefield Haskell.

'What will happen to Mrs Mack's beloved cottage?' asked Mrs Garret.

'What about her even more beloved hens?' asked Eliza Garret. 'Could we take them?'

'I'll keep feeding the hens,' said Masefield Haskell. 'I'll keep selling the eggs, too . . . Although . . .'

'What is it, Masefield?' asked Elizabeth Garret, placing a sympathetic hand on the geologist's arm.

'I couldn't possibly go on living at the cottage,' said Haskell, 'and, without a job, I couldn't possibly stay in Prospect.'

'What about all your work with the Native lands?' asked Pius Garret.

'All gone,' said Haskell.

'It would make a wonderful book, though, wouldn't it? Such an amazing discovery,' said Garret.

'If I could get it back, it might,' said Haskell.

'You could draw new maps and collect new samples!' said Eliza Garret. 'You could have your adventure all over again!'

'I do have some savings,' said Haskell. 'I want to stay in Prospect for long enough to see that justice is brought to those who attacked Mrs Mack, at least.'

'Stay then,' said Eliza. 'I could come to the Land of the Red Moon with you. I'm old enough, and with you and Jake to look after me, who could object?'

'Your mother, that's who,' said Mrs Garret. 'What with Mrs Mack, and the burglary, and with Jake gone away, I've had quite enough interruptions.'

'You live for interruptions, Mama,' said Eliza.

'That still leaves accommodations,' said Masefield Haskell, his floppy fringe falling in front of his face.

'You could stay in Mrs Mack's cottage,' said Nathan McKenzie.

'On whose say-so?' asked Masefield Haskell.

'On my say-so,' said Nathan McKenzie, 'acting on behalf of Mrs Mack's brother.'

Everyone turned to look at Nathan McKenzie as he sat on his stool at the end of the bar. No one spoke for a moment. Then Pius Garret said, 'So, Mrs Mack didn't just have a secret name then? She had a secret family too?'

'I don't know if it was a secret,' said Nathan McKenzie. 'After all, I knew that Mrs Mack had a brother, and I knew who he was . . . who he is.'

'Well,' said Mrs Garret, always a practical woman, 'are you going to tell the rest of us, or not?'

'Very well,' said Nathan McKenzie. 'Mrs Mack's brother is my good friend, Trapper Watkiss, and I'm sure he won't mind you staying in his sister's cottage until he returns from his travels.'

35

The sky had turned a steely grey by the time two Appaloosas rode into town, late on the afternoon of Merry Mack's funeral.

Her cottage was shut up and dark, and so was the mercantile. The lamps were lit in the saloon, though, where many of the townsfolk were still telling stories about the old woman who had been part of the community almost since before there'd even been a community.

Nobody could remember a time before Merry Mack had arrived in Prospect, and that included Nathan McKenzie. They'd been surprised to find out that she was Trapper Watkiss's sister, until they started to remember little things about them. Trapper Watkiss had always taken his hat off to her whenever he saw her, and she had always had a kind word for him, or a cross one, depending on his needs and her moods. She also had soft little wisps of red hair among the white ones that escaped from beneath the house cap that she wore indoors or the bonnet she wore outdoors. She was small and stocky, like her brother, and her skin was just as fair.

When they began to talk about it, some of the townsfolk were surprised they hadn't put two and two together and realized that the pair must be related.

They were still talking about Mrs Mack and Trapper Watkiss, and about the hens, when Yellow Cloud and Black Feather tied their horses to the tether post outside the saloon and walked in.

Pius Garret was out of his chair and shaking Yellow Cloud's hand within moments.

'You're back!' he said. 'It's wonderful to see you!'

'Winter is over,' said Yellow Cloud. 'Our training is complete.'

'How's Jake?' asked Mrs Garret, stepping forward to stand beside her husband.

'When can we see him?' asked Eliza. 'Can we come back to the settlement with you, now? Please?'

Eliza grabbed Yellow Cloud's hand as soon as her father let go of it, not to shake it, but to clasp it, to beg the Native to take her back to the plateau.

Yellow Cloud looked over the girl's head to where her parents were standing, a silent question on his face.

'Not now, Eliza,' said her mother, pulling her daughter gently back beside her.

Then, suddenly, Masefield Haskell had taken hold of Yellow Cloud's hand and was shaking it vigorously.

'It's marvellous to have you home!' said the geologist. 'A return to the plateau would be most welcome!'

'I can go with Mr Haskell,' said Eliza, jumping back in while she had the chance.

'There'll be no more talk of visiting until we've heard news of Jake, and shown Yellow Cloud and Black Feather some hospitality,' said Pius Garret, pulling out a chair for his friend to sit down. 'Let's have a fresh pot of coffee, at least.'

Nathan McKenzie stayed on his stool at the end of the bar. He never took his eyes off Yellow Cloud, knowing very well that if Horton Needham found the gems that were going to make him and the Hudson's Bay Company rich, then he was bound to cause no end of trouble for the Natives. However, from the look of Yellow Cloud, Horton Needham certainly hadn't caused the Natives any problems, yet.

Nathan McKenzie began to wonder whether Masefield Haskell's maps had been accurate. Then he began to worry that Trapper Watkiss might be lost, or, worse, that Trapper might be in some sort of trouble with Horton Needham and his cronies. Nathan McKenzie was beginning to feel very uncomfortable, and there was nothing at all he could do about it. He resolved to sit on his stool and listen to the blacksmith and the Native, and find out whatever he could.

*

The Garrets soon found out that Jake was fit and well, and that he'd made good progress at his dragoncraft over the winter.

'Dragon Sight is almost a man,' said Yellow Cloud. 'He is strong of mind and body, and he is making many decisions.'

'What do you mean?' asked Mrs Garret. 'He isn't fourteen yet, and he hasn't finished school. He still needs guidance.'

'That is true,' said Yellow Cloud, 'and I promised that I would return him to his family, but we must work together to persuade him of what is right.'

'The sooner we go up to the plateau the better,' said Eliza. 'He'll listen to me!'

'Eliza,' said her mother. 'It isn't as simple as that. Jake has to make a new life.'

'Well, he'll have to learn to share it with us,' said Eliza. 'It's not fair! I've been sitting in a classroom all winter.'

'Perhaps Eliza should come with us,' said Yellow Cloud.

'I don't mean to interrupt, but, now that we know that everyone's safe, we really do have much more important things to talk about,' said Masefield Haskell.

Yellow Cloud looked at the geologist, who had swept back his floppy fringe, and whose large eyes looked extremely serious.

'What is so important?' asked Yellow Cloud.

Masefield Haskell looked over his shoulder at Nathan McKenzie. The two men's eyes met for a moment. Then Haskell looked back at Yellow Cloud.

'We can't talk here,' he said. 'Can we go back to the plateau now?'

'Yes,' said Yellow Cloud.

'Me too,' said Eliza, her mouth set in a determined line.

Pius and Elizabeth Garret looked at each other. Elizabeth finally sighed and tilted her head at an angle, and Pius nodded to Yellow Cloud.

'Will you carry Miss Garret?' Yellow Cloud asked Black Feather, who had remained silent throughout the conversation. Black Feather nodded solemnly. He had never forgotten the day that Trapper Watkiss had stabbed him, but he had also never forgotten how Eliza had been on the side of right and good.

'Yes,' he said, 'I will carry Miss Garret.'

'Thank you,' said Eliza, smiling broadly.

'Do you need anything for the journey?' asked Elizabeth Garret, fussing around her daughter.

'No, Mama,' said Eliza. 'I wore my winter coat and hat for the funeral, and White Thunder will help me with anything else I need.'

'We should go,' said Haskell. 'I'll get my knapsack.' He hurried out of the saloon, and was waiting with the horses when the others emerged a few minutes later. He always kept a knapsack packed, because he liked to be the sort of geologist who was always ready for anything.

Haskell was about to climb up behind Yellow Cloud on one of the Appaloosas when Nathan McKenzie appeared from around the side of the building, leading a fresh horse.

'You'll be better off with a horse of your own, if you can ride,' he said, offering the reins to Haskell.

'Of course I can ride,' said Haskell, 'but why would you lend me a horse?'

'I've been a leader of men in Prospect for as long as this has been a town,' said Nathan McKenzie. 'I've got a spare horse you can ride, so take it.' With that, McKenzie turned to climb the steps of the saloon. Then he looked back.

'If you hear any news of my old friend Trapper Watkiss, just let me know that he's safe,' he said. He didn't wait for an answer, but carried on up the saloon steps, carefully, one at a time, because of his bad leg.

36

Trapper Watkiss ducked, and started to make frantic hand signals as soon as the vast shadows swept over him. Ground cover was sparse and there were no trees at all, but he was determined not to be seen.

After weeks of travelling through the forests, the six men had finally emerged, sometime during early March, into a flat-bottomed canyon. The ground was covered in crystalline orange sand. Trapper had picked up some of the larger pieces and dropped them in his pocket. There were great, hot pools of purple mud, too, and evidence of the Natives. There were two fenced enclosures that Trapper guessed might be corrals for horses, or for the other terrible creatures.

Trapper inspected the joints in the fence posts and was convinced the enclosures had been built by Natives. Then he spotted something sticking out of one of the joints. He reached in with two fingers and pulled out a glossy blue-green feather. He looked at it closely for a minute or two, and then ran it between his forefinger and thumb to feel its texture. It shimmered in the winter sunshine.

This don't belong to no bird I've ever seen, thought Trapper Watkiss.

He carefully placed the feather behind his right ear, took a small sketchbook out of one of his pockets and looked at the geologist's drawings. Haskell had sketched the dragons' neck and wing feathers.

Trapper took the feather from behind his ear and placed it on the page next to Haskell's sketch. All of a sudden, he dropped the sketchbook, complete with the feather, and he hopped from one foot to the other. The sketchbook fell straight to the ground, but the feather floated down, and Trapper Watkiss was hopping to try to avoid it landing on any part of his trousers or boots. He didn't like dragons. They were as wrong as a creature could be.

Once the feather had safely landed, Trapper Watkiss lifted the brim of his hat, and peered long and hard into the sky, turning full circle to make sure that he didn't miss anything.

'Them there dragons don't belong in the mountains, or in the sky or anywhere else,' said Trapper Watkiss to no one in particular. 'The only place a dragon belongs is in a child's storybook.'

Trapper was relieved that his map-reading skills had been as good as they should be. He was more relieved that Masefield Haskell's map-making skills had been as good as he'd hoped. He didn't know exactly how far the six of them had travelled, because the terrain had been very difficult in places. He did know that the map only had to be slightly inaccurate and they wouldn't have a hope of finding the Land of the Red Moon.

Trapper Watkiss had also satisfied Horton Needham that he was well on the way to finding the Land of the Red Moon. Things had grown a little less tense since Christmas Day when Needham's men had sung with him and eaten his bacon. They'd needed him to learn to forage and stay warm through the worst of the weather. Some of them had even grown to like him, although they remained loyal to their boss. Needham's opinion of Trapper Watkiss had not changed.

The six men scurried into the scrub and ground cover, at Trapper's hand signals, flattening their bodies to the ground. They tried to hide behind bushes that were too small to mask them, and Trapper encouraged them to camouflage themselves with rock dust.

Trapper was the first to find good cover. Hiding had been part of his job as a fur trapper for the Hudson's Bay Company, and he could always spot a good place. Besides, being a small man helped. He brought Sarah down beside him, and, between her and the shrubs, he was well camouflaged. In fact, the little mule, sitting low in the undergrowth, looked more like a shrub than some of the shrubs did.

From his hiding place, Trapper Watkiss watched the shadows that had first frightened him into hiding. It was morning and the sun was low, so the shadows were big and distorted. He could see the bodies and wings, and he could make out the heads and tails, but there was something else. It looked as if each dragon had something hanging from its body.

Trapper Watkiss followed the shadows along the ground and around the cliff that surrounded them, but, for some reason, he couldn't tell where the dragons were coming from or how many there were, because there always seemed to be more of them.

He turned and looked up into the sky. All the dragons were flying in the same direction, and each one of them had a harness slung beneath it, carrying what looked like a man. Trapper cast his eye down the line of half a dozen or so of the beasts, and saw another emerge from what looked like a solid black cliff.

Everything he feared about the dragons, and everything he feared about the Natives, was coming true. Trapper Watkiss didn't want to believe that the dragons were magical, and he didn't want to believe that the Natives weren't real men, but he had to believe what he was seeing with his own two eyes.

Trapper jumped, and then realized that the tap

on his shoulder was only Othniel Seeley trying to get his attention.

'What?' he asked in a gruff whisper.

'Why are you whispering?' asked the geologist. 'They can't hear us from all the way up there.'

'They be dragons!' hissed Trapper Watkiss. 'You don't know what they can do!'

Mr Seeley dropped his voice to a whisper, saying, 'That's a very unusual rock formation. If you look at it from just the right angle, the rock actually forms two walls that pass one another.' He suddenly grasped Trapper's shoulder again as Trapper hitched himself up on one elbow and took another look at the cliff.

'Look!' said the geologist, pointing. 'Here comes another one.'

They both watched as first the head and neck, and then the shoulders and front legs of a bright green dragon emerged through the rock. It wasn't until Trapper Watkiss moved his head further to the left that he could see into the gap in the cliff. Then the rest of the dragon appeared, complete with its swinging harness. It was the ninth.

The six men lay in cover and watched as a total of twelve dragons flew through the gap in the cliff, and gathered for the rest of the journey back to the plateau. They were the first twelve riders carrying Chief Half Moon and his warriors back to the plateau settlement, after their long winter in the Land of the Red Moon.

When they were clear of the valley, Trapper Watkiss and Othniel Seeley planned the route up the cliff and through the fissure, which would take Horton Needham's band into the Land of the Red Moon.

'What's the point if the Natives are leaving?' Trapper Watkiss asked. 'We won't have any guides. We won't know what we're looking for, or where to look.'

'That's why we brought miners,' said Horton Needham. 'We don't need Natives getting in our way. We don't need to ask their permission, and worry about what *they* want from *us*. No! It's much, much better this way!'

The dragons returned every hour or two, depending on how long it took to reload the harnesses or to stop for a rest or a meal. When the dragons were in the sky, Trapper Watkiss insisted that Horton Needham's party laid low.

By the end of the afternoon, the party approached the fissure, and could see how wide the gap in the cliff actually was, even though the two sides overlapped. It was as if someone had drawn a circle, but instead of the two ends meeting, they had passed, like the start of a spiral.

A single harnessed dragon had left about an hour before, followed shortly afterwards by a dragon carrying nothing but its rider. The old mountain man had a hunch that there were no more Natives and no more dragons beyond the gap.

Trapper Watkiss stepped on to the flat section of rock that would lead him through the gap. A ledge wove a curving path through the fissure and down into the valley below. He couldn't sense the presence of dragons any more. Their smell had gone from the air, but he could still feel the hairs on the back of his neck sticking up, and he knew that his arms were covered in goose-flesh.

It took several minutes to cross the distance between the two sheer cliffs, but, when that was done, Trapper Watkiss stepped into the sunlight.

He could not believe his eyes. He stopped, and blinked hard. The five men behind him wanted to keep moving, and began to grumble that they couldn't get around him. All Trapper Watkiss wanted to do was turn around and go home, and he didn't care if it took another three months to get there.

The sand was blue and the sky was green, and the air was too hot and too dry for spring, and Trapper didn't understand the feel of the rocks or the smell of the plants, and heaven only knew what animals they'd find. If this was where the dragons came from, and Trapper Watkiss was suddenly very sure that this *was* where the dragons came from, then the old man wanted nothing to do with the place.

'Keep moving!' said Horton Needham. 'Why have we stopped?'

'Look!' said Othniel Seeley, taking off his hat and spreading his arms wide to take in the entire landscape. There was a long silence, and nobody moved for what felt like a very long time.

Then Sarah brayed, and the spell was broken.

'I saw the maps and the samples,' said the geologist, 'but did he tell anyone about that sky?'

'I don't like it one little bit!' said Trapper Watkiss, rubbing Sarah's neck, trying to reassure himself. 'Ain't natural!'

37

Jake wasn't gone from the Lodge for long. Match was soon settled in the corral and fed gleaming fish by the dragon handlers. Winter was over, spring was on its way, and the dragons would soon get used to being back at the settlement. Until then, fires would be lit in the corrals in the evenings.

When Jake returned to the Lodge, he was amazed to see the Native girl sitting by the fire with Tall Elk and White Thunder on either side of her. She was holding a bowl, and eating hungrily from it. The food was very hot, and puffs of steam kept escaping from her open mouth. She smiled when she saw Jake, and waved at him with her left arm, obviously showing off her brand-new tattoos.

'How has she recovered so fast?' Jake asked Tall Elk. 'She's awake. She's eating!'

'She says her name is Hen's Tooth,' said White Thunder, leading Jake towards the girl.

'Hen's Tooth?' asked Jake. 'Hens don't have teeth.'

'Not here,' said Tall Elk.

'She's never been here, has she?' asked Jake. 'Hen's Tooth was born in the Land of the Red Moon and has never lived anywhere else.'

'Yes,' said White Thunder. 'That is what she says.'

'Who are your people?' Jake asked Hen's Tooth. 'Where are you from? Where did you find my sister's doll?' Jake had spoken the Native language with ease. Now that the girl felt better, she understood much more of it. It wasn't the same as her language, but there were many similar words. Gestures were important too. When Jake didn't know the Native word for 'doll' or 'toy', he used the English word, pointing at the rag doll cradled in the girl's lap.

The child smiled and held the doll out for Jake. He tried to touch it, but she snatched it back again, giggling, as if it was a game.

'She likes you,' said White Thunder.

'Good,' said Jake, 'because I need her help.'

Then the girl began to speak fast and loudly in a high voice. Jake couldn't understand most of what she was saying, but White Thunder listened carefully, and translated.

'She says she feels better,' said White Thunder. 'She says she ran away. Her family was hunted by . . . She means dragons, but not like our dragons. She is calling them dragons with the hearts of evil men . . . Does she mean Dragon Lords?'

White Thunder looked from Hen's Tooth to Tall Elk, her eyes suddenly wide. She said nothing, but Jake knew that she was scared. He felt a chill run through his blood as he heard the words 'Dragon Lords' on the lips of another human being. He had heard the words in his visions, and he had known these men existed, but now he had proof.

Jake thought that he saw Tall Elk nod slightly, but Hen's Tooth was still talking, and he didn't want to miss anything.

'What's she saying?' he asked, almost frantically.

White Thunder put her hand on Hen's Tooth's arm, and the girl stopped speaking.

'Slow down and tell me again,' said Jake. 'Where did you find the doll?' He reached out and pointed at the toy again. Hen's Tooth wiggled the doll in front of him, and then pulled it back, giggling, when Jake tried to touch it. It was a game she obviously enjoyed.

Hen's Tooth ate some more food from her bowl, and then started her story again.

'She got lost, separated from her family, and she travelled too far east. She did not know the land, and there was no shade, so she could not forage. She starved in the wilderness for days.'

White Thunder reached out to touch Hen's Tooth again, as the girl stopped talking to eat.

'Poor Hen's Tooth,' said White Thunder. 'She must have been very lonely and afraid.'

'Where did you find the doll?' asked Jake again, pointing once more at Emmie's rag doll.

Again, Hen's Tooth played the game with him, snatching the doll away, and giggling.

'It was only when she saw the Crest Mountains and knew there would be shade that she had any hope of surviving,' said White Thunder. 'That is when we found her. She wanted the groundnuts, and she had been in the sun so long that she needed the shade.'

'I have to take her back to the Land of the Red Moon,' said Jake. 'She has to tell me where she found Emmie's rag doll.'

He held Hen's Tooth's arms, firmly, so that she was looking into his face.

'Where did you get the doll?' he asked. He didn't reach out for it, this time, but just used the word. He knew that she understood him, because he'd said it several times before.

Hen's Tooth looked at Jake and shook her head.

'She does not know,' said White Thunder. 'She lost her way a long time before she reached us. She does not remember where she found the doll.'

'If we take Match and fly home, if I take you to find your family, can you show me where you found the doll?' asked Jake.

Hen's Tooth looked Jake in the eyes and smiled.

38

There was a commotion as Eliza Garret burst into the Lodge, dashed across to the fire and threw her arms around White Thunder.

Once she had embraced her friend, Eliza turned to Jake, and said, 'Stand up, Jacob Polson, and let me look at you.'

Jake thought that she sounded rather bossy, but he did as he was told. He wasn't expecting to see her, and he was pleased, but a little bit put out. He was trying to make plans with Hen's Tooth, but they would have to wait, because of Eliza.

'Your hair's gone a funny colour, and it needs cutting,' said Eliza. 'Mama will have something to say about that.'

'You've just said something, Eliza,' said Jake.

'How did you get so brown?' she asked, taking his hand to compare the colour of it to her own pale skin.

'The sun's big and dappled in the Land of the Red Moon,' said Jake. 'It's like a long, hot summer every day.'

'Don't describe it to me,' said Eliza. 'Show it to me!'

'Maybe one day when you're old enough,' said Jake.

'I'm as old as you,' said Eliza.

'You're a girl,' said Jake, and then he blushed. He remembered that Hen's Tooth was a girl, and that he'd insisted her burn scars should be tattooed just as if she was any other rider.

'So?' asked Eliza.

'I'll take you,' said Jake. 'Just as soon as Mr and Mrs Garret give me permission.'

'Promise?' asked Eliza, beaming.

'Promise,' said Jake, smiling back. 'It's good to see you. Are the twins all right?'

'David and Michael have grown about two inches since Thanksgiving, and David has started parting his hair on the left, so that people will know he's not Michael. Except, now, people can't remember who has which parting, so nobody's any wiser.'

They both laughed.

Then, behind them, Hen's Tooth, who had finally finished eating, began talking again. Jake sat down to listen to her. He didn't mean to ignore his friend, but it was White Thunder who made Eliza feel welcome, and gave her food and drink.

Jake listened to every word that Hen's Tooth said, and, when he couldn't understand, he made White

Thunder translate. He wouldn't leave the girl's side, even when she was too tired to speak.

Finally, Tall Elk insisted that Hen's Tooth rest, and he found a quiet place for her to sleep, close to White Thunder and Eliza in the Lodge.

Jake had only just left the Land of the Red Moon, and, already, he couldn't wait to go back. He needed to take Hen's Tooth home. She was his only clue to what had happened to his family, and he was determined to follow that clue wherever it might lead.

Eliza was simply pleased to see Jake, and she was delighted when he promised to take her to the Land of the Red Moon. She wasn't at all pleased when she saw how interested Jake was in Hen's Tooth. Who was the strange Native girl? And why was Jake so interested in her?

Eliza would try to ask White Thunder as soon as she got the chance.

39

Yellow Cloud took Masefield Haskell straight to Chief Half Moon when they arrived at the plateau. The two men had talked for most of the ride from Prospect.

Haskell had told Yellow Cloud what he knew about Horton Needham's plans. He had also told him about the burglary. Yellow Cloud knew about the geologist mapping the Land of the Red Moon and the landscape between the settlement and the winter training grounds.

Chief Half Moon asked his questions, which Yellow Cloud translated.

'Are you a good map-maker?' translated Yellow Cloud. 'Could a man read your maps and make a path from one place to another?'

'Yes,' said Haskell. 'I make very fine maps. I was taught by one of the best cartographers in England. I'm sorry to say, I believe that anyone could follow one of my maps successfully.'

'Do not be sorry,' said Yellow Cloud. 'It is a worthy skill.'

'The men that stole the maps are bad men?' asked Chief Half Moon.

'Bad men and foolish men, I'm afraid,' said Masefield Haskell.

'Never be afraid of bad or foolish men,' said Yellow Cloud, translating. 'Bad men can be overcome with goodness, and foolish men can be charmed with wit.'

'I hope so,' said Masefield Haskell, 'because I fear that making those maps may have been the most foolish thing in the world . . . in *two* worlds!'

Yellow Cloud and Chief Half Moon began to talk to each other, turning to Masefield Haskell for his opinion.

'Have our people ever travelled to the Land of the Red Moon on foot or on horseback?' asked Yellow Cloud.

'It would be impossible for a horse to cross the land. A mule could, or a strong man with a good map,' said Chief Half Moon. 'There are legends from the vision quests.'

'The legends say it takes a hundred suns to cross to the Land of the Red Moon,' said Yellow Cloud.

'I know no man who has made the journey,' said Chief Half Moon. 'I believe Mr Haskell's maps would make it possible.'

'Could a man walk the land in less than a hundred days?' asked Yellow Cloud.

'No boy on a vision quest ever had a map,' said Chief Half Moon. 'Our legends are our truths, but these men with their maps . . . I do not know.'

'Mr Haskell,' said Yellow Cloud, 'do you know how long it might take a company of men to cross to the Land of the Red Moon, on foot, using your map?'

Mr Haskell took a pencil and a notebook from his pocket and began to make calculations.

'I mapped the land very carefully, and my memory is sharp,' he said, 'although I say it myself, and shouldn't.'

'Do you know how long it would take?' asked Yellow Cloud again.

'I might be able to work it out,' said Haskell. 'I know the distances and the route, and I can estimate snowfall and wind speed. I know who's travelling, and their guide, but researching a landscape, scientifically, as I did, is very different from travelling through it, you understand?'

Chief Half Moon and Yellow Cloud watched in wonder as Masefield Haskell wrote a series of numbers and symbols across two pages of his notebook. After five minutes, Haskell took a long look at his calculations, and breathed out hard.

'I should say, three months and a fortnight,' said Haskell, 'give or take as much as a week.'

Chief Half Moon looked at Yellow Cloud, who shrugged. They both looked at Haskell again.

'One hundred and ten days,' he said. 'No fewer than one hundred and five days, but perhaps a hundred and twenty days.'

Chief Half Moon closed his eyes and dropped his head back slightly.

'They have not crossed into the Land of the Red Moon, yet,' he said.

'On the contrary,' said Haskell, taking out his diary, 'I believe they might very well be entering the Land of the Red Moon right now!' He showed the pages of the diary to Chief Moon, pointing to the day marked as Thanksgiving and then to that very day's date, and running his finger along all the days in between.

'It rather depends on how religious Boss Needham is,' said Haskell. 'He might have stopped to celebrate Christmas, or to say a prayer on Sundays. On the other hand, he might be in the Land of the Red Moon, right now.'

'Why would any man who is not our friend, or our foe, want to visit our home?' asked Chief Half Moon.

'He is not our friend,' said Yellow Cloud. 'He

thought he could buy us with cheap goods and bad whisky.'

'He might be your enemy,' said Masefield Haskell.

'He is a wealthy businessman,' said Chief Half Moon. 'What does he want from us?'

'More,' said Masefield Haskell. 'Men like Horton Needham always want more.'

40

Hen's Tooth was eating hungrily again, this time from a bowl of hot maize porridge, when Jake left her with White Thunder and Eliza to find Yellow Cloud.

It was early and the sun was low in the blue-grey sky. Jake had almost forgotten how the colour of the sky, over the plateau, could change from grey to purple to bright blue, during the course of one morning. He had forgotten all the different shapes the clouds could be, from the wispy, feathery, almost transparent clouds, to the great, lumpy, fluffy ones. It was all so different from the green, almost cloudless sky of the Land of the Red Moon. He wasn't sure he'd ever get used to it again.

It was damp too. Everything was moist with spring dew; everything was lush and green. There was grass everywhere, and fresh shoots. The trees on the horizon were a rich green, and everything was flourishing anew with the spring.

Jake soon found Yellow Cloud, tending to the

dragons in the corral. The fire was a pile of glowing embers, giving off whiffs of grey smoke, and the creatures were rousing from sleep.

'We must return to the Land of the Red Moon,' said Jake, approaching his teacher. 'If I take Hen's Tooth back to her home, she might be able to show me where she found Emmie's rag doll.'

'Hen's Tooth has been through a terrible ordeal,' said Yellow Cloud. 'You do not understand about the Dragon Lords.'

'I'm not afraid,' said Jake. 'I've seen the Dragon Lords in my dreams.'

'You are not afraid because you do not understand,' said Yellow Cloud. 'You are not one of us. You have not lived with the legends.'

Jake snorted in fierce anger.

'But I *am* one of you,' he said. 'I am Dragon Sight, and, if I work hard enough, I hope to be one of the *best* of you! Tell me the legends of the Dragon Lords. Help me understand!'

The boy stood before the man, defiant. He felt that he had earned his place among the Natives.

'I am sorry, Dragon Sight,' said Yellow Cloud. 'You cannot go.'

Jake fought to stay calm. He couldn't believe Yellow Cloud would deny him this opportunity to find his family.

'Then go with me,' he said, following Yellow

Cloud out of the enclosure. 'I must find my family, and, if you won't help me, I'll find them on my own.'

'There are the Rites of Spring,' said Yellow Cloud calmly. 'We will celebrate the rising of the spring moon, and then you will return to your family in Prospect.'

'You can't send me back to Prospect,' said Jake, his cheeks flushing with anger. 'I belong in the Land of the Red Moon with Hen's Tooth.'

'The child cannot return to her family if they have been hunted by the Dragon Lords,' said Yellow Cloud.

'Then she belongs with us,' said Jake. 'Besides, she's a rider!'

'That is not your decision. She is not a toy for you to take or leave to suit you,' said Yellow Cloud. 'One day you will be a leader of men, Dragon Sight, and then you will understand what it is to balance the needs of many. Until then, Chief Half Moon, Tall Elk and I make the decisions. We know what is best for the Cloud People.'

'She's one of us,' said Jake.

'You do not understand,' said Yellow Cloud. 'If the Dragon Lords hunted her family, next winter, they will hunt us.'

'Then we'll defeat them,' said Jake.

'No one has ever defeated the Dragon Lords,' said Yellow Cloud. 'For hundreds of years they were our brothers. Then the troubles began. Brother turned against brother, and only those who could stand alone survived. Any who left their homes returned to find their families enslaved and their possessions stolen or destroyed.

'The Cloud People turned east and made a new life close to the colony, across two lands: the Land of the Red Moon and the Land of the White Sun.

'We live with the dragons and with the land and the earth and the seasons. We live with the creatures and the plants. We live for each other and for our families. We have simple lives.

'The Dragon Lords live soulless lives of the mind,' explained Yellow Cloud. 'They live for hatred and to do battle. They live through the dragons and not with them, and they live separate lives, one from another. Everything they need to live comes from outside. They enslave men, as they enslave dragons, as if they were beasts of burden, men like Hen's Tooth's brothers, who feed them and clothe them, and fight their battles for them.

'They join forces only to satisfy the old legends,' said Yellow Cloud. 'Hen's Tooth has crossed the Crest Mountains, and it is a sign that cannot be ignored. The legends will come true.'

Jake stared at Yellow Cloud in disbelief, but he knew that his teacher was telling the truth.

'What does it mean?' he asked.

'It will be the end of times,' said Yellow Cloud.

'Yes, but what exactly does that mean?' asked Jake, confused. 'The brood queen will die, but what will happen to our people?'

'We will lose our homes,' said Yellow Cloud. 'It has happened before. It is destined to happen again.'

'If it is the end of everything, I'll never find my family,' said Jake. 'If I don't take Hen's Tooth back to the Land of the Red Moon, all the clues will be lost. I know they're out there, Yellow Cloud. I know it!'

'To go back now is to face certain death,' said Yellow Cloud, and he turned to leave.

Jake watched Yellow Cloud walk away. The boy was breathing hard, trying to stay calm, but he was only getting more and more angry.

Before he knew what he was doing, he ran at his mentor and launched himself on to Yellow Cloud's back. The two went sprawling into the dewy grass. In a split second, Jake was on top of his teacher, his chest heaving and his cheeks flushed.

Yellow Cloud did not resist. He was by far the stronger man, but there was only sadness in his eyes as he stared up at Jake.

'Promise that you won't stop me! Promise you'll help me find my family!' Jake yelled.

'I will help you find your family,' said Yellow Cloud, 'but I will not let you risk your life.'

'I'm going back to the Land of the Red Moon,' said Jake. 'I know my family's there.'

'It is no longer our home, Dragon Sight. Our tribe must find a new place of safety,' said Yellow Cloud, 'but, once we are all safe, I vow that I will lead a search party myself.'

Jake dropped his head into his hands and breathed hard. He was angry and upset, and it wasn't what he wanted to hear, but he knew it was the best that Yellow Cloud would offer him.

He didn't know why Yellow Cloud was so afraid of the Dragon Lords, and he didn't care. Not for the first time, Jake's thoughts were fast filling with more questions than answers.

He got up off Yellow Cloud's chest just as Tall Elk was walking towards them, a question on his face. Jake left his teacher on his back, on the ground, and strode towards the Lodge, straight back to Hen's Tooth.

'Did Dragon Sight attack you?' asked Tall Elk as Yellow Cloud stood up and straightened his clothes.

'It was nothing,' said Yellow Cloud.

'Do we need to talk to Chief Half Moon?' asked Tall Elk.

'No,' said Yellow Cloud. 'Dragon Sight is upset, but I have made him a promise and he knows that I will keep it.'

'I hope you are right,' said Tall Elk.

The two men walked back to the Lodge, to discuss the war party that would ride to the Land of the Red Moon to find Horton Needham and his cronies.

'What of the Dragon Lords?' asked Tall Elk.

'First we must find the boss and Flame Beard,' said Yellow Cloud.

'What does Dragon Sight call him?' asked Tall Elk.

'Trapper Watkiss,' said Yellow Cloud, the name sounding strange from his lips, 'but we have been calling him Flame Beard for much longer. Black Feather will be in the war party, and I am sure he will want a chance for revenge.'

41

Jacob Polson didn't know that it was March 17th, 1851, and he didn't care. He hadn't even remembered that he would be fourteen in six weeks' time. He did know that it was time to celebrate the first spring full moon on the plateau. The Natives returned to their summer settlement on the first full moon after the first full ground mists on the plains.

Jake had slept in the Lodge in the Land of the Red Moon for two weeks because of those mists, and now was the night of the first full moon over the plateau. There was no moon, though. The sky was a dirty grey, because of the dense cloud coverage. The air was thick with moisture, and the only sight of the moon was a thick, pale haze in the sky that was trying to cut through the clouds.

It didn't matter. The Natives celebrated the full moon whether they could see it or not. They also celebrated the rain. There was no rain in the Land of the Red Moon, and the Natives counted the richness of their blessings in all their forms.

Everyone had a job, before, during and after the celebrations, except for Masefield Haskell, Eliza Garret and Hen's Tooth.

Jake had won back his position as top apprentice before the end of winter training, and it was his job to fly Match over the huge bonfire, during the celebrations.

While the fire was being lit and the food prepared, and while Chief Half Moon, Tall Elk and Yellow Cloud were putting together a war party to fly back to the Land of the Red Moon, Jake was making plans of his own.

'Good boy, Match,' he said, feeding the dragon gleaming fish, and stroking his shoulder. 'Eat well; you've got a long flight tonight. We're going on an adventure, Match, to the Land of the Red Moon.'

Then Jake left the dragon, and, avoiding the others, went to speak to Hen's Tooth.

He beckoned to Hen's Tooth from the entrance of the Lodge, but he heard someone behind him, and ducked inside the door flap, so that he couldn't be seen from outside.

'What are you doing here?' asked Eliza. 'I thought you were feeding your dragon.'

'I just wanted to speak to Hen's Tooth,' said Jake, gesturing towards the girl, who was playing with Emmie's doll. She was holding it at arm's length, swooping it and swirling it around, as if it could fly.

Then Jake realized that Hen's Tooth was playing dragons.

Jake and Hen's Tooth whispered together, and Hen's Tooth's voice soon became loud, and she started to speak more quickly, so that Jake couldn't understand. Jake tried to slow her down, taking hold of her arms, and making eye contact with her, but she was excited and he couldn't stop her chattering.

Then Jake snatched the rag doll from Hen's Tooth, and she yelped at him.

Eliza hurried over to them. Masefield Haskell also raised his head from where he was poring over his notebook, to make sure that everything was all right.

'Leave her alone,' said Eliza. 'You're upsetting her.'

Hen's Tooth had stopped yelping, and was quiet. She was watching Jake swing the doll, at arm's length, just as she had done. He was showing her a flying doll, and talking to her in the Native language.

Eliza took the doll from Jake and gave it back to Hen's Tooth, but Hen's Tooth only smiled at Jake. Jake smiled back, nodded, and got up to leave the teepee.

As he reached the door flap, someone grasped his arm, and whispered at him, 'If you don't want me to tell Yellow Cloud what you're up to, you'd better let me in on your plan. I know it's got something to do with the dragons, so you'd better tell me right now!'

42

'I can't tell you,' Jake hissed at Eliza. 'It's too risky, and I'm already in enough trouble.'

'What on earth are you up to, Jake?' asked Eliza. 'What's going on? Why is everyone so tense?'

'The rag doll that Hen's Tooth is playing with,' said Jake, 'it belonged to my sister.'

Eliza gasped.

'Where did she get it?' she asked.

'That's what I want to know,' said Jake. 'I'm taking her back to the Land of the Red Moon, to find out.'

'Why the secrecy?' asked Eliza.

Jake just glared at her, and Eliza suddenly realized what was happening.

'Yellow Cloud doesn't want you to go!' she said.

Jake's head dropped.

'Well,' said Eliza, 'if you want me to keep your secret, you'll have to take me with you.'

'I can't!' said Jake.

'You haven't got a choice,' said Eliza.

'What's going on?' asked Masefield Haskell,

looking up from his notebook, aware of the intense whispering.

'Nothing,' said Eliza, 'it's just been so long since we've talked, and Jake's supposed to be feeding Match. You won't tell, will you, Mr Haskell?'

'You'd better run along, Jake,' said Mr Haskell.

'Meet me by the corral after my fly-past,' whispered Jake, leaning towards Eliza one last time. 'Keep Hen's Tooth happy. She knows what to do, but she mustn't tell anyone.'

Then he turned and ducked out of the Lodge, and Eliza was left alone. She wanted to jump for joy, and she would have if Masefield Haskell hadn't been in the teepee. She'd been jealous of Jake for too long, but she'd also missed him terribly. The promise of an adventure made up for all of it, even if she did have to share it with Hen's Tooth.

'I'm keeping my eye on you,' said Masefield Haskell, from behind his notebook.

'No need, Mr Haskell,' said Eliza. 'Everything's perfect. Jake's well, Hen's Tooth is playing with her doll, and we're all looking forward to the feast. What could possibly go wrong?'

'Are you soft-soaping me, as my mother, Mrs Haskell, would say?' asked the geologist, peering at Eliza.

'I don't know what you mean, Mr Haskell,' said Eliza.

'I don't know what Mrs Haskell meant, either,' said Masefield Haskell, 'but, whatever she meant, I suspect that's exactly what you're doing, and I don't like it.'

'Don't worry, Mr Haskell,' said Eliza.

'Those words fill me with dread,' said Haskell, but Eliza wasn't listening.

She had wandered over to where Hen's Tooth was playing with Emmie's rag doll. She was determined to make the Native girl her best friend over the next hour or two, even if they didn't speak the same language.

43

The sky was a penetrating grey with its thick covering of clouds, and it was impossible to see the edges of the full moon that was hanging high above the plateau. It was impossible to see anything that was more than a few feet away from the two fires that had been lit.

The dragon handlers had a fire burning in the corral to keep the dragons warm, and there was a large bonfire at the centre of the settlement. Various Native groups were taking it in turns to perform their ceremonial dances around it.

The warriors were first, with their slow, heavy steps, their knees bent, their weight low, their rhythm slow and even. They looked strong and regal, and their war cries rang across the plateau as they danced, almost without moving from the spots where they began.

Then came the men and women with families, who danced for renewal, for the plants to grow and for the animals to produce their young. They wove paths around the fire, faster and lighter than the warriors. They twirled and sang, and whooped joyful, high-pitched calls.

White Thunder took Eliza's hand, and Eliza, in turn, took Hen's Tooth's hand, and the three girls took a turn around the bonfire, swirling and whooping. It didn't seem to matter that Eliza didn't know the dance, or that Hen's Tooth threw her arms up high and tossed her head. Everyone smiled at them, pleased that they'd joined in.

When their dance was coming to an end, Eliza made sure that she pulled Hen's Tooth out of the circle on the same side of the bonfire as the corral. That would make it easier when it was time to sneak away.

Next it was the riders' turn. Their dance was so energetic that it was performed only by the oldest apprentices and the youngest riders. The older riders sang. At this point, the best apprentice of the winter performed a fly-past over the bonfire, almost as if dancing with the riders below.

There were eight dancers, all wearing neckbands and armbands, decorated with dragon feathers. The riders took up various stances, using their arms as wings. They made themselves very tall, by standing on tiptoe, and some of them raised one knee so that it looked as if they were walking into the air. Then, when the drumming and the singing began, they swooped and glided and beat their arms, as if they were dragons. They stretched their necks and lifted their knees. They turned and swirled, and they passed each other in the circle.

Eliza had never seen anything so extraordinary in her life, and the strong voices of the older men blended and soared to form a wall of sound in the night air, the like of which she'd never heard, not even in church.

Suddenly, Hen's Tooth was no longer by her side. Eliza looked left and right, panicking, knowing that she must find the girl before it was time to meet up with Jake. She couldn't let him down.

Then there was a light in the sky, and Eliza looked up to see Jake riding Match. He was turning circles and figures of eight above the bonfire, matching the patterns that the dancers were performing, except that Match was breathing fire.

Jake turned Match, and, as the dragon swung his head, a great burst of flames lit up a figure who was barely half the size of some of the riders. Nevertheless, the little dancer was performing all the same moves, turning and swooping and gliding around the bonfire. Eliza caught sight of the dancer and gasped.

She kept an eye on the figure as it danced towards her, and, when it was within arm's reach, she swung out and grabbed hold of its waist. She didn't try to stop it. She knew that would be a disaster. She swung the little dancer up in her arms and twirled it around. She danced with it, twirling and swirling and laughing, all the time moving closer to the corral, hoping that no one would notice.

Minutes earlier, Hen's Tooth saw the riders dance, and she knew that she was meant to dance too. All the boys had the same burn scars and tattoos that she had. She could see the colours and patterns of their tattoos dancing in the bonfire flames. She was one of them, and she wanted to dance so badly that she couldn't help herself.

She danced twice around the bonfire, and then, suddenly, she was flying through the air.

When Eliza put her down, Hen's Tooth wanted to get back to the dance, so she darted towards the fire. It took her a moment to realize that she wasn't looking at the bonfire. She was looking at another fire.

Hen's Tooth hadn't left the Lodge until the evening of the celebration. She didn't know the layout of the settlement. She didn't know the dragons lived in a corral, or that the corral had its own fire.

She leaned against the corral fence, and peered in. By the light of the flames, Hen's Tooth could make out the shapes of several dragons lying on the ground. One or two of them had been brought back from the colony and were very young. They would be paired with their riders during the next few years. Hen's Tooth looked through the fence, making odd clucking noises.

Eliza couldn't stop the girl, because she didn't know how to tell her to stop. Hen's Tooth clucked again, and one of the smaller dragons lifted its head and turned towards the sound. Hen's Tooth opened the corral gate. Eliza reached out to stop her, but the Native girl had already entered the corral, and Eliza didn't dare follow her.

'You've got to wait for Jake,' said Eliza.

Hen's Tooth didn't listen, but at least Eliza could tell Jake that she'd tried. She wished that one of the dragon handlers had been here, but they were all at the ceremony. Besides, if even one of them had stayed at the corral, Jake's plan would have been ruined, and Eliza really wanted an adventure.

Eliza watched Hen's Tooth walk into the corral as if it was nothing. She wandered between the dragons, and even patted their necks.

Eliza wished that Jake would come back. She could still see him, in the bonfire light, weaving circles and figures of eight over the crowds of Natives. She'd seen the dance, though, and it required a lot of energy. The riders couldn't possibly keep it up for long, however fit and young they were.

Eliza watched with growing alarm as the little

dragon that had turned its head lifted its shoulders and forelegs, so that it was sitting with only its back legs and tail on the ground. Its wings were furled, but it seemed remarkably alert. It was watching Hen's Tooth intently as she walked towards it.

Time almost seemed to stand still for the next ten minutes as the most extraordinary scene unfolded. Eliza didn't have a clue what it all meant, but she knew it meant something.

When it was over, a hand fell on Eliza's shoulder, and she almost jumped out of her skin.

'How could you let this happen?' he asked.

She turned to see Jake's eyes boring into her.

'How . . . How could I have stopped it?' Eliza stammered.

44

Ten minutes earlier, Jake had finished dancing over the bonfire with Match while his brothers performed the ceremonial dance. Then he'd flown back to the corral.

He hoped no one had noticed that Eliza and Hen's Tooth were missing. His entire plan relied on being able to get the Native girl off the plateau without anyone realizing that she was gone.

As he was landing, Jake saw that only one figure was standing by the corral. He slipped off Match and looked around for a second girl.

He soon became aware that Eliza was standing outside the corral, watching what was happening inside the enclosure. He followed her gaze and took in the scene unfolding before them.

Hen's Tooth was standing in the firelight, among the dragons, perfectly relaxed. All was calm and quiet, except for one little dragon.

Jake recognized it as one of the new dragons, fresh from the colony. He was a beautiful creature with very glossy, dark blue-green scales. He reminded Jake of Yellow Cloud's description of Starling's dragon.

As Eliza and Jake watched, the young dragon stood up, pawed at the ground, swished its tail and tossed its head. Then it flexed its wings, making the scales gleam and shimmer. Finally, it snorted puffs of sulphurous breath from its nostrils, which formed yellow clouds in the air.

Suddenly, the little dragon lowered its forelegs to the ground and placed its head flat on the earth. Hen's Tooth hardly hesitated. She placed her left hand on the little dragon's snout and rubbed and patted it. The creature opened its eyes and breathed a yellow whiff of smoke from its nostrils. Then Hen's Tooth removed her hand, and the little dragon stood up.

Now, Jake watched Hen's Tooth with the startled Eliza standing next to him.

'How could you let this happen?' he asked.

She turned to see Jake's eyes boring into her.

'How . . . how could I have stopped it?' Eliza stammered.

Jake called gently to Hen's Tooth, and, when she crossed the enclosure, her dragon followed her. Jake couldn't help thinking he'd been right about having her tattooed; she was a rider, after all.

'It's time to go,' he said.

Hen's Tooth smiled and began to lead her dragon out of the enclosure.

'No!' said Jake. 'There's room on Match for you and Eliza.' It was true that Match had grown in the warm climate of the winter training grounds.

Hen's Tooth frowned and shook her head, and said something that Jake didn't understand.

'You ride with me,' said Jake, more firmly the second time.

Hen's Tooth reached under her cloak and pulled out Emmie's rag doll. She swung it through the air, and Jake knew that she hadn't been using the doll to mean the dragon. Emmie's rag doll was supposed to be Hen's Tooth. She'd always known that she would be a rider.

Jake snatched at the doll, and he managed to tear it out of Hen's Tooth's hands. He shook it at her, and then stuffed it inside his jacket.

Hen's Tooth's face fell, and then her lip stiffened. It was clear she could be just as stubborn as Jake.

The Native girl put her hands on her dragon's shoulders, dug a toe into the joint of his foreleg and hoisted herself up, so that she was sitting on his back, clutching the feathers at his neck.

Fearful of what might happen next, Jake mounted Match, and reached down to take Eliza's arm.

'Come on, Eliza, it's quite safe,' he said.

He could see that Eliza was still a little fearful of Match, but the look of dread on her face soon turned to one of determination, and Jake felt a tight grip on his arm as she sprang into position in front of him.

In another moment, Hen's Tooth had pulled her dragon up into a rampant position, and began to walk him into the air. When it was obvious that there was absolutely nothing he could do about it, Jake gave her clear instructions so that she would, at least, be safe.

Match was right behind Hen's Tooth's little dragon, and they both climbed into the sky in a great arc. Jake only counted his blessings that the girl had the sense not to fly over the settlement. She took a wide detour to avoid the bonfire, and, in a grey, moonless sky, she used her instincts to fly west, towards the Land of the Red Moon, and home.

45

When they were clear of the plateau, they flew side by side. Jake kept a close eye on Hen's Tooth, but her flying was instinctive, and her relationship with her little dragon seemed very natural. Jake was reminded of himself and Match when they'd met only months before. He knew that Yellow Cloud had said it was rare, but Jake trusted Hen's Tooth, and he trusted his dragonsight.

When they approached the crossing point between the Land of the White Sun and the Land of the Red Moon, Jake took the lead, flying Match in a tight circle around Hen's Tooth on her little dragon, and then hovering ahead and above her. He turned his arm in the air, telling Hen's Tooth that he would fly through, and then come back. His gesture was firm, because he wanted to be very clear that he was in charge. He had not flown with a total novice before, and he wanted to ensure her safety.

Jake tipped Match on his side, aware of Eliza's body tensing in front of him. Match spread his wings, above and below his body, and they glided, effortlessly, through the gap. Then Jake made a turn, so tight that Match never straightened up, and he flew them back to where Hen's Tooth was waiting.

Her back pressed against his chest, Jake could feel Eliza's heart thumping, and she gasped as they levelled up. The two dragons flew around for another pass. Hen's Tooth showed Jake that she was confident by turning her dragon on to its side and making it spread its wings. She flew a short distance in that position, and straightened up.

The next time Hen's Tooth's dragon tilted its body and spread its wings, it flew through the gap in the cliffs, and out into the Land of the Red Moon, where the big bright disc hung low in the dark green sky. Everything was lighter, and brighter, and Jake could see the grin on Hen's Tooth's face as Match joined her dragon over the blue sand dunes.

Only minutes later, they flew over the plains and the swirling ground mists. Match began the landing circles. Hen's Tooth tried to resist, continuing to fly west, but she'd been flying for some time, and she was tired.

They landed on the plains, close to the Lodge and the colony.

'Something's wrong,' said Jake, feeling his stomach tighten with nausea as soon as they were on the ground. 'It's too quiet, and there's a bad smell.'

Hen's Tooth suddenly sat on the ground, almost disappearing in the yellow mists that came up to their knees.

'You can't sit,' said Jake, trying to lift the girl by her armpits.

Suddenly, Hen's Tooth vomited.

'We must get her in the Lodge,' said Jake. 'She can't get ill again.'

Eliza looked at Jake with a strange expression on her face.

'You have no power over her health,' she said.

'She's ill because of what's happened here,' said Jake. 'It's got something to do with the colony, and with that terrible smell.'

'I don't understand,' said Eliza, lifting the door flap of the Lodge.

'There isn't time to explain,' said Jake, laying Hen's Tooth on a mat on the floor, and covering her with a skin. He looked around. No one had lit a fire for several days, but there were dishes with half-eaten meals in them, and people's belongings were all over the place. The small band of Natives that stayed with the colony had clearly left in a hurry, and Jake had a horrible feeling that they'd been driven out of the teepee or were even being hunted.

'What should we do?' asked Eliza.

'There's nothing we can do,' said Jake. 'We must make Hen's Tooth comfortable, and we must eat and sleep. Tomorrow, I'll visit the colony and see whether the brood queen is alive or dead.'

Eliza heard a squeak, and she yelped and stamped.

'Can we clean up first?' she asked. 'Rodents have got in, because of all the rotting food, and, if the sky's green and the sand's blue, I'm not sure I want to know what the rats are like.'

'I'll do that if you build a fire and cook something,' said Jake, waving a hand. 'There should be nuts and flour and salt meat, over there.'

The two busied themselves while Hen's Tooth rested.

Ten minutes later, Eliza went over to where Jake was burning rubbish on the fire she'd lit. She had a bundle of wood from the pile outside the Lodge. She'd found something, and she held out her hand to show him.

'Gun cartridges,' said Jake. 'There's only one place they could have come from.'

'The Natives carry guns,' said Eliza.

'Not in the Land of the Red Moon,' said Jake. 'No one else here has guns, so the Cloud People don't need them. Besides, they use old American guns. These cartridges are for new, fancy European guns. There's only one place a man would get a gun like that.'

'Mr Haskell said Boss Needham and Trapper Watkiss stole his maps and came to the Land of the

Red Moon to find gems and make a fortune . . . and it's all true,' said Eliza. 'Sheriff Sykes can arrest them now!'

Jake smiled slightly, and said, 'These cartridges didn't come from Trapper Watkiss's old Hawken rifles.'

'I'm glad to hear that,' said Eliza.

'Sheriff Sykes won't need to arrest anyone either,' said Jake. 'The Natives have their own justice.'

'He doesn't want to arrest them for stealing gems,' said Eliza Garret. 'Sheriff Sykes plans to arrest them for killing Mrs Mack.'

'That's terrible,' said Jake.

'It's worse than that,' said Eliza, 'because Mrs Mack was Trapper Watkiss's sister.'

46

A flash of lightning filled the sky with bright light. Then thunder rolled over the plateau. The rain, which had been threatening all day, poured down on the Natives and their bonfire.

Some of the Natives continued to dance, revelling in the tempest. The storms in the Land of the Red Moon were hot, dry and windy, and the lightning came in small, fizzing balls rather than great forks and bolts.

Masefield Haskell and Yellow Cloud entered the Lodge together.

'Have you seen the children?' asked Haskell.

'No,' said Yellow Cloud, his face a mixture of concern and controlled fury. 'I will find White Thunder; she will know where they are.'

Five minutes later, Yellow Cloud returned with White Thunder.

'Tell Mr Haskell what you know,' he said.

'I danced with Eliza and Hen's Tooth around the bonfire,' said White Thunder. 'They were happy.'

'They were together?' asked Haskell.

'Eliza insisted on being with Hen's Tooth, because she was Jake's particular friend,' said White Thunder. 'Did I do something wrong?'

'No,' said Yellow Cloud. 'You did nothing wrong.'

'*I* did something wrong,' said Masefield Haskell.

'What happened?' asked Yellow Cloud, deep concern on his face as he remembered how much Jake wanted to return with Hen's Tooth to the Land of the Red Moon. That didn't explain why Eliza was missing, though.

'Eliza and Jake were talking,' said Haskell, working through everything he knew logically. 'At least, properly speaking, Jake and Hen's Tooth were talking. Then Jake took her doll away. She got upset, but she calmed down when he flew it through the air.'

'He flew it through the air?' asked Yellow Cloud.

'I think they were pretending it was a dragon,' said White Thunder.

'Eureka! I've got it!' said Haskell. 'Jake and Hen's Tooth were plotting to fly away . . . That's why he made the doll look like it was flying. Eliza realized what was happening, and she made him take her with them.'

'I promised him I would send out a search party,' said Yellow Cloud. 'Why could he not wait?'

'It's dangerous out there!' said Masefield Haskell.

'Horton Needham is after the gems, and goodness only knows what he could do to three children.'

'Jake is taking Eliza and Hen's Tooth right into the jaws of the Dragon Lords,' said Yellow Cloud. 'We must go after them!'

Yellow Cloud folded back the door of the Lodge with one sweep of his arm. The rain was pouring down so hard that the last of the dancers were running, soaking wet, towards the Lodge for shelter. The bonfire was smouldering and smoking, and would soon die in the downpour. Another great flash of lightning lit up the plateau, so that Yellow Cloud could see all the way to the corrals. The thunder came almost instantly behind the lightning. Soon, the storm would be directly overhead.

'There's nothing to be done,' said Haskell, peering over Yellow Cloud's shoulder. 'Do you think they're safe?'

'If they left after the riders' dance, they arrived in the Land of the Red Moon before the storm broke,' said Yellow Cloud. 'They are safe from it. I do not know whether they are safe from the evils of men or of the Dragon Lords. We will find out tomorrow, Mr Haskell.'

47

Trapper Watkiss looked into the green sky and over the blue dunes, and he knew there would be no trees on which to leave his mark for a long time. He looked towards the horizon, at the wide open spaces, and he made a mental note of the shape the cliff made against the sky. He wanted to know exactly where the gap in the mountain was when he decided to go home. He wanted to go home right now.

The path down on to the blue dunes sloped gently, and the men were able to gaze around to their heart's content as they made the descent. When they reached the blue dunes, Othniel Seeley pushed his hands into the glittering blue sand, and let it run through his fingers. Great cascades of sparkling grit caught the light as it fell back into the dunes. Larger pieces of crystal caught between his fingers, and he held them up to the light to examine them.

'These are gemstones, right here in the dunes,' he said to Boss Needham. 'We won't even have to dig!'

Horton Needham had taken off his squat, felt hat,

not the top hat he'd been wearing in Prospect, and was wiping his sweaty head with a large square of linen. It had been a beautiful handkerchief when he'd put it in his pocket on leaving Prospect, but it was now little more than a rag. He stopped, and peered down at the sand. Then he picked up a handful and began to sort through it until he found a crystal large enough to satisfy his interest. He put it in his pocket and began again.

'These are really precious gems?' he asked Seeley.

'Semi-precious,' said Seeley. Then he hesitated before saying, 'Almost certainly.'

Horton Needham tossed the crystals away.

'I won't waste my time with semi-precious,' he snarled.

'I'm sure there's plenty more,' said Othniel Seeley. 'There's evidence in Haskell's samples of precious stones of all kinds.'

'Why are we wasting time on sand then?' asked Needham.

'Which way?' asked Trapper Watkiss.

'It's *your* job to tell *us* that,' said Boss Needham. '*You're* the map-reader.'

'The sun's all wrong,' said Trapper. 'There ain't no east nor west. I ain't got a clue where I'm s'posed to be going, and I don't like it one little bit.'

'We go forward,' said Boss Needham. 'Set a course, or I'll send you back.'

'I'll be very happy to *go* back, thank you very much,' said Trapper Watkiss.

Somebody coughed. When Needham couldn't tell who'd made the noise, he said, 'If someone's got something to say, they'd better come straight out and say it.'

'We wouldn't have got here without Mr Watkiss,' said Pennyworth. 'He knows the land, and he knows maps, and he's kept us straight.'

'Let's see how much difference a gap in a cliff makes then, shall we?' asked Boss Needham, pointing away from the mountains. 'After you, *Mr* Watkiss.'

Trapper looked at Haskell's map. It had landmarks clearly drawn on it with colour references for rocks, plants and features like the sand dunes. There were no compass directions on the map, but there was a diagram, showing the Land of the Red Moon in relation to what was directly the other side of the gap in the cliff. Haskell had labelled it as 'the Land of the White Sun'.

The Land of the Red Moon lay to the west of what Trapper Watkiss called home. Trapper looked into the green sky and noted that the large, dark, speckled sun appeared to be in the southern part of the sky. It was not setting in the west, where it ought to be setting, and that fact bothered him more than he would ever admit.

Trapper Watkiss took out his compass and looked

at it, facing in the direction that he assumed was north. The compass needle swung back and forth and then around and around. When it wouldn't settle, Trapper shook the compass and looked at it again. He scowled.

'By God, a man needs to know which direction his life is going in,' he muttered. 'For once, I couldn't agree more with them nuns!'

Everything in this unfathomable place was bothersome and wrong and troubling.

Then it crossed his mind that Masefield Haskell hadn't put compass points on his map of the Land of the Red Moon, because it was impossible to plot them if the needle in the compass was never still.

Trapper Watkiss reasoned that if they'd travelled west into the gap, and if Needham wanted to go deeper into the Land of the Red Moon, then they should continue to head west. If the sun moved across the green sky from north to south, he should keep it on his left.

Without compass bearings, and with only the landmarks and guesswork, Trapper Watkiss was relieved to find that, with the sun on his left, the gap in the cliff was behind him. So, if he'd been in the Land of the White Sun, he'd be travelling west.

Trapper took the stub of a pencil out of his pocket, licked it and made a note on Haskell's map. He would have liked to make a note on the map he'd drawn on his silk handkerchief, but, unless he got the chance to do it in private, he wouldn't do it at all.

Two mules and six men headed in the direction that Trapper Watkiss decided was 'west', until they were following under the shadow of a great crested ridge of mountains, looking out on to misted plains.

'Look yonder,' said Marcus Mimms suddenly. 'What's that, rising out of the mists?'

Trapper Watkiss had seen the Lodge, several minutes before, but had decided to hug the ridge and keep to the shade. The strange sun was very low, and the mists on the plains looked sinister. It didn't help that they smelled of old eggs, rotten mud pools and dragons' breath: three things that Trapper Watkiss didn't want anything to do with.

He knew that, if Boss Needham got wind of a Native settlement, he might want to attack it. Trapper Watkiss was many things, but he did have a broad streak of loyalty. Once upon a time, the Natives had saved his life, and it was impossible for him to actually hate them.

Sometimes, Trapper Watkiss feared the Natives, and, when he was afraid, he lashed out, which was how he'd come to stab Black Feather. He wouldn't attack a Native in cold blood, though, not even if Boss Needham said so.

The sun was very low in the sky, but the moon was rising, and it really was red. What's more, it was large and bright. The green sky began to turn an odd, sludgy colour, but it certainly wasn't black. The cloudless sky, the last of the sun and the uninterrupted moonbeams meant that the night was almost half as bright as the day.

'We're following the mountain ridge,' said Trapper. 'A man can get lost in a mist.'

'It looks like the top of one of those Native tents,' said Anthony Mimms, pointing at the Lodge with its skirts shrouded in purple mists.

Horton Needham peered out across the plains.

'There's no chance of getting lost,' said Othniel Seeley. 'We can see for miles.'

'What about the mists?' asked Trapper Watkiss, trying one last time to draw attention away from the teepee.

'No one ever got lost in a knee-deep mist,' said Seeley. 'As a geologist, they don't look like weather to me. They look like a chemical vapour being produced from the rocks.'

'Ain't chemicals dangerous?' asked Trapper.

'It's just sulphur,' said Seeley. 'We'll only be walking through it. I don't see the harm.'

Horton Needham had been listening to the men, trying to make a decision, when two great purple flares reached into the sky to their left.

'What in blue blazes was that?' asked Trapper Watkiss, before he could stop himself.

'That's rather funny,' said Othniel Seeley.

'You think great purple flames are funny?' asked Reginald Pennyworth.

'Well, no,' said Seeley, 'I imagine the flames are rather serious. The fact that Mr Watkiss chose to swear with the expression "blue blazes" is funny, though.'

'Are you making fun of me?' asked Trapper Watkiss, blushing slightly behind his red beard.

'Blaze means fire, after all,' said Seeley, 'and those flames are purple. Anyway, I thought it was funny.'

'It ain't funny,' said Trapper Watkiss, 'and p'raps we should take a look at that teepee, after all.'

'Lead the way,' said Boss Needham. 'If the Natives are gone, we'll use it as a base camp.'

48

The Natives that remained with the brood queen and her colony, while the rest of the tribe returned to the plateau, were surprised by the sounds of footsteps and mules approaching the Lodge. They had done their chores, and returned to the Lodge once the mists had set in at the end of the afternoon. They were eating a meal when they first heard people approaching.

They didn't use mules or horses in the Land of the Red Moon. They walked short distances or rode on the dragons. The settlement was small, and the winter was a short season, so travelling distances was less important. Besides, their settlement was bordered by the cliff that separated them from the Land of the White Sun, and by the Crest Mountains, which were difficult to cross.

No one else lived between the Land of the White Sun and the Crest Mountains. Beyond the Crest Mountains lived nomadic Native tribes that offered no threat to the Cloud People, and beyond them lived the Dragon Lords.

With curiosity more than with fear, the Natives lifted the door flap of the teepee, and stepped through to greet their visitors.

They were surprised to see Boss Needham and his men. No one from the Land of the White Sun had ever travelled into the Land of the Red Moon, and there were no rules for greeting them.

Straight Arrow, who was in charge of the colony, and had not left the Land of the Red Moon for five summers, did what he had seen Chief Half Moon do long ago: he held out his right hand. When Boss Needham failed to take it, Othniel Seeley leaned past him, and shook hands with the Native.

'Good evening,' he said. 'Pleased to meet you. This is Horton Needham, our patron, and I'm Othniel Seeley, geologist.'

Straight Arrow had never spoken much English, and the little he had once known he'd forgotten.

Horse Tail stepped forward, while the two men continued to shake hands. Straight Arrow finally loosened his grip on Seeley when Horse Tail began to speak.

'Why are you here?' he asked.

'That's not the warm Native welcome I've heard about,' said Boss Needham. 'You should be ashamed of yourselves. Invite us in and feed us, and we'll tell you why we're here.'

The Natives didn't understand Needham's manner and tone, but it wasn't hard for them to take an instant dislike to him.

Strangely, it was Trapper Watkiss who smoothed things over between the visitors and the Natives. He coughed, and slowly said the few Native words he could remember. They included a friendly greeting and the words for food and drink. Soon, everyone was smiling, even if some of the smiles were uneasy, and the men were invited into the Lodge.

As bowls and beakers were handed to the visitors, Boss Needham kept a sharp eye on the hands holding the dishes and doing the serving.

'Look at their wrists,' he said to Othniel Seeley.

'Ankles too,' said the geologist.

The Natives wore shin-length trousers and sleeveless shirts in the warm climate. The beads they wore around their wrists and ankles as ornaments, and as whistles to call their dragons, were clearly visible.

'Are those beads what I think they are?' asked Needham.

'I believe you're looking at sapphires and emeralds, and even rubies,' said Seeley. 'These men are wearing jewels worth more than a working man's wage . . . for a year . . . each.'

'Ask them where they came from,' said Needham.

'I don't think it's as simple as that,' said Seeley. 'Besides, I don't speak their language.'

'Then ask Watkiss to do it,' said Needham, his face turning red, 'and, while you're at it, find out what the hell I'm eating.'

Trapper Watkiss was sitting quietly, steadily eating the food in his bowl. Some of the flavours were new to him, but he'd been surviving for three months on what he could forage, and on the smoked and salted meat he'd packed. It was a pleasure to eat fresh meat, even if he didn't know what it was. The vegetables were fleshy, but tasted fresh and sweet, and had a delicious nutty flavour. Not knowing when he would eat a fresh meal again, he devoured as much food as he was offered.

He was chewing a small bone, similar to a chicken leg, when half of the Natives began to gather together.

Needham jumped up.

'Where are you going?' he asked.

Straight Arrow shrugged, picked up a knapsack and headed for the door flap. Needham shoved Pennyworth.

'Nobody leaves until I know why, or until we all leave!' he said.

Pennyworth was on his feet, blocking the door flap, in a moment. A few seconds after that, the

Mimms brothers had been allowed out behind him so that they could grab their guns off the mules, where the Natives had insisted they left them.

Trapper Watkiss wanted nothing to do with it, but he was the only one who had any Native words, and the Natives who remained with the colony spoke little English.

With more gestures than words, Trapper was able to work out what was happening.

'They have to tend to the dragons,' he said.

'So that they can fly away?' asked Boss Needham. 'They're not going to get away with that!'

'You said yourself that we don't need them,' said Trapper Watkiss. 'We've got the jolly-gist's maps, and I brought you here, so we don't need a Native guide.'

'You haven't found the jewels, though, have you, Master Map-reader?' yelled Horton Needham, his face turning a terrible colour. He pulled Trapper towards him, and rummaged around in the old man's pockets, until he found Haskell's map. He spread the map out and pointed.

'Where do you see anything on that map that shows where the jewels are, *Mr* Watkiss?' asked Boss Needham. 'Where do you see "X marks the spot"?'

'I don't see it,' said Trapper Watkiss.

'You don't see it, because it isn't there!' said Horton Needham. 'Masefield Haskell didn't know where the gems were, but these people do! They're wearing more jewels than you've seen in your entire life!'

'That's why we brought miners,' said Trapper Watkiss. 'At least, that's what you said . . . boss. "We don't need Natives getting in our way," you said. "We don't need to ask their permission, and worry about what *they* want from *us*. No! It's much, much better this way." That's what you said,' said Trapper Watkiss.

Needham stared at him, for a moment, turning purple.

The Natives looked at each other, wondering what the two men were arguing about, and why the fat, bald one was turning such an unlikely colour. Some of them wondered whether he was quite well.

'Dimwit!' scolded Boss Needham. 'Why should we do the hard work when we can get them to do it for us? We take charge and make the Natives do what we want. Do you understand?' He glared at Trapper Watkiss, daring him to complain.

'Perfectly,' replied Trapper Watkiss. 'I suppose you want me to tell *them* that?'

'You suppose right,' said Boss Needham, pulling his felt hat down over his ears.

49

Two gunshots rang out in the still night air.

Marcus Mimms had shot his gun close to where wood was stacked for the fire that was in daily use in the Lodge.

Trapper was having a hard time explaining to the Natives why his boss was being so aggressive. Although they remained polite and helpful, Trapper could tell they were tired of being ordered around in their own home. They did, after all, outnumber the visitors five to one.

Marcus Mimms had also noticed that he was in a minority. He'd learned long ago, however, that authority didn't depend on numbers, but on a show of power. He left the hubbub of conversation behind him, in the Lodge, and stepped out on to the misty plain. Aiming his gun at the sky, he pulled the trigger twice, revelling in the noise of the explosions reverberating around the campsite. Then he flipped the remains of the home-made paper cartridges out of the gun and loaded two more.

Silence fell inside the Lodge, and, soon, everyone was filing out of the teepee, and gathering outside.

Straight Arrow reached out a hand and placed it on Trapper Watkiss's shoulder, making him jump.

'What d'you want?' asked Trapper. Straight Arrow gestured and said two or three words, very slowly. Trapper nodded to him.

'They just want to feed the dragons,' he said to no one in particular.

'It won't do any harm if we go along then, will it?' asked Horton Needham.

'Dragons ain't natural,' said Watkiss.

Horton Needham made a strange, high-pitched noise in the back of his throat. The Natives stared at him for a moment, before realizing that the boss was laughing.

'Look around,' said Needham. 'Does anything here look natural to you?'

Trapper Watkiss merely grunted. He didn't want any part of it, so he was carrying his rifle over his arm and walking with the Natives. The Mimms brothers and Pennyworth had their guns up, ready to shoot. Boss Needham was armed with a fancy English rifle too, although Trapper Watkiss doubted the man knew how to use it.

Othniel Seeley wasn't carrying a rifle, but Trapper knew that the geologist kept a revolver in a holster, under his jacket. He'd seen him shoot a rat in the forest with it.

Trapper kept a wary eye on the men while they walked across the plains. He also checked his bearings. He realized the Natives were walking directly towards the place where they'd seen the great purple flares rising high into the murky green sky, in the shadow of the vast crested ridge.

Trapper Watkiss hesitated, stopping in his tracks as the mists swirled around his knees. The others kept moving, until all he could see were the grey shapes of almost two dozen men, walking into the darkness. The dull glow of the red moon lit the swirling mists around their legs. The old man shuddered.

A purple flash illuminated the face of the mountain, and the grey shapes of the men turned to black silhouettes. Then Trapper saw the necks, heads and tails of more than a dozen vast dragons. What's more, he saw scores of smaller ovoids, like piles of smooth boulders, all similar shapes and sizes. He didn't want to think about what they were and what they might become, but, somehow, he knew that this was the dragons' breeding ground.

Trapper Watkiss knew that the Natives weren't just going to feed any dragons. The Natives were going to feed the breeding dragons. This was the heart of everything. These dragons were laying and brooding their eggs, and they would hatch and there would be more dragons in the world . . . in both worlds.

Trapper Watkiss didn't want to take another step towards the creatures, and he wasn't alone in his terror.

When the purple flames hit the sky, and bounced off the great rock face of the Crest Mountains, shedding light on the colony, Reginald Pennyworth broke out in a cold sweat. He was rooted to the spot, his face pale, his hands rigid and sweating, and his gun at his shoulder, ready to fire.

A second purple flash hit the rocks, and light bounced off the eyes of the brood queen as she turned to look out over the plains, checking that her handlers were coming to feed her.

As the second flare went up, Trapper Watkiss saw the barrel of Pennyworth's gun buck, and heard a shot. He shouted before he realized what he was doing. His shout was drowned by the sound of the gun firing. By the time Pennyworth had fired his second shot, Marcus and Anthony Mimms had also begun shooting, and Horton Needham had raised his gun to his shoulder and was swinging wildly.

Trapper Watkiss brought his gun up, but he didn't point it at the dragons. He didn't like dragons, but he couldn't bring himself to raise his gun to them, not with five other men already taking potshots.

The Natives did nothing. There were more than twice as many of them as there were of the visitors, but they were unarmed, and Trapper could see the shock on their faces that anyone would fire guns at the colony.

Horse Tail was the first to move. He dived at Pennyworth's legs, bringing the big man down hard. Reginald Pennyworth was full of adrenalin, which can make a man very dangerous. Pennyworth pulled himself quickly to a sitting position, and swung his rifle hard at Horse Tail's head.

He knocked the Native out with the butt of his rifle, and got back on his feet. When another Native rushed towards him, Pennyworth shot from the hip, without even raising his rifle to the firing position. The shot was wide and low, causing a flesh wound above the Native's hip that sent him sprawling to the ground, clutching his side.

The old brood queen could do nothing but send up her flares and count her eggs. Trapper heard her brood sisters' squawked assurances, but their voices were drowned out by the explosions from the guns. They lifted their heads and necks, and tried to add their puffs of purple flame to the air above the colony, but it was too full of the flash and smoke of gunfire, and they were so afraid that their flames were mostly strangled in their throats. He watched as they extended their bodies into more upright positions, and began to unfurl their wings for the first time in decades or scores of years to form a shield around the colony of eggs and hatchlings, and around the queen. They must protect her, if they could, but the gunfire penetrated nevertheless, and the desperate cries of the handlers made them more fearful than ever.

Shots began to penetrate, either accidentally or on purpose. Trapper saw one sister take shots to the eye and the nape feathers, and collapse among her sisters. A second stood high on her hind legs, and, with the blessing of her sisters, she unfurled her wings and began to step into the sky.

She was old and heavy, her scales had begun to fall away and her feathers were not as lush as they had once been. Her walk into the air was ponderous, and Trapper watched as Marcus and Anthony Mimms swung their rifles, making her their next target. They pulled the guns firmly into their shoulders, sighted their prey, took aim, and four shots were fired in quick succession.

Trapper watched with horror. Almost as if it was happening in slow motion, he saw the puffs of smoke from the barrels of the rifles, the jolts to the men's bodies as the guns recoiled into their shoulders, and then the smiles of triumph on the men's faces as the bullets hit their targets.

Then Trapper watched a second brood sister

begin her walk into the sky, and then a third, while their sisters sent flares up around them to light their way.

The first brood sister began to make a wide, wobbly circle over the colony as Trapper watched the Mimms brothers reload their guns. The action of her wings beating the air and of her body streamlining had caused her to rain scales down on her sisters. Trapper saw them sparkle in the light of the flames that her sisters breathed up at her. The naked patches on her skin also made her look vulnerable.

When Marcus and Anthony Mimms began to shoot at her again, Trapper noticed that so much of her naked flesh was exposed that the next four shots to her belly were fatal. She fell out of the sky in a heaving, roaring mass, her limbs thrashing and her wings curling around her dying body. Trapper could hardly bear to watch.

She fell among the eggs, which would now have no chance of hatching.

Trapper could only stand by as the Natives tried to intervene. Some tried to stop the men, and some put themselves between the men and the dragons. Nothing worked. Violence only leads to violence, and the men with their guns threatened the Natives, and fired at the dragons.

One of the Natives came so close to being shot by Horton Needham that Trapper Watkiss wondered whether the boss had missed his target by accident. Watkiss saw the feathers attached to a leather band around his neck flutter as the bullet flew close enough to make them move. Trapper was so concerned for the Natives that he began to point his own rifle at them, hoping that they'd run away rather than risk being shot.

When one of them bravely stared Trapper Watkiss down, Trapper aimed his rifle into the air and shot over the man's head. Then he pointed the gun at the man's chest, once more, and made a gesture with his head to suggest that he run away.

Finally, the Native turned and walked towards the colony. He took the knapsack from his back, and emptied its contents on to the ground. Then he lifted one of the eggs from the colony and squeezed it inside the bag. Trapper Watkiss watched as the Native put the knapsack on his back and jogged away.

Only when all the dragons were dead or had flown away, and only when they could carry no more eggs, did the Natives leave, helping one another, the fit carrying the wounded.

Horton Needham didn't see the men leaving. He didn't care.

Horton Needham's strange, high-pitched cackle filled the air. He was on his knees, surrounded by dragon eggs, both bulging fists clutched in front of him.

'It's all about the dragons!' he said.

A shriek raged through the air, and Trapper Watkiss shuddered once more. He stood at a distance from the others, away from the eggs and the dragon corpses. He would not be part of the mayhem these men had caused.

Trapper Watkiss heard a shot, and knew that one of the men had put the last of the dragons out of its misery, if it had not already died with its final desperate cry.

He wanted nothing more than to walk away from this wretched slaughter, but he knew that the boss would never allow that, so he stood at a distance. He was only grateful that none of the Natives had died.

'Seeley, come and look at this!' said Needham.

Othniel Seeley held out his hands, and allowed Horton Needham to empty some of the stones he was holding into his outstretched palms. They were smooth, polished precious gems, exactly like the beads the Natives wore on their bracelets.

'We've found them,' said Othniel Seeley.

50

The baying and moaning in Jake's head was unbearable, and he awoke with his hands clutching at his head, and a groan bubbling from his lips. He felt sick to his gut as he remembered the dream that had awoken him, the gunshots and the death throes of the dying brood dragons.

The sun had barely begun to rise when he shook Hen's Tooth from her disturbed sleep as she rolled around under her blanket, clutching her stomach.

'We must do a fly-past of the colony,' he said to her. 'We must make sure that the brood queen and her sisters and all the eggs and hatchlings are safe.'

Hen's Tooth did not need to be told twice. She felt sick and weak, but she also felt a bond and a duty.

Jake stood by to help as Hen's Tooth mounted her little dragon, but, even in her weakened state, the girl didn't need his assistance, and they were soon mounted and walking into the air.

Match took the lead and flew over the plains and

into the shade of the Crest Mountains. Every second he flew, the knot in Jake's stomach grew tighter, his head grew colder and heavier, and dread filled his bones. Once they were over the colony, Jake could feel death and destruction all around him. He knew that if he looked down his worst fears would be confirmed.

Then he heard a scream and a low moan, and he saw Hen's Tooth's little dragon sweeping down in a steep dive towards the colony. Hen's Tooth was slumped on his back.

Jake turned Match in a dive, and, as he drew level with the little dragon, Jake concentrated very hard. He stopped pressing his thighs and heels into Match's shoulders and sides, and he let go of Match's nape feathers. Then he closed his eyes and he searched in his mind for the little blue dragon. When he found it, he reached out to the little dragon's mind and soothed it.

Jake knew that, even with his dragonsight, he couldn't control two dragons at the same time, but he also knew that his friend would do the right thing. He closed his mind so that Match could not enter, and then he stepped into the mind of the little dragon so that he could save Hen's Tooth. Its mind was smaller and darker and warmer than Match's. Jake found Hen's Tooth's little dragon sad and serious, and he knew that he wouldn't be able to stay there for long. The dragon's mind was a bad fit for his and made him feel as if he was wearing a suit of clothes two sizes too small.

All he needed to do was land the little dragon, for the girl's sake. So, he did it as fast and efficiently as he could.

Match followed Jake's lead, and landed side by side with the little blue dragon, with Jake and Eliza still safe on his back. Jake slid off Match and strode over to lift Hen's Tooth from her dragon. She was coming round as he took her in his arms.

'Did you see?' she asked.

'I couldn't bear to look,' said Jake, 'but I know what I would have seen.'

'They're all dead,' said Hen's Tooth, 'or gone.'

'What do you mean, *gone*?' asked Jake.

'There were not enough bodies,' said Hen's Tooth, 'and not enough eggs. Some of them must have got away.'

Jake put Hen's Tooth down gently, among the nut plants. He was grateful that they'd sorted out their language problems and were talking freely, at last.

'So, they're not all dead?' he asked.

'I don't know how many there must be,' said Hen's Tooth, 'but our legends speak of a brood queen and her sisters, and of a sea of eggs. That's not what I saw.'

'How many *did* you see?' asked Jake.

Hen's Tooth put her face in her hands, and Eliza knelt beside the girl and put an arm around her.

'I don't know,' said Hen's Tooth.

'Let me look after her,' said Eliza. 'Don't put her through any more pain.'

They had landed deep in the shade of the Crest Mountains, and the edge of the colony was only a dozen strides away. Jake walked purposefully towards where the brood queen and her sisters had spent their lives. He could hear nothing, and, with the sun rising steadily in the green sky, he could see no signs of any dragons. He couldn't see their stretching necks or their bobbing heads, and he couldn't see the great purple flares that they sent skywards as they greeted the riders.

The smell was wrong too. Hen's Tooth's face was looking decidedly green, and Jake saw her cover her mouth as if she might vomit. He also noticed that the smell of sulphur was not as strong or as fresh as it should have been.

Jake noticed that plants had been uprooted, and he could see bootprints in the soft earth. Then he caught sight of something, and stooped to pick up another gun cartridge like the ones Eliza had found outside the Lodge. Then he found two more that were slightly different, because they'd come from a different gun. They looked too new, too bright.

Everything that Jake remembered from his winter training somehow seemed dull. The once-familiar odour was dull on the air. When he reached them, the surface of the eggs, usually leathery and shiny, was dull. Jake soon realized that the creatures inside had died, for the want of brooding.

There were hatchlings too, lying lifeless among the eggs. Jake couldn't bear to look at them. His stomach felt watery and in turmoil, as if some strange storm was brewing in his gut. He swallowed, but it didn't help.

Then Jake saw the great curving backbone of a large, adult dragon. It was one of the brood sisters brought down by a barrage of gunfire. The dragon's body was only half covered in scales, and the scales she did have weren't blue and green and iridescent, but grey and cloudy, and the sight of them brought a lump to Jake's throat that was impossible to swallow, and a bucketful of tears to his eyes.

A second dragon lay at an awkward angle, her wings battered and her back broken as she'd landed among the eggs. There was nothing left alive.

Jake touched several of the eggs, but their leathery surfaces had grown cold, and were beginning to wrinkle, and he took his hand away, distraught.

Then he heard a click and a puffing sound, and he turned suddenly, still squatting. He looked over the tops of perhaps a dozen eggs, and came face to face with Eliza, who was sitting, cradling something in her arms.

'What do they eat?' she asked quietly.

'What?' asked Jake.

'The little ones,' said Eliza. 'What do they eat?'

51

'Brother, sister,' they heard Hen's Tooth cry.

Jake and Eliza turned to see two Natives, wearing thick cloaks that were far too heavy for the hot conditions of the Land of the Red Moon. The three came together in a fierce embrace moments later.

'We've found you,' said the short, stocky man, tears of joy rolling down his cheeks.

Jake and Eliza approached them, cautiously, curious to meet Hen's Tooth's family, but careful not to interrupt their happy reunion.

As Jake and Eliza got closer, both adults drew long, curved knives, which glinted in the light. When Jake got a good look at them, they appeared to be made of some transparent blue stone. He put his hands in the air to show that he was unarmed.

Hen's Tooth grabbed hold of his hand, and said, 'This is my friend Dragon Sight. He is looking for *his* sister. He saved me. I'm a rider because of him!' She showed her family her left arm, and they knelt on the ground before her.

'Get up!' said Hen's Tooth. 'There isn't time. The brood queen and her sisters are dead. I am sick, and something terrible is happening.'

Jake held the gun cartridges in his hands that told him Boss Needham and his cronies had come to the Land of the Red Moon. He knew they had destroyed the colony, driven away or slaughtered the brood sisters, and killed the brood queen. Then he heard Hen's Tooth's sister say something, and he understood two words that would change everything.

He heard the words 'Dragon Lords' spoken by the Native, who knelt before Hen's Tooth, because she was a rider, and Jake didn't know what to think.

'Men did this,' he said. 'Men destroyed the colony.'

The Natives looked at him, only half-understanding what he was saying.

'It is the end of times,' said Hen's Tooth's sister.

Jake knew that she was right. He knew that the sick feeling in the pit of his stomach was to do with the brood queen and her sisters. He knew that Hen's Tooth was sick because of the deaths in the colony, and that it all meant the end of times.

'The legends are wrong,' said Jake. 'The end of times does not come *because* of the Dragon Lords. These dragons were killed by ignorant men with guns.'

'What are you talking about?' asked Eliza. 'And

what do babies eat? It's going to die if you don't tell me!'

She held the tiny hatchling out for everyone to see. There was no doubt that it was alive as it tried to get close to Eliza, to steal her warmth. It blinked, and tiny puffs of yellow smoke curled out of its nostrils. The Native woman took the knapsack from her back, and reached inside for something wrapped in leaves. She partly unwrapped the parcel to expose a yellow paste. Then she took some of it in her fingers, and held them up to the little dragon's snout. The tiny hatchling sniffed at the Native woman's fingers and then licked greedily from them. Eliza sighed with relief.

'Our legends say that the Dragon Lords come at the end of times. They say that we'll lose our homes, that our brood queen will die, and that there'll be a new dragon age. I believed that the end of times would come *because* of the Dragon Lords. Yellow Cloud told me that no one could defeat the Dragon Lords, and so I believed *they* would kill our brood queen,' said Jake. 'This wasn't done by other dragons, though. Look! This was done by men with guns! If Yellow Cloud could be wrong about this, then maybe he's wrong about finding my family too.

'I know who killed our brood queen. The Dragon Lords come in defiance and in power. They come because it *is* the end of times, not to *cause* the end of times.'

'Does that make it better?' asked Hen's Tooth.

'It gives me two enemies instead of one,' said Jake. 'It gives me two chances to defeat them.'

'What about Emmie and the doll?' asked Eliza. 'What about this little dragon? What are we going to do, Jake?'

'You must go back to the Lodge,' said Jake, 'while I go after Needham. Hen's Tooth is sick, and her brother and sister might get sick too, because of what's happened to the colony.'

'What about you? You can't go alone,' said Eliza. 'They've got guns!'

'I'm stronger than they are,' said Jake, 'because I believe that I can change the future. Besides, Yellow Cloud and his warriors are on their way. Haskell knows all about Boss Needham and his villains. I'm surprised he's not here already.'

'You'll have to tell them what to do,' said Eliza, pointing at the Natives. 'I don't speak their language, remember?'

'Keep them busy with the hatchling,' said Jake. 'I think he's making Hen's Tooth better already.'

'Her,' said Eliza.

'What?' asked Jake.

'I think,' said Eliza, adjusting the little bundle of

dragon in her arms, 'that she's a girl. I'm going to call her Sarah, after Trapper Watkiss's mule, because she was stubborn enough to live through all of this.'

'Yellow Cloud might have something to say about that,' said Jake.

'We'll see,' said Eliza.

52

There was nothing to be done about the complete devastation of the colony.

Jake simply followed the trail of destruction. He knew it must lead him into the paths of Horton Needham and his cronies. He needed to find the men who had killed the brood queen and her sisters, and an entire colony of eggs and hatchlings.

He didn't know what had happened to Straight Arrow or Horse Tail or the other Natives who tended the colony, but he'd found no bodies. He did know, however, that one of the prospectors had killed Merry Mack.

Jake found bootprints and one or two more cartridges, but not much else. The ground was soft, so the lighter footprints left by the Natives had mostly disappeared, and Jake was not an expert tracker like Trapper Watkiss. He followed the trail all morning. The men had kept close to the rock face, and never strayed on to the plains.

Jake didn't know how long the colony had been

occupied, but Yellow Cloud had told him the queen had been brooding for a thousand years. There was evidence of the queen and her sisters, and of their occupation, for miles. The base of the mountain was piled with the detritus of the colony along with the shale and shingle that the brood sisters used as their nesting material.

Jake idly picked up a handful of shingle as he followed the line of the cliff. The pebbles were perfectly smooth, like glass beads. He looked at the shingle in his palm. It was dirty from being mixed with the earth, broken shells and rotten food, and other waste from the abandoned hatcheries.

Jake took one pebble from his handful of shingle, and spat on it. He rubbed his thumb over it, and looked at the gleaming, glassy blue surface. The piece of shingle was a bead like the ones on his bracelet. He picked up another pebble at random and did the same. It was greener than the first, but it was another perfect gem.

'If Horton Needham wants to make money,' said Jake, 'this is all he needs.' He tossed the bead back into the wave of pebbles that had built up against the side of the mountain, and cast his eye along the shingle bank.

He saw the barrel of a gun, first, pointing up out of the shingle, the sun glinting off it.

53

Horton Needham and his cronies had done most of their walking during the night. The boss wanted to see the full extent of his riches, once the excitement of killing the dragons had worn off. He also wanted to make sure the Natives didn't come back.

He'd eventually got bored with walking, but he hadn't got bored with the gems, and he couldn't imagine ever tiring of them. Of course, he'd forbidden his men from taking any of them. He'd called it theft, and produced some legal papers from his pocket to prove his ownership of the land.

Trapper Watkiss sat at a distance from the others, chewing on a piece of dry cured meat.

'Hey!' shouted Jake.

Marcus Mimms put his gun to his shoulder and pointed it straight at him.

'Put that gun away,' said Trapper Watkiss. 'He's just a boy.'

'You're not the boss,' said Horton Needham.

'Neither are you,' said Jake, 'not of me.'

'I'm the boss of these five men,' said Horton Needham, his cheeks turning pink.

'My name's Dragon Sight,' said Jake. 'This land has been home to the Cloud People for a thousand years.'

'Well, now it belongs to me,' said Horton Needham, waving his legal papers, 'and I plan to mine it for gems.' He pushed his documents back in his pocket, picked up a handful of gemstones and scattered them in Jake's direction. Then he laughed his high-pitched cackle.

'You can't kill our dragons and steal our land!' said Jake. 'You can't take what you want and not expect consequences!'

'Dragons are dangerous,' said Pennyworth. 'They attacked us, and we defended ourselves.'

'There's no law in the world against it,' said Needham.

'No law in whose world?' asked Dragon Sight. 'We have our own laws.'

'Oh, shut him up!' said Horton Needham. 'Tie him up, and we'll take him back to Prospect.'

The Mimms brothers stood up to follow the boss's instructions. Dragon Sight did not resist or fight back.

'He's just a boy,' said Trapper Watkiss. 'What harm can he do?'

The Mimms brothers tied Jake's hands and feet, and left him sitting at the edge of the shingle bank.

'I could do a lot of harm,' said Jake. 'I could tell you about your sister.'

Trapper stared at the boy, his eyes widening.

'How do you know I've got a sister? I know she didn't tell you. It was her secret more than it was mine. I was a disgrace to her . . . Not honest enough, not by half.'

'Everyone loved Mrs Mack,' said Jake.

'What do you mean, loved? Don't they still love her?' asked Trapper Watkiss. 'What's happened to my sister?'

'I'm so sorry, Mr Watkiss,' said Jake.

'No one calls me mister,' said Trapper Watkiss. 'Only the sheriff when he's arresting me, and the doctor when somebody dies . . . Oh no . . . Oh dear Lord!'

'Every single person in Prospect came to her funeral,' said Jake.

'What did she die from?' asked Trapper Watkiss.

'She was hurt during a robbery at her cottage,' said Jake. 'She died from her injuries.'

Trapper Watkiss stared at Jake.

No one spoke. Othniel Seeley dropped his head and stared at his feet. He dared not look Trapper Watkiss in the eye, knowing that his guilt was written all over his face. The Mimms brothers looked at each other, and then looked away again. Horton Needham's eyes never wavered.

Trapper Watkiss turned his gaze on the five men. His silent assessment of them didn't take long and it ended with a sigh that turned into something like a growl. He stood, slowly, put the piece of dry cured meat he'd been chewing in his pocket, and checked his gun was loaded. He hooked it over his arm, strode down the shingle slope to where Jake was tied up, and cut the ropes with his pocket knife.

'What's next?' he asked.

'That's what's next,' said Jake, gesturing at the sky as a great, black dragon swooped overhead.

'Oh my Lord!' said Trapper, his face turning an unnatural white, making his beard appear even redder than usual. His eyes grew so big that the whites of them were visible all the way around his irises.

All five men turned and looked up into the bright green sky to see the monster approaching, its wings at full stretch, beating the air. Then the dragon tossed its head and breathed a great burst of flames in an arc across the sky. The flames glowed orange at their centre, but the edges were a shimmering purple where they burned the sulphur in the atmosphere.

'That's a rogue dragon,' said Jake.

'Take aim!' said Needham, his voice a hard, high rasp.

'You can't kill it with guns,' said Jake.

'Then what can we do?' asked Boss Needham.

'You can face your consequences,' said Jake.

Jake had met Boss Needham on only two occasions, and both times the man's face had been some shade of red. This time, though, all the colour drained out of Horton Needham's face until it was a pasty white, and only the rims of his eyes showed pink.

'Aim for its belly,' said Needham, his voice suddenly sounding feeble.

The Mimms brothers and Reginald Pennyworth had raised their guns and were aiming at the black dragon. Even Othniel Seeley had unholstered his revolver and was pointing it into the air. Then they saw another dragon coming up over the ridge behind the first.

'It's useless,' said Jake.

Trapper Watkiss stood next to Jake, making no attempt to raise or aim his gun. Horton Needham glared at him.

'I told you to take aim,' he said in his rasping whisper. He didn't sound sure of himself, but he did sound desperate. 'We killed dragons yesterday, and we can kill them today.'

'You killed old, female dragons, who'd lost their strength and their scales,' said Jake. 'You took potshots, and you destroyed a thousand years of brood history.'

'They were dangerous,' said Pennyworth, firing his gun.

'You killed the females and the infants,' said Jake. 'You deserve to face their fighting males. Let's see how long you last!'

As the five men fired their weapons, Jake removed his bracelet from around his wrist and held it above his head. Then, as the men began to reload their weapons, he started to spin the bracelet. Soon, air began to pass through the large red gem at its centre, sending out a clear, high-pitched note.

Jake felt the vibration of the gemstone in his hand as the note sang out, and he sensed Match responding to it. Then he closed his eyes and opened his mind, and he projected himself out over the ridge of the Crest Mountains. He soon found what he was looking for. He found a creature responding to loss and pain. He found empathy.

Jake felt the change in air pressure as Match circled around the small group of men. He also felt a sharp twinge of panic.

Jake anticipated Pennyworth's turn almost before he'd made it. He took two long strides towards the big man, and grasped the barrel of his gun in his right hand, close to the stock, and pushed it upwards. When Pennyworth pulled the trigger, the gun fired, harmlessly, into the air.

Jake wrenched the gun out of Pennyworth's hands.

'Never point a gun at my dragon!' he said.

The big man's lip was quivering. He was unarmed

and surrounded by dragons, and he was utterly terrified.

Jake handed Pennyworth's gun to Trapper Watkiss, and then mounted Match in one easy movement. He grasped his nape feathers, and Match was rampant one moment, and walking into the air the next. In less than a minute, the little green dragon was circling up into the sky to meet his enemies.

The Mimms brothers aimed their guns into the sky. The little green dragon was flying away from them, but the great black dragon had cleared the ridge of the mountain and appeared to be descending. It was followed by two others, and there could be more.

Fingers tightened on triggers. There was a boom as a shot was fired, a ping, and an echoing ricochet as the bullet hit rock and flew off in another direction.

Marcus Mimms jumped out of his skin. The sound startled him very badly, preventing him from shooting his gun, but the shot was also fired at his feet, and he and his brother could both feel the vibrations as the bullet struck the rock they were standing on and ricocheted away. For a moment, he was convinced that the bullet had bounced off the rock and right into his flesh.

A tiny whiff of smoke curled from the barrel of Trapper Watkiss's old Hawken rifle.

'The next man that shoots at them there dragons won't be so lucky,' he said.

'Are you defying my orders?' asked Boss Needham.

'Do you want to stand trial for my dear sister's death?' asked Trapper Watkiss with real menace. 'Or maybe you'd prefer I skip straight to your execution?'

He glared at Needham, and then at the Mimms brothers. He didn't know why, but he wasn't afraid. He was angry and his heart was broken, but he wasn't afraid of Boss Needham or his cronies.

54

Jake blinked slowly and concentrated, slipping easily into Match's mind as the little dragon circled and climbed into the sky.

He could feel Match's sadness. Match knew that the brood queen was dead, and that the end of times was upon them. Jake soothed Match's mind and reassured him that all would be well. He reminded Match of the hatchling that Eliza had saved and of the brood sisters that had escaped.

The moment it took to soothe Match made a huge difference to the dragon, preparing him to fly out to meet the big black dragon.

Jake could feel its pain, just as he had felt Match's pain. He knew that, if he concentrated, he could also feel his way into the dragon's fragile mind. It was not his job to soothe the dragon. It was his job to save his people, and his home. More than anything, it was his duty to hold the Dragon Lords at bay.

Jake reached out and touched the black dragon's mind. He felt pain there, and he knew the dragon was being used. He turned Match in a sweeping curve around the beast. As he swept over and around the great, black dragon, Jake used his dragonsight to dig deeper into the creature's mind.

He found more pain.

The animal was bigger and slower than Match, and was also keeping several other dragons in formation, so Jake was able to steer Match around for another pass, bringing Jake face to face with his foe. Match hovered in front of the black dragon, and Jake stared into its purple eyes.

He caught a glimpse of something there, before Match had to pull away in a hard climb to avoid the burst of searing flames that the black dragon exhaled.

Jake saw a large, straight-backed man with silver in his hair and a determined, downturned mouth. He was sitting on an elaborately carved throne, adorned with crystal spikes and reached by a flight of curving steps.

Jake shuddered. These were the Dragon Lords of his dreams, the evil men who controlled the dragons. Somewhere in the west, these men existed in their strange mountain settlement. What did they want? And how could he keep them away?

Jake left the black dragon's mind. He concentrated on riding Match, and on cutting elaborate paths through the formation of riderless black dragons in the sky. He flew between them, around them, and under and over them. He got them to break formation, and, once he'd divided them, he found that the connections between them were weak.

Jake targeted a dragon at the edge of the formation. He wove Match between it and its neighbour, and flew them around it until it began to follow them in circles at dizzying speeds. Soon, it didn't know where it was, and Match flew west for three minutes before peeling off. The dragon was so confused that, realizing it was on course for home, it simply kept flying.

Jake flew Match under another of the dragons, and then forced it upwards until it was flying so high above the rest of the formation that it could no longer see or feel its leader. Then Match turned on it in a loop the loop with a half-turn, so that, suddenly, it was face to face with the little green dragon. Match breathed a stream of fire into its face, and it coughed uncontrollably, and dropped out of the sky. It crashed, hard, into another dragon in the formation, and soon they were both tumbling, thrashing their wings and trying to balance with their tails as they craned their necks and paddled furiously with their legs.

The dragon that had been crashed into was so angry that it turned on the other, spraying it with flames, and clawing and lashing out at it in mid-air. The two dragons were well matched, and fought on as Jake and Match pursued another victim.

55

Jake turned Match in the sky as the black dragon swung around to meet him, smaller dappled grey dragons to left and right. They breathed streams of orange flames into the green sky that turned purple as the heat burned up the sulphur over the colony.

Jake did not expect them. He thought he had the upper hand, but he'd underestimated his opposition.

The great black dragon hovered for a moment. Then it raised its front legs in the rampant position, half-folded its wings, extended its head and neck, and plunged towards Match. Its nostrils flared and filled with yellow smoke, before it exhaled another burst of flames.

In that moment, Jake saw something. A split second later, he blinked and entered Match's mind. When he opened his eyes, he was seeing through Match's eyes, over the black dragon's shoulder. Match's streamlined body, his wings pushed back, glided past the bigger, slower dragon. A tight turn and a controlled swish of his muscular tail brought Match past the dappled beast to his right. Match spat a well-aimed fireball under its wing, where it joined its body, scorching the flesh. The creature folded its wing to extinguish the flame, making it drop and spin away.

As the black dragon lumbered around for another pass, the grey dragon on Match's left flew underneath Match, trying to force him into the black dragon's path. Match simply stayed low, and then stopped, unexpectedly.

The shot of flames, which the grey dragon had aimed at Match's belly, missed. They appeared right in front of the black dragon's snout, spoiling his view of Match. The black dragon's next attack was ruined, and, while he turned, high and wide, Match and Jake regrouped. It was one dragon against three. Jake and Match had speed on their side, but not strength nor numbers. The fight was going to be tough.

Jake was still in Match's mind, but part of him was trying to remember what he'd seen in the black dragon's eyes. There was a flash of something. He was sure he'd seen something . . . no . . . *someone* familiar.

Suddenly, Match dropped, and Jake was almost unseated. He could not feel Match between his knees or under his feet, and his hands barely held on to his neck feathers.

Then Match stopped dropping, and Jake landed heavily on his back.

'Remember your dragonsight,' said Jake.

Match squealed and puffed yellow smoke from his nostrils, and Jake could feel his panic. He tensed his legs and adjusted his hands in Match's nape feathers, constantly scanning the skies for their enemies.

The black dragon's face loomed impossibly large before him. Jake held Match steadily, in a hover, while he stared into the creature's eyes. Then he pulled up hard on Match's nape feathers, and let the dragon open his wings fully and fast.

The black dragon was so close that Match almost kicked him in the snout as he flew over him. The black dragon's burst of flames nearly singed Match's paws, but he pulled his back legs under his body at the last moment. In return, Match breathed a stinging line of fire all along the ridge of the black dragon's back as he passed over him.

There was no time for Jake to collect his thoughts. He simply concentrated on the picture in his head and flew Match high and wide over the Crest Mountains. In his mind, he was looking down at the faces of his ma and pa buried in a sea of Native faces, his heart gladdened to see them alive. Jake's ma and pa were together, and they were with a group of Natives that looked like Hen's Tooth.

Emmie was not with them.

In the distance, Jake could see riderless, black and dappled dragons patrolling a sea of people.

56

Jake jolted back to reality as he heard rifle fire filling the air. Half a dozen shots were fired, including the snap of a revolver.

He was sitting comfortably on Match's back, but he realized that he'd been thinking deeply for longer than he'd intended.

Without Jake to steer him, and with three angry dragons chasing him, Match had flown out over the plains. West, where the black and dappled grey dragons had come from, was not safe. If he had any allies, they would come from the plains and the blue dunes, and from the Land of the White Sun.

Match could smell his brothers in the air. He could even smell the little blue dragon at the Lodge.

Jake patted Match on the neck, and tightened his hold on his nape feathers. He turned Match west, to face the foe, and watched as Needham and his cronies reloaded and fired their guns. With Match and Jake out of the way, it was safe to attack the evil, riderless dragons, even if they couldn't be stopped.

Jake settled his mind. It was time to prove to Yellow Cloud that the Dragon Lords could be beaten. It had to be possible to defend their home and rebuild the colony, and to find his family, with Hen's Tooth's help.

Jake slipped into Match's mind once more. He intended to attack the three dragons flying over the Crest Mountains. They appeared to be performing a fly-past of the colony, making figures of eight where the brood queen had hatched and brooded her last batch of eggs.

Dragon Sight was ready to attack, but Match seemed to be fighting his master's will. There had never been any question of who was in charge, and for a second Jake couldn't understand what the dragon was doing. It wasn't like Match to be disobedient.

'What is it, Match? What can you sense?' Jake asked. Then he spotted them.

Flying towards them over the horizon was a formation of a dozen dragons. Jake's heart soared.

'Yellow Cloud!' he said.

57

As Gale flew to the Crest Mountains with Yellow Cloud, two of the dragons peeled off over the plains. They landed at the Lodge where they'd seen Hen's Tooth's little blue dragon. They were not surprised to find Hen's Tooth and Eliza, but the strangers were also welcomed.

When they told the Natives that they would all return immediately to the Land of the White Sun, Hen's Tooth ducked away from them, mounted her dragon, and walked into the air before anyone could stop her.

The riders were not expecting her to mount so easily or so quickly, nor to be able to fly without help. They had no choice but to follow her. They shared a few words, but quickly decided that they should all fly to the colony. Eliza and Hen's Tooth's sister flew with one of the riders while the two Native men flew together.

High up in the sky, Yellow Cloud had thrown himself into battle, flying Gale with complete control.

The noise of wing beats and the shrieks of angry dragons filled his ears as he swooped down to meet the vast black dragon. Out of the corner of his eye, he could see Match forming a pincer movement, and in an instant they'd crossed paths, confusing the giant beast, causing it to spin and wobble precariously in the air.

Yellow Cloud could feel the powerful updraught created by Match as he passed barely a hand's breadth below. Then the dappled grey creatures attacked Match's flanks.

Black Feather sideswiped one of the dappled greys, and shot a blast of flames across the back legs of the other, causing it to peel off, screaming in pain, the stench of its singed scales filling the air.

At the top of his climb, the black dragon stalled, dropped and hovered. Jake and Yellow Cloud had to brake and turn and weave a path around one another. The black dragon had the advantage, and he came in fast behind Match, chasing him into the mountain. Match swung his tail hard, turned and dropped to where the cliff scooped into the mountainside, and found room to turn and fly out of harm's way. The black dragon could not turn, and had to fly along the inside edge of the ridge before it could escape the curve and turn back towards the fray.

Black Feather and Yellow Cloud continued to

duck and weave around the dappled grey dragons, driving them into one another in a tangle of legs and tails. Their streams of flames met and crossed, and so much heat so close to their snouts caused the sulphur around them to flare and ignite purple. The air was starved of oxygen, and the dragons grew light-headed and sluggish.

Black Feather flew in front of the grey on his left, luring him along the ridge and into the shadow of the mountain, before bringing him into sunlight. The cool sunbeams gleamed off the rock face and off the myriad gems banked up against the cliff. For a moment, the dappled dragon was blinded by the reflected light.

Black Feather turned his mount and came at the dappled grey in a broadside, first blasting it with a spray of flames and then ripping into the beast's wing with his dragon's foreclaws. The dappled dragon turned its head, trying to bite and fend off the attack, but its wing was already badly torn. It flailed its paws and beat hard with its one good wing, but it couldn't turn away from the rock face.

Yellow Cloud was mesmerized by Black Feather's prowess in the air. He had never seen such deft flying, nor such extraordinary skill in battle.

Black Feather attacked with another blast of flames, this time aiming under the other wing, scorching its tender underside. The dappled grey shook its head, half-folded its wing, and coughed a fireball in response. It was beaten. It tried to extend its wings, but one was broken and the other badly singed. It tried to gain height by paddling its legs, pawing desperately at the air, but it was already falling.

Black Feather ducked the fireball and peeled away from the cliff, as the dappled grey dragon lost its fight to stay in the air. It tumbled down the face of the mountain, rolling through the shingle that the brood queen and her sisters had nested in.

The six men on the ground watched the great grey dragon fall out of the sky, and tumble down the rock face only twenty or thirty strides from where they stood. The crash of its body against the rocks and the rumbling groan that emanated from its throat seemed to make the very air throb.

Pennyworth took several steps towards the fallen creature, lifted his gun to his shoulder and aimed it at the beast's head. He did not hear the man come up behind him, so he didn't defend himself when the gun was taken from him.

'No!' the Native said.

'Shoot them!' shouted Horton Needham, his face a deeper, darker purple than seemed humanly possible.

His cries had no effect on his men.

Pennyworth was more afraid of dragons than he ever thought it was possible to be afraid of anything.

Somehow, the news of his sister's death had changed Trapper Watkiss. He sat on the soft earth, surrounded by strange, fleshy plants, with his gun across his knees, and he thought about Nathan McKenzie. He had been his friend and his boss for a long time. Trapper didn't think he wanted McKenzie to be his boss any more, and he wondered whether that meant that McKenzie would stop being his friend. He decided that it didn't matter.

Marcus and Anthony Mimms had their guns slung over their shoulders. They had no consciences, and whoever appeared to be in charge was the man they'd take their orders from. It didn't matter to them, one way or the other. Besides, there was a spectacle going on, and the Mimms brothers loved a spectacle!

Part of the performance was the little dark blue dragon that was darting around, spiralling towards the big black dragon.

Yellow Cloud had given his orders. Two riders were to secure the Lodge and then land at the colony. Two more might also land at the colony, depending on how many were needed in the air.

Yellow Cloud and Black Feather were Jake's main back-up. Too many dragons in the sky would only confuse things.

Hen's Tooth was merely a child on a dragon, who had never had a lesson, or heard a legend. She hadn't even been properly introduced to her dragon, but she didn't know or care about any of that.

Hen's Tooth knew all about the great black dragon and its masters. She had run away and hidden from them. She had been burned by them, and she had been denied the right to ride because of them. Her people had suffered for generations, because of them, and she was filled with anger.

Hen's Tooth drove her little mount up behind the great black dragon as it flew into the air, chasing Match, swinging west over the ridge of the mountain and then turning back over the colony in a figure of eight. She snapped at its tail as it swept past, and made her dragon cough a ball of fire, which rumbled over the tip and spines of its tail. The black dragon twitched and flicked away the flames, altering its course just enough to prevent a great gout of its flames from setting fire to Jake's shirt and hair.

Yellow Cloud swooped low under the black dragon's belly, belching flames under its wings as he passed. The black dragon turned its head, and another stream of fire flew from its maw, searing the scales along Gale's flanks. Then the flames licked so far out that Hen's Tooth's hair caught alight, and she shrieked and began to bat at her head with her hands.

Hen's Tooth had let go of her dragon's nape feathers, to put out the fire, and the last dappled grey dragon saw that she was in trouble. It flew around to meet her coming over the ridge, and came at her head-on. Hen's Tooth was still shaking her head and batting at it with her hands, unaware of the danger she was in.

Jake was aware. He also knew that Yellow Cloud had taken a hit, and that Black Feather was turning wide and would take too long to return to the fray to be of any use.

Jake could either save Hen's Tooth or continue to attack the black dragon. He had a sudden, flashing memory. He could see his favourite book and Emmie's rag doll bobbing in the river in front of him after they'd fallen out of his parent's wagon. He could not save both, so he'd saved Emmie's doll.

Jake tugged on Match's nape feathers and kicked Match's foreleg joints, and he brought his dragon around to attack the dappled grey. Jake willed Match to blast the dappled dragon with a stream of flames down its side, and whip it with his tail as he passed behind it. The angered grey turned away from Hen's Tooth and followed them down the side of the mountain. Jake doubled back, and drove Match at the grey from behind, blasting the dragon in the rear. He was elated at the direct hit, and spurred Match forward to snap the dragon's muscular tail between his teeth. Jake could see the purple blood welling up between Match's teeth, as he leaned forward to see what damage he had done. Then he twisted Match's nape feathers, and the little dragon wrenched his head around, throwing his opponent off balance.

Jake ordered Match to let go, and the grey dragon paddled his legs furiously, and beat his wings to try to get some lift in the air. Jake flew Match in a spiral around the dragon, confusing it still further, until the dragon began to panic. Match was taking every instruction, responding perfectly to every command, they were winning, and Jake could not be more content.

There was no room for the grey dragon to expand its wings, and, every time it tried, it beat them against Match's chest as Jake flew circles around the beast. Finally, the creature could not maintain its hover and it could not breathe. Its eyes glazed over, its legs stopped paddling and its wings stopped trying to beat, and the creature dropped out of the sky.

The corpse landed with an almighty thump. A vast spray of shingle was forced out in all directions, flying through the air, in a display of gleaming colours, and a tremor spread far and wide through the earth, shifting the mists across the plain in new and extraordinary patterns.

Jake didn't see the jewels and the colours the shingle made as it flew through the air, because he was at Hen's Tooth's side. The Native girl's hair was almost all gone, but the fire was out, and she obviously had control of her little blue dragon and was out of danger. Jake flew beside her and made a sign for her to land.

Hen's Tooth nodded, solemnly, and Jake was reassured that the girl would do as she was told. Then he and Match peeled off in a hard turn, swung around and up, and turned to face the Crest Mountains. Jake wanted to remember the scene of the lost battle with the evil, riderless black dragon. He had given it up to save Hen's Tooth. He had done what would have made his pa proud.

As they turned, Jake remembered the scene on the ground below. Why had there been so few Native warriors? What had happened?

58

The great ridge of the Crest Mountains cut a familiar line across the endless green sky. There were no clouds, and the dull, dappled sun sat huge and heavy halfway up the sky.

Jake wondered if he'd ever been so tired. He knew that Match had never worked so long or so hard. The little dragon was singed and sore, and he'd been through a great deal in a short time, but Jake knew that he was up to the task.

He also knew that it must soon be over.

The vast green firmament should have been empty. The dappled grey dragons were dead or had fled, and the black dragon was being herded by the other dragon riders. Jake knew that the Dragon Lords controlled the great black dragon and his companions. He knew that the deaths of the brood queen and her sisters had brought them to the Crest Mountains, and he knew that they had come for the end of times.

He also believed what no one else had believed:

that legends could be wrong, and that Dragon Lords could be defeated.

Now, Yellow Cloud knows the Dragon Lords can be defeated too, Jake thought.

The vast green firmament should have been empty, so Dragon Sight was amazed to see that it wasn't.

The sky over the ridge of the Crest Mountains was full of dragons. Jake could see eight warrior riders on the backs of eight yellow, green and blue dragons, dipping and weaving in a great circle. They looked as if they were performing a ceremonial dance, like the one the riders had performed around the bonfire on the plateau.

At the centre of the ring of dancing dragons was a ninth: a riderless, angry, fire-breathing, purple-eyed, black dragon. It was writhing, and weaving figures of eight, and, every so often, it lunged at one of the other dragons, baring its teeth and breathing fire.

Jake breathed a long, deep breath, and he blinked slowly. He let his body melt into Match's back and he let his mind find Match's, slipping into it as easily as a hand into a silk glove.

'Come on, boy,' he said, soothing his friend. 'One last job, and then we can rest.'

When Jake opened his eyes again, he did so through the clear, powerful vision of his dragon.

He could see the black dragon approaching fast in the great ring of Native riders, and he could smell the burnt scales on its back where it had been caught by Match and Gale. Jake noticed that the black dragon favoured his right side and preferred attacking from above. It should have been dead, but, instead, it was exhausted. Its tail was slow to respond, and it was becoming easier to confuse the beast.

Jake reassured Match that everything would be fine before he blinked slowly, and gently left his dragon's mind. Then he relaxed his feet, his knees and his thighs, so that he barely had contact with his mount. He needed to know that Match would continue to do his job without guidance. Nothing changed. Match turned hard to the left and over the black dragon's right shoulder, just as Jake expected him to.

After the black dragon had breathed a vast stream of fire, Match came face to face with it, knowing that there would be no more flames for several seconds. Jake looked the dragon hard in the eyes. He thought he would have to beat his way in, but it was almost easy to see past the purple irises. It was almost easy to work his way past the reflections of himself and Match, and into the great black cavities of the glossy pupils.

Suddenly, he saw dragons nesting on their isolated ledges, on the sheer sides of a mountain. It was as if he was flying around the mountain, higher and higher in a great spiral. Then the picture blurred, and he saw the tall throne with its narrow flight of steps and its spiky jewels. He saw the man with the silver in his hair, sitting on the throne, and he saw his grim face with its deep frown and its unnaturally downturned mouth.

Jake pushed his face close to the face of the Dragon Lord, until they were almost nose to nose, and he looked into his eyes. He saw nothing there but hatred, despair, hostility and evil. He had never looked into a man's eyes before and seen such a dark past and such a bleak future.

Jake pulled back just a little and began to conjure pictures in his head of all the things that he loved. Suddenly, he was standing next to his pa with his kind face and his large, smooth doctor's hands, always ready to help anyone who needed him. Then his mother was laughing and tossing her shawl around her shoulders, wearing her pink, Sunday-best dress and her jewelled brooch with its ruby and its green enamel dragon scales. Then Emmie was there, running around her father's legs, waving her rag doll at him and calling his name.

In no time, he was surrounded by his new friends too, introducing Yellow Cloud and White Thunder to his family, watching Emmie and the twins laughing and playing and climbing all over Match.

All the time, Jake looked into the Dragon Lord's face, and, all the time, his wonderful imaginings, and all the people he loved, passed around him and between them.

Suddenly, it was clear to Dragon Sight what he must say.

'Your hatred and despair do not belong in a dragon's mind, Dragon Lord,' he began. 'You have no right to bring your misery into these dragons' lives, nor to use them for evil.

'Leave!' he declared. 'You have no right to wield power over such fine and beautiful creatures. Leave their minds, now and forever!'

The Dragon Lord did not flinch. Jake was bringing hope into dark spaces filled with evil, and the Dragon Lord was fighting him hard.

'You know not of what you speak,' said the Dragon Lord. 'Dragons have done our bidding for a thousand years.'

Jake did not give up.

'That doesn't make it right!' he said.

All the pictures and words, and all the feelings that built up inside him gave Jake strength and pride, and they filled him with hope and love.

The more he looked at the Dragon Lord, the more fierce Jake felt, the stronger he felt, and the more in charge of the situation he felt.

Finally, Jake used the only language that the

Dragon Lord understood. He fed all the energy that he'd gathered from all his positive thoughts into his anger.

Jake felt calm, but ferocious. He stared the Dragon Lord deep in the eye, and, with all his anger and all his hatred for the evil that the Dragon Lords stood for, he bellowed at him.

'Leave this dragon!'

It was a battle of wills. It wasn't like wrestling with Horace McKenzie or being punched by one of his cronies. It wasn't like defying Mr Garret or arguing with Yellow Cloud. It wasn't like being humiliated by Eliza Garret or like being scolded by Masefield Haskell. It was like none of those things, and yet, in a way, it was like all of those things rolled into one. It was like every petty squabble and every grown-up decision. It was like every fistfight and every war council.

Jake Polson had never fought a battle like it in his life, and he didn't know if he could win. He hoped that, if he couldn't win it, perhaps Dragon Sight could. He was becoming someone new, someone who was braver than he'd ever been, stronger and more resolute.

Two yellow puffs of smoke obscured the black dragon's eyes, and Match beat his wings and lifted his tail. He turned his body on its side and sailed over the black dragon, tucking his legs underneath him so as not to collide with the creature's back ridge.

Jake flew Match wide of the black dragon, which hovered for a moment, but didn't try to follow him. Then Match came around in front of the beast, face to face with it. It seemed not to know where it was or what it was doing. Then Jake felt the sudden movement of air as the black dragon began to thrash and writhe uncontrollably before him. Its wings spasmed out of synch with one another, its neck twisted in an unnatural rictus, and its back arched. The beast appeared to be in agony.

Jake wanted to reach out with his mind, to soothe the beast, but it was too late.

Suddenly, the great, black dragon's muscles softened, and its body was as slack and inanimate as it had been rigid. There was a rush of air, and its corpse fell out of the sky.

The black dragon did not, however, die in vain. Its death proved that the Dragon Lords could be defeated, and that legends could be changed.

EPILOGUE

Jake, Yellow Cloud and Black Feather sat in the Lodge on the misty plains, deeply saddened by the loss of the colony.

To one side, Hen's Tooth sat quietly with her brother and sister, and Eliza tended to the fire and kept out of things, not knowing quite what to think.

The rest of the riders had returned home and taken the prospectors with them. Boss Needham had put up some resistance, but Trapper Watkiss had cuffed him around the head with the butt of his rifle, knocking him out cold so that he could be tossed over a dragon's back, no questions asked. Then the old man had taken a large nip of Othniel Seeley's whisky, for courage, before he'd agreed to be strapped to his rider.

'Boss Needham can't be allowed into the Land of the Red Moon to destroy everything,' said Dragon Sight. 'It's because of him that the end of times has come.'

'Yes, and he will face justice,' said Yellow Cloud,

'but the end of times would always have come. Nothing lasts forever. The brood queen reigned for a thousand years.'

'Men like that shouldn't be allowed,' said Dragon Sight.

'Men like that have always existed,' said Yellow Cloud. 'They helped to build your great country. It is because of men like Boss Needham that you are a rider, that you came home to us.'

'But he's a bad man,' said Dragon Sight.

'He is a bad man,' said Yellow Cloud. 'We will do what we can to stop him, and so will Sheriff Sykes. You will learn that nothing is all bad and nothing is all good, Dragon Sight, and you will learn patience.'

'You must learn something too,' said Dragon Sight. 'You must learn that things can change.'

Yellow Cloud frowned, a confused look on his face.

'You'll help me find my sister now, won't you?' said Dragon Sight, pulling out the rag doll from inside his jacket. 'We've banished the Dragon Lords from the plains, for now at least, and we can fight them again, if we must. If my ma and pa and Emmie are in the Land of the Red Moon, I'm going to need you to help me find them.'

The rest of the day was spent quietly discussing the Dragon Lords, tending to the animals, and preparing and eating a meal.

As they were packing the Lodge, and preparing to leave, Hen's Tooth ran over to Dragon Sight and took the rag doll, holding it out for her brother and sister to see. They got up and joined the three men.

Hen's Tooth's sister took the doll and held it between her hands. Then she held it to her face for a moment, smelled it, and smiled.

'We found a girl in the desert. We did not understand her clothes, her skin, her golden hair. They all looked like this,' she said, holding out the doll. 'Some thought she was a goddess, some a demon.'

'You saw her?' asked Dragon Sight. 'Tell me your name, and tell me where you saw my sister.'

'My name is Desert Serpent and we found her wandering,' she said. 'We left her with our people, in hiding.'

'Can you take us there?' asked Yellow Cloud.

'They might have gone,' said Desert Serpent. 'The Dragon Lords . . .'

'We can fight the Dragon Lords,' said Dragon Sight, 'but we must save my sister, and your people too. Will you show us the way?'

'Yes,' the woman replied. 'Hen's Tooth has told us how you saved her life. It will be our honour to take you to your sister.'

Hope rose in Dragon Sight's heart. Suddenly, he

didn't feel tired, his muscles didn't ache and his mind was as alert as it had ever been. His sister was alive and he'd do whatever it took to track her down.

Dragon Sight nodded to Desert Serpent.

'Then we prepare to leave,' he said.

HOW TO DRAW A
DRAGON

BY ANDY LANNING
CO-CREATOR OF *DRAGON FRONTIER*

ANDY LANNING

is a veteran comic-book inker and has worked on almost every major superhero including **Spiderman**, **Batman**, **The X-Men**, **Wonder Woman**, **The Fantastic Four**, **The Ultimate Avengers** and **Superman**.

He has worked with **DAN ABNETT**, author of **Dragon Frontier**, for more than twenty years. In that time they have written some of the most famous superhero comics in the world, including **Iron Man**, **Thor** and **The Punisher** at Marvel, and **Superman**, **Batman**, **The Justice League of America**, and **Wonder Woman** at DC Comics.

Now Andy uses his inking skills to reveal how to draw a dragon – just like Match, Jake's dragon in **Dragon Frontier** . . .

Share your dragon picture with other fans at
Facebook.co.uk/DragonFrontier
(or ask an adult to do this if you're not thirteen yet).

DRAGON FRONTIER
HOW TO DRAW A DRAGON

STEP
A good starting point is to draw so
basic shapes that form the framework
your dragon. The two lower rings fo
the body and the oval is the he

STEP 2:
Continue with the framework by adding basic
shapes for the neck, legs and wings. Always draw
these bits in light pencil so they can be erased
later. They are the basis for the details. In
Dragon Frontier the dragons are four-legged
(like horses) and are therefore easier to ride!

STEP :
Once you have the framework, you c
begin to flesh out the dragon's shape
detail. Start with the head and neck – y
can design this to look any way you wa
This is a young dragon, like Match from
story, and is lean and fast so its head
more like that of a bird, streamlined a
sleek. Use the line you've drawn in t
framework as a guide and fill out the ne
with curved lines. The underside of t
dragon is a different texture
the topside: it's ridged a
scaly, made up of tough th
skin to protect

STEP 4:
Next, add detail to the legs and body of the dragon. Again,
use your guidelines and draw in curves. Notice that the
dragon's legs are bent like those of a dog: double-jointed
with a claw-spur on the elbow joint. The fourth leg is not
seen as it is hidden by the other leg and the body. You can
add as many or as few toes as you decide. This dragon has
three toes on each foot, two at the front, one at the rear.

STEP 5:

...esh out the tail. Again, this is ...mething you can add as much or as ...le detail to as you want, but start by ...tting the basic shape worked out by ...lowing the line of your framework. ...otice this dragon has a 'devil's' spiked ...l but it could have another spike at ...e tip or even end in a feathery tuft.

STEP 6:

Finally draw the wing (we've hidden the second wing behind the first to keep things simple but you can always mirror the first wing behind it). Using your framework, draw a thicker 'arm' joint with a spiked elbow then follow that thick line down to the wing tip. Then join up the other wing joints with curved lines that make up the wing folds. These should look like the folds of an umbrella.

STEP 7:

...w you have sketched out the basic shape of your dragon, the next step is really fun! You can add all sorts ...details to customize your dragon to look like whatever you want. This dragon is one of the breed the Cloud ...ople in *Dragon Frontier* ride. It has a feathered mane at the back of its head and down its neck. It also ...s feathers on the line of its wings and scales down its back and tail. It is also patterned with spots like ... Appaloosa horse, which were traditionally ridden by Native Americans in the Bitterroot Mountains of the ...cific Northwest where the story takes place.

NOW IT'S TIME TO HEAR FROM THE AUTHOR OF *DRAGON FRONTIER* HIMSELF, DAN ABNETT

Q. Did you know a lot about the Wild West before you started writing *Dragon Frontier*?

A. As a kid I played cowboys and Indians, and my favourite TV western was *The Virginian*! I also liked to read about the Wild West. The West I imagined was probably quite different from the truth, but I have made sure that the West in this book is, at heart, very realistic.

Q. How did you research *Dragon Frontier*? It's hard to find a dragon these days!

A. The Dragon Frontier is really easy to find . . . It's right here in my imagination. That's where I do most of my research when I'm dealing with things that are not from our world.

Q. Did you take inspiration from any other books or films?

A. Yes, the western TV shows I loved as a kid, and I still love monster movies. The best dragon stories are the oldest, in my opinion. The myths and legends from the ancient civilizations are hugely inspiring.

Q. Have you ever been flying, apart from in a big aeroplane? Would you like to ride a dragon?

A. I've been on planes of all sizes, including one almost the same size as the bigger dragons in my book. Of course I'd love to ride a dragon . . . Who wouldn't?